COREY ANN HAYDU

THE WIDELY UNKNOWN MYTH OF APPLE & DOROTHY

KATHERINE TEGEN BOOKS
An Imprint of HarperCollins Publishers

Katherine Tegen Books is an imprint of HarperCollins Publishers.

The Widely Unknown Myth of Apple & Dorothy
195 Broadway, New York, NY 10007.
www.harpercollinschildrens.com

Library of Congress Control Number: 2023933827
ISBN 978-0-06-297693-2

Typography by Amy Ryan
23 24 25 26 27 LBC 5 4 3 2 1

First Edition

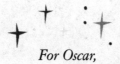

For Oscar,
and the way you were always nestled next to my desk,
a white fluff of comfort and sweetness,
in so many different homes over the years,
and all the books we wrote
together.

THE WIDELY UNKNOWN MYTH OF APPLE & DOROTHY

PROLOGUE

Here's what I want to say about the silver ladder to the sky: It's long and thin and it shakes in the wind and it's the sort of thing the gods could have made sturdier, better, but they didn't. And that means something, I think, even though no one is saying what it might mean, or why it is that the gods have made our journey skyward long and tiring in the way that rubs blisters into your skin, gathers sweat on your neck, makes your feet wonder if they are only bone now, because they feel so worn. I don't know what it means that it's so impossibly hard to get to the sky, to the place we're supposed to belong.

It is mythological. Which is another way of saying impossibly difficult, overly complicated, destined to hurt.

That's what Mama's always said, with a roll of her eyes, the same way she used to roll her eyes at everything up in Olympus—winged Eros always flying around the trees, the laurels stuck behind everyone's ears, and, of course, the twelve marble thrones, in their perfect arc, the gods, straight-backed and silent, sitting upon them.

I'd always remind Mama that we have laurels and marble down on Our Hill, too. And togas. We have tall white columns making paths all over, circling the school, the river, our own home. And we have immortality. And fate. She'd never say much to that. Just look out the window at our little bit of earth—the silver ladder always squarely in the distance, bending but never breaking in the wind—like she was wishing it was some other bit of earth.

On our last trip to the sky, I go first, then Dad behind me, which is the way we've always climbed—me, then Dad in case I fall, then Mama because she moves a little slowly and doesn't like to be rushed. This morning, Mama's best friend, Heather, and her nearly perfect daughter, Apple, are ahead of us. Which means we are the end of the line, the last family to take the annual climb to Olympus on this winter solstice. We are the last ones who will take a bite of golden apple, the last family to ensure our immortality for another year, to renew our near-god status. I feel Dad behind me for the first few hikes of my legs up the rungs, the first few slips of my hands. The ladder shakes and settles, shakes and settles.

"Penny!" Dad calls down to Mama when we are half-way to the sky.

"Is Mama okay?" I ask. I make the mistake of looking down. We are so high that the world below us looks make-believe—grassy knolls and jagged rocks and yellow flowers decorating our lawns, and a river running through it all; the descendants of water nymphs are always knee-deep in its rush, like their legs won't take them too far from the water, too far from their past. The statues loom largest of all—Zeus and Aphrodite and Athena and the rest of them built in marble and metal and wood below us. We make them with every kind of material. We build them again and again and again, a promise to remember where we've come from.

"Penny, what are you doing?" Dad calls, not answering me. I try to lean my head this way and that to see Mama. Her hand should be right below Dad's foot. I should be able to hear her breathing, which gets fast and hard this high up. I don't see her hand. I don't hear her breath.

"Is Mama hurt? Is something wrong?" I need Dad to answer. I can't keep climbing until I know where Mama is, why this day isn't like other days. I look up—a hundred near-gods in blue are almost all the way to Olympus, ready to eat their apples and come back down to earth. But we're

3

hanging here, the ladder swaying from the wind: from the people above us, or from Dad's panic, it's hard to say.

"Penny. You can't stay there," Dad says. His voice is stern now, but panicked, too, like she's not listening to something very important he's trying to tell her.

"Stay where? Dad, what's going on?"

Above me, Apple's mom, Heather, shouts my name, her voice high and screeching. "What's going on? Is everything okay?" She's nearly all the way into the clouds, ready to climb off the ladder and say a quiet hello to her ancestors Zeus and Hera. They honestly barely ever acknowledge us when we arrive, sitting on their enormous thrones. They wait for us to thank them, and they make sure we are in blue. They remind us it's our way to stay connected to our home in the sky, a home that is really only our ancestors' home.

"I don't know. Dad's not answering." I tilt my chin up to her so that my voice will carry. The ladder feels even narrower, even wobblier, so I have to grip harder. So hard my palms hurt, my knuckles hurt, my head hurts. "Dad. Where's Mama? What's going on? Everyone's worried."

"Penny," Dad's saying, "you have to come up here. You have to have apple. It's solstice. You have to— Penny, you *have* to." When my parents argue, Dad gets stuck in a loop. Mama says new things, makes complicated arguments that feel a little like dances, and Dad just keeps sputtering out the same few words over and over.

I hate when they fight.

I hate whatever this is.

"Dorothy, you need to come up here right away," Heather yells to me. She can't hear Dad and I can't hear Mama and the whole game of telephone is awful and scary and wrong. "They're asking where you are. They're saying you need to get up here right away." There's wind and distance and panic and all those things make it hard to hear, hard to be heard.

"I— Something's happening," I call back up, and I know that's not enough. Heather will ask a hundred different questions that I can't answer, so I tune her out, look down again. The ladder shivers. The statues below make Our Hill look crowded, busy, messy. I lean my body out a little, to get a better look at where the ladder meets the earth. And right there, in that place, is my mother. Penny Hardy. Dressed in a royal blue sleeveless jumpsuit, her hair in two braids pinned at the top of her head, her shoulders bare, her eyes wide and teary. I strain to hear what she's saying. Her hands wave, shooing me up, up, and away, but she doesn't move toward the ladder, she doesn't grab on, she doesn't climb.

A hundred years pass, or maybe three seconds, and Dad sighs. "Go, Dorothy," he says.

"When's Mama going to get on the ladder?" I ask.

"We have to go, Dorothy," Dad says again, his voice a straight line, an arrow through all the things I'm feeling and wondering and worrying over.

"Shouldn't we wait for her?"

"Dorothy. Now. Climb." He is growling, a sound he never makes, and I lean to look at Mama again and she's nodding, her mouth is maybe saying *go go go* but it's hard to hear what's being said on earth when you're in the sky.

"But—"

"NOW!" It isn't Dad this time. It's a voice from above, it's *the* voice from above. It's Zeus. And he means it.

I think my heart stays where it is, but my body moves, and I don't know why or how, exactly, except that Zeus and my father are both telling me the same thing, which is to climb, to get to the sky, to do it fast, to stop waiting for whatever it is I'm waiting for, which is my mother, who isn't moving. So I do what they say and a few blue and blistery and blustery minutes later, I am in the clouds, I am at the top of Mount Olympus, the real top, away from the earthbound mountain that mortal humans visit in Greece, and up where the gods live. The place we left behind. The place we return to every year to make sure we are still near-gods, we are still immortal, we are still ourselves.

At the top of the ladder, Heather takes my hand, helps me onto the cloudy ground, then helps Dad, too. Apple, who is my age but made of something entirely different than the quiet and wild things I'm made of, straightens my blue dress, smooths down my hair. She's done it a hundred times before. We have touched like this more than we've talked, I think.

"Penny?" Heather asks, my mom's name now just a question.

"She didn't come," Dad says. "She just— She didn't come."

We are still. Everything but our hearts and our hands, which shake and shake and shake.

We eat apple. We look at Olympus and declare it beautiful. We promise to come back next year. We say again and again and again that no, we don't want to stay, we love Our Hill.

And then we climb back down. It is simple.

It is supposed to be really simple.

Simple things are made awkward and heartbreaking when essential things change. Essential things like Mama climbing up the ladder with the rest of us.

When we are all back on earth, made immortal for another earthly year, our near-godship renewed and sturdy and easy, it snows. Like every other year except also nothing like those other years at all.

The snow is meant to tell us something, I guess.

Maybe it's all of them—Apollo and Poseidon and the rest—telling us we are theirs. We can slip into human towns and cities from time to time, to visit and observe and even interact once in a while, like our humanness is a thing to be practiced, tried out in public. And occasionally humans will find themselves on Our Hill, confused, always, be it because of our blue clothing or our endless statues and the ways we hide from them.

We are a little bit human, but we belong to the gods. They don't let us forget.

Which is why it is the same every solstice, a series of reminders of whose we are. Blisters, blue, apple crunch, snowfall. We do what we have done, and they do what they have done, and Our Hill remains the same. Until it doesn't. Until it shifts.

It's funny. Or, well, not funny, but it's the awful kind of true that's actually pretty impossible to understand. How little it takes to shift the whole world, until it happens.

You'd think, as near-gods, we'd know that the world is always ready to shift, to break, to be rebuilt. Columns can crumble, after all. Rivers can dry up. Apple trees can wither if there isn't enough rain or sun.

But we never think of those things. Maybe no one really does.

Back on earth, the snow catches in Mama's eyelashes. She doesn't wipe it away. Dad stands next to her and me next to Dad. Heather paces around. Apple tells her mother a dozen times to calm down, to please calm down.

"I don't want to be a god anymore," Mom says at last. Her smile is a sad one, but it's there. "I just— I wanted to know what would happen. If I stopped doing a thing I never really wanted to do to begin with." She shrugs, like it's nothing. Like magic and immortality and history and Olympus mean nothing. "I want a life that is all mine, that doesn't belong to them. With their rules and their judgments and— I mean, look at this place. I just want to be here. On earth. A real person on earth. People live long and beautiful and full lives, and that's what I want. To live a long and beautiful human life looking up at the clouds, not climbing into them."

So she does. Look at them, I mean. And that's really all she does for a good long while.

The clouds seem close when you're looking up at them like we do all year. Because even though Olympus isn't visible from earth, from the bottom of the ladder, you know it's there, the way you know all sorts of invisible things are there—seasons and power and history and love.

And tradition.

Except that's not here anymore actually, after all.

Mama took care of that.

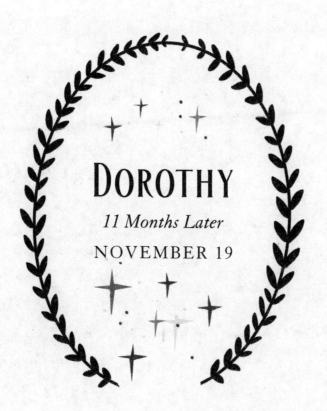

DOROTHY

11 Months Later

NOVEMBER 19

1.

The sun comes up early on Our Hill this morning.

It does that sometimes, the whim of one near-god or another, trying to sneak in an extra hour with their family, worrying about this patch of roses or that of cucumbers, or maybe just missing the sun's light because of sadness or sickness or the funny sort of longing that comes from having two homes, two places to belong.

Our powers here on earth are limited, and the timing of the sun in the sky is one of the few things we can control, usually.

Whatever the reason, I'm happy to see it. An extra hour of sunlight means more time outside, more time to myself, more time to climb into a tree or throw rocks in the river or to hole up in the attic, where Mama had just begun the tapestry she was weaving. Maybe, if enough spare hours of sunlight appear, I might finish it for her someday.

I'm listing all the things I could do with the extra time while I wander into the kitchen, hoping to grab a clementine and a mug of hot chocolate to take with me on a long walk before school starts. Dad shouldn't be up yet. The sun can't sneak its way into his heavy-curtained room. He's never wanted extra sunlight.

Until today I guess. Because he's standing at the kitchen counter, an apron tied around his waist, covering his red pajamas. Dad used to sleep in togas, even though most of the rest of us prefer the nightgowns and pajamas of humans—flannel and fleecy and footed. But lately he's taken to wearing a pair of red pajamas Mama made him.

Dad looks good in red. Mama always said that. She wished other people could have known that about him.

"Morning, buglet," he says.

"Morning."

He sees the confused look on my face and gives a sad sort of smile.

"It's her birthday," he says. "I rose the sun early for her. For us. So we could have more of the day."

It's rare for him to do much of anything godlike here on earth, so I hadn't imagined it could be him. And I'd

14

forgotten the date, too. November 19. Mama's birthday. Nearly eleven months since the climb she didn't take to Olympus.

"Big day," Dad says, but it isn't. Not anymore. So I don't know why my heart squeezes at the thought of it. I sit down; my body suddenly feels too heavy to hold up. I would have told the sun to rise even later, would have asked it to set early, would have made the day short and dark and chilly. We're not much alike, me and Dad. Maybe I'm not really much like anyone.

I was a little like Mama. But I don't know if it counts, to be like someone who's gone.

Dad's baking bread. It used to be Mama's job, but now it's his. Except it isn't a job—it isn't something that has to be done. We could get bread at the store. We could whirl a hand around in the air and make it appear. Another magic we are allowed—the magical making of bread, cake, soup, sandwiches.

But Mama loved to make it all by hand, like mortals do, the bread especially, so I guess it feels like something that has to be done. A floury smell that has to haunt the house, a warmth in our home's heart that we need in order to survive.

It has been eleven months since the climb she didn't take.

But it has been ten months since the accident.

Mama would never have refused the climb if she'd known. But how would she have known? We miss so much of what it is to be human, and when we learn something new it shocks us, always.

Always.

"You want a slice with honey?" Dad asks, waiting for me to say something, anything, I guess. I shake my head. "Heather and Apple are bringing some cheese. There's jam in the fridge, can you get it?"

"Bread and cheese and jam?" I say, still trying to join this version of the morning after imagining an entirely different one for myself. "That's the whole thing?"

"That's the whole thing, Dorothy," Dad says, "unless there's something you'd like to do. To honor her. Or to—"

"No, thanks." When Mama was here, we celebrated her birthday the regular way. With cake and candles, balloons and presents. Dad would sing "Happy Birthday" in the beautiful voice he's known for, Mama and I would try to keep up, attempt harmonies or even a little bit of the prettiness of his singing, but we'd fail and apologize and he'd grin and say we sounded like muses, and we'd say he was lying, and he'd shrug instead of admitting the truth. Here, we can only be what the gods have made us. Here, we are all shadows of the more powerful gods and muses from which we descended.

Maybe that's something else Mama wanted to free herself from.

Without Mama here, there's no reason to have cake, but Dad insisted Heather and Apple had to come. *It's what Mama would have wanted*, he said. So I had to agree.

And then, of course, I forgot.

Something I didn't know about death—because I know nothing about death—is that it makes the rest of you foggy. Even if I'm not actively missing Mama, my brain isn't totally available to me. So I forget things like math tests and Dad's coffee order when I offer to pick some up for him, and a planned birthday party, I guess, for the only person from Our Hill who has ever died.

My heart does something that feels like a hiccup. When I remember how much I hurt, my heart startles and my head swims and I get a little bit lost. Dad sees it happen this time and puts a hand on my shoulder. It's steadying. But I still wish I could leave this moment and end the day before it has a chance to really begin.

"I don't know how to do this," Dad says. We both realize at the same time that his hand on my shoulder has an oven mitt on it, and we laugh, which weirdly is a thing we can still do sometimes. He takes off the mitts and straightens Mama's old apron. It's polka-dotted and all wrong on him. "No one can tell me what to do for this day. Penny loved fresh bread and good cheese. And who doesn't like jam? I don't know. It's breakfast. It's her birthday. I'm sad. I'm doing my best."

It's hard to be mad at Dad when he says things so plainly, which is what he does lately. Sometimes he lists his feelings like he's a little kid learning what they are for the first time. *Look at this frowning mouth and downcast eyes. This is sadness. Sadness feels sleepy and gray and heavy.*

I get the jam from the fridge and find the wooden cutting board Mama liked to place her bread on. I lay out delicate pink-gold plates brought down from Mount Olympus generations ago and a fading white pitcher that Mama said our ancestor Pandora used for her own morning milk back in her day, before she opened the box, before she brought misery to earth.

"This?" I ask Dad. We don't use the plates, the pitcher, often. Most everything in our kitchen is from stores in town—the sorts of places real people have in their towns, too—a bookstore with a tabby cat inside, a clothing store for people who like their blue dresses to be floral and silk, a home store that sells heavy jewel-toned plates and spatulas that look too fancy to actually use. So much of the town is normal enough that if regular people came by, they'd think it was a town like any other. We're here to live human lives, mostly. We're here to understand them and be like them.

Except for the columns. The statues. The blue dresses and togas and sweaters and swishy pants.

Oh. And the ladder. And the way it gives us immortality. If we climb it.

Heart. Hiccup. Heavy sigh.

"Sure, let's use the good stuff," Dad says. The bread is done, so he scoops it out of the oven with two bulky mitts back over his hands and I make room for the steam, the toasty presence of it, like it's something sacred. Which it sort of is. It's ours. Other families here don't bake their own bread. They don't let their homes get cluttered. And they don't have dead mothers.

Heather and Apple come right in like always, without knocking. They are a gust of wind in our house, which smells like sourdough and the promise of melted butter. With them comes the early fall breeze, light and chilly today. We haven't been out in it much. We haven't been much of anywhere. Just school and home. Dad plays piano in one corner of the house and I read books about other people's sadness in the windowed, starlit corner, or work on Mama's tapestry upstairs where the roof slopes the perfect amount to make me feel cozy, and I think about doing the sorts of things I used to do with Mama—dipping my feet in the river or climbing a tree or hiking.

Those were Mama's things. That's what Mama liked

about living on the mortal earth. That's why she wanted to stay, I think. To be human. To promise herself to earth instead of having to belong to the sky.

Her not-here-ness has turned those things heavy and sad.

"Beautiful sun, George," Heather says instead of hello. I wonder how she knows it was his doing. Heather always knows things, though. About who said what, and what the gods on Olympus think of it, and which earthly matters we should concern ourselves with, and why some days feel too long or too short or too rainy or not rainy enough.

Which I guess makes it even harder to understand why she didn't know what Mama was going to do on the last winter solstice.

Or what would happen a month later.

"We brought Havarti," Apple says. We all know it was Mama's favorite. History matters a lot on Our Hill, and we memorize things like what Zeus liked to eat and do and say and what Apollo wore and how Aphrodite moved through the world. It matters—that Pandora wore her strawberry-blond hair long and wavy, that the box she opened was bronze and heavy, that she tried to close it but failed, that she loved beautiful things. That her curiosity was dangerous. That her greed brought misery.

And that she loved soft, mellow cheeses and the rising of the sun.

Like Mama.

Like me, too.

"Thank you," I say, and it sounds weird. Formal. Like we've never met before.

Heather and Apple, with their long dark curls and bright blue eyes and airy voices, have been in our home hundreds of times, but today they don't quite fit. They wear blue dresses and long gold chains and look exactly the way we are supposed to look. Bright. Powerful. Happy. Immortal.

It's been a while since we've all been in our kitchen together for longer than a moment. Every month they drop off something delicious to eat and a bouquet of flowers that Heather arranges in a vase while she asks Dad how he's holding up. Maybe this is what humans do when someone dies. I wonder how it feels to them.

Apple comes too on these monthly check-ins. Sometimes she asks if I've done the homework yet, or whether I've listened to a certain song that everyone else is listening to. But mostly we don't know what to talk about or even what to do with our hands, so we just stand at the kitchen counter and trace letters, shapes, whole paragraphs maybe, onto the marble surface.

Today is different. Today they are here for this strange, sad birthday breakfast, not just to drop something off.

"Wow," Heather says, and I'm not sure if she's talking

about the state of our house—messy—the state of my hair—messier—or the bigness of the day—huge or nothing at all, I guess, depending on how you look at it. Apple's eyes are wide and her hand is over her heart like something hurts right there.

"Sorry, we aren't good at cleaning," I say, piling some papers on top of each other like that will make a difference. "Mama always said Pandora was probably the messiest one in those days. Messy and curious in every way, good and bad. So, I'm probably the same."

"It's not that," Heather says. "Messy is fine. You know that. We don't mind messy." This must be true, because Heather and Mama were so entwined, so deep in friendship, that they had tea every morning on the tallest point of Our Hill, right under the silver ladder, and had lemon cake every evening by the river. They talked about everything, except of course her plan to not climb the ladder, to stop being a near-god and start being just a regular human.

I look at Heather now for signs that she knows something I don't about the day Mama didn't climb, but she's the same Heather she's always been. Straight nose, straight back, elegant and austere and exactly the sort of person you'd think was descended of Zeus and Hera.

Apple is her spitting image. Heather, but a little smaller. Almost as intimidating. Almost as perfect.

"It's like she's here," Apple says, her voice shaky and small in a way I've never heard. She loved my mom. Not as much as I did, but strongly in her own way. She was dedicated to letting my mother teach her to cross-stitch. She ate Mama's crooked loaves of bread and declared them her favorite food. She begged my mother to braid her hair, to lend her a bracelet, to tell her, again, the stories from the past that everyone knows by heart but my mother told with a particular flair, a little less reverence, a little more bemusement.

"It smells just like it used to," Heather goes on, putting her hand on my dad's arm.

"Perfect," Apple says, and she smiles softly now too. Sometimes I was a little envious of how she and Mama were together. How similar they were. They had the same easy way about them, like finding the right words for the right circumstance was no problem at all. Like they knew they belonged in any room they entered, and if they didn't, they'd figure out a way to.

"Well, not perfect, I'm sure," Dad says, but he's blushing, and I can tell the compliment means something to him. I inhale, trying to smell it too, trying to get a sense of her being with us the way they all seem to.

I don't know much about dying—none of us on Our Hill know much about it. We climb the ladder and have the slice of apple from the tree that Apple's ancestor, Hera, nurtured and protected, and then we return to earth, immortal like the rest of the gods, hanging on to bits and pieces of our inherited powers—diluted over time by generations passing and the trip back and forth from earth to sky every year—but still there is enough to make a cherry pie, to stop a blizzard, to wake the sun a little early. Then we live, as generations before us have, right here. In blue dresses and blue sweaters and blue bows in our hair or hats on our heads. Blue like the sky, a reminder of where we come from, a bit of the heavens down here on earth. Mama was always quick to remind me we wore blue like the sky, yes, but also like Athena's eyes: "Zeus granted her one wish, and she wished that the whole world could encounter her beauty every day. So he turned the skies the color of her beautiful eyes."

I told Mama this didn't seem that wise, for the celebrated goddess of wisdom. We have always been told to honor her the most, since wisdom is what we seek here on earth.

"Making the world beautiful has a wisdom to it," Mama said. And like so many things she said, I was still trying to understand exactly what it meant.

I have time to figure it out, I guess. Because we live and live and live, and we don't die. We feel out all the different ages, then go back and freeze ourselves at whichever ones we fall in love with. Sixteen or thirty-seven or eighty-two. And then we stay there forever. Some of the kids in class with us are generations older, but they don't act any different. Their bodies and minds are eleven. Sometimes they seem a little bored in class, having learned the same things thousands of times over, but that's all any of us are really doing anyway. Learning the ancient myths. Honoring the gods that we left in the sky.

Sometimes, not often but I can think of a few examples, there is an eighty-year-old person who is the child of a twenty-year-old, and it can look a little funny, I guess, their bodies in familiar shapes, their mouths saying parent and child words, but at the wrong ages. We're used to it, though, because we have forever to get used to the strangeness of living this weird mishmash of godly and human life.

Except for Mom.

The evening after the climb she didn't take, she tried to talk to me about it, all watery-eyed and shaky, like she'd just woken up from an important type of dream. "We think we know more than the humans," she said, "but they know more than us. About living. And I want to live. You get that, right? I want to live the way they do. I don't want to be half of something and half of something else, and not really fully anyone at all. I want to be someone. I want it to have meaning. I don't want to choose an age and stay there forever. I want to know life. The real kind." She went on about how wonderful it would be, to be old and wise, how every day would matter, how she loved the earth and the humans muddling along on top of it.

It almost made sense. It was starting to make sense, and she was so happy, and her happiness made sense.

And then a car from out of town came around a corner too fast, and it zipped away without stopping to check the woman who had taken the full force of it. And then she was gone.

Now nothing makes sense.

She'd never talked about how humans don't all get to live to be one hundred and wrinkled and smiling at the lives they lived. I don't know that she'd ever considered it. We'd never had to consider it. Human life was a story we told each other, not a thing we actually understood. There is so much we never considered, so much that is now thrumming around, right here, right now, even in our kitchen with warm bread and the way Heather talks a little too fast and the missing piece of Mom who knew just how to slow her down. Apple tries now, with a hand on her elbow, but Heather plows forward, not noticing, because Heather never notices things like that.

My legs ache and I don't want bread and the sun is hurting my eyes, the way it's coming in through the windows.

I don't know much about dying, but everyone else seems to sense my mother somewhere around us—in the smell of bread or the color of the wildflowers that grow on the steepest parts of the hill. Even, they say, in my voice, which sometimes growls and breaks like hers used to, an unexpected roughness when otherwise our voices are sweet, decent at carrying a tune, hard to hear in a crowd. But I don't feel her anywhere.

Sometimes I don't feel me anywhere, either.

So I just keep waiting. And waiting. And waiting.

2.

The bread is still warm.

"Honestly, it really is perfect," Heather says.

"Mom, you've said that already," Apple sighs. "We both have." Her voice is airy with a pinch. Apple herself is airy with a pinch—she's so popular, so beloved, that it almost feels strange to be in a room with her, except I've been in rooms with her my whole entire life. She's so popular that I think she doesn't even notice popularity, like she's floating above it, like maybe part of her is up on Mount Olympus with Hera and the rest of her is down here on Our Hill with us, a little annoyed that we keep pestering her with questions about vocabulary and dishwashing and where she got her prettiest blue dress.

It's a funny thing to ask, really. There is only one dress store in town. Otherwise, it can be assumed that it was made by magic. And it doesn't matter much, who is wearing what. We are all in blue, to honor Athena's wisdom, in the hopes we find our own by being down here. And to remind ourselves we are from the sky. Usually our blues are draped like togas or fashioned the way we've seen humans do. Sometimes we stick flowers in our hair, in the summer we have gold sandals, and in the winter we pull on tights and boots and wonder what the gods think of us, playing in the snow and bundling ourselves in wool and fleece when we could just as easily ask the winter not to come.

I asked Mama once why we don't use magic much down here, why we let things be, most of the time. She smiled, like it was her favorite part of Our Hill. "We choose this life," she said. "We choose the earth, and this is what the earth does. It rains and snows and makes a mess of dinner if you keep the rice too long in the pot and it makes some days hard and others easy depending on silly things, like what time your body wakes you up or whether or not the tree you are allergic to is blooming."

"Up there, there aren't bad days?" I asked.

She shrugged. Sighed. "Our families came down here because there were other kinds of bad days. They're gods, of course. They're wonderful and powerful but also . . ." She shook her head and let the sentence drift away. "It's different up there," she said, and then her cooking timer beeped us away from our words, and I thought the conversation would continue but time ran out in ways that weren't supposed to be possible.

Now we live in this house that is absolutely crammed with unfinished conversations, things that were supposed to be said someday but were never said because someday doesn't exist anymore.

"Your mom loved birthdays," Heather says. She's the only one sitting at the counter—the rest of us are leaning against it, like we haven't decided if we're going to stay. Apple's chin quivers. Shivers.

Something inside me does too, even though I keep telling it not to.

"I'm sorry, Dorothy," Apple says. "It's awful. It's completely awful."

It's weird, because it's been ten months and I guess she's said some version of this from time to time since my mom died a few weeks after the solstice. I remember her at Mom's funeral, giving me a hug and whispering in my ear, "How do humans survive this?" as if I knew the answer. The funeral was awful, a bunch of near-gods pouring tea for me and Dad and draping black scarves over their blue dresses, trying to remember how grief was done, what it looked like when we'd watched it from afar. Our families have been living on Our Hill for generations, trying to get closer to human life, trying to understand the very people gods are meant to help and guide. But not a single person knew what to say or where to look, as if we'd forgotten to study this one especially vital part of the human experience.

Now Apple's hand reaches out for mine and I let her hold it. No one's held my hand since my mother, whose was cool and soft and always reaching for mine—when we crossed streets, when we read books, when we did Happy and Sad, our end-of-day ritual when we told each other one good and one bad thing from our day, when we drank hot chocolate by the river on fall mornings, the way she liked to do.

My whole body wants hot chocolate and to know the best and worst part of my mother's day and to have her hand wrapped around mine.

"Yeah. It's awful." I don't know what to say, so I just take another bite of bread, wishing I'd spread more honey on it.

Apple's hand squeezes mine and hers is cool and soft like Mama's, just smaller. I hang on to it. I don't let go.

"We're glad you could both be here," Dad says, and I notice he has flour in his beard, sunk into his knuckles, on the collar of his shirt. Mama would have had him clean himself up. She would have put him back together. We are all kinds of messy without her. And the gods don't like mess, at least not the kinds of mess they haven't made themselves. "You remember on her last birthday, she asked for three cakes since she couldn't decide on a flavor? Vanilla, chocolate, and— What was the third, do you remember?"

I don't. My heart sinks at the empty space where the specifics of the memory should be.

"Lemon," Apple says.

"Lemon!" I repeat, my whole self lighting up with knowing, with having a new fact that is true, that I can hold, that I can be sure of. "Lemon cake." I smile and Apple squeezes my hand again.

"I remember," she says.

Maybe this is why Apple is the most loved person on Our Hill. Or at least the most loved twelve-year-old. Her voice, which knows how to be sure, and her hand, which knows how to be strong, and her hair, of course, which knows how to curl and hang and stay in place. She is practically Hera herself—dark haired and elegant in a way kids aren't supposed to be. Meanwhile, I've dripped honey on my toga already. I have always been a little too human.

Mama liked it about me. But she's gone. Now I'm just the human mess without the love she wrapped me all up in. I try to rub the honey from my dress with my free hand and it only makes it worse. Now my fingers are all sticky too.

"I'll remember when you can't," Apple says. She must notice my sticky honey fingers and the blotch on my dress, but she doesn't say anything else. We've never been exactly close, Apple and I, or at least not close the way our mothers wanted us to be. She has a hundred friends and I don't really have any. She looks like a true goddess in a blue dress and I always look too small and too itchy in whatever I put on. She can say she misses my mother like it's something simple and pure, and I don't say it at all, because I know if I did it would come out messy and snotty and ugly.

But right now, holding my hand, reminding me about lemon cake, Apple feels close. Like a friend.

"Happy birthday, Penny," Heather says to the ceiling.

"Mm," Dad hums. Like me, he doesn't ever find the words to say, so we settle for sounds and gestures and the heft of silence.

"I brought flowers," Apple says. She pulls two cherry blossoms out of her pocket. On Olympus, Apple's family protects the tree that grows golden apples of immortality. Here on earth, they have a cherry blossom tree that is always in bloom in front of their home.

Mama loved it.

I mean, everyone does. But Mama maybe most of all.

Mama knew how to love beautiful things harder than everyone else.

She loved me harder too. Loved that I am quiet and strange. Loved that my hair only gets messier if you try to brush it, that my dresses don't fit right, and mostly loved that I don't care.

She said other people would get me too, someday, but it sounded like the sort of thing said to cover up the truth, which was that I would never fit in.

Apple stands behind me now. Without hesitation, she puts her fingers to my hair and braids it into two plaits, which she crosses up and over my head. She sticks the blossom into the weave, then does the same to herself. Her fingers move fast; I don't have a chance to decide if I want my wavy strawberry-blond hair in something so elaborate. I mostly opt for a low, slowly twisting bun that undoes itself during the day, my uneven bangs lazy on my forehead.

"It looks good," Apple says, and I catch sight of myself in the oven's reflective surface, and she's right. It looks good, simple and befitting of an almost-god, similar to pictures I've seen of Pandora thousands of years ago. She always looks delicate and innocent, despite the stories about her mistakes, despite the misery she brought to earth.

She looked exactly the way the gods wanted her to look, I guess, because they made her. And then when she made a mistake, she was hated. We've been told the story a hundred times a year, at least, for our whole lives, but it's still hard for me to understand.

The tapestry in the attic that Mama began was supposed to be of Pandora, too. "Everyone else around here is celebrated through art," Mama said, sunny but also serious. "Statues and paintings, and I mean, gosh, Heather wears that golden charm of Hera's face around her neck. Apple has their names on bracelets. I want something beautiful showing who we come from too."

I didn't argue. Mama had heard all the arguments. That we don't celebrate someone who ruined the perfect place that earth was supposed to be. We don't make beautiful artwork of someone whose actions caused something so ugly.

Mama would hear those arguments, shake her head, and say, "Your premise is faulty," and move right along, like she knew something we didn't, like her tapestry was meant to tell us what that was.

"Why do you like Pandora so much?" I asked her when she started what was supposed to be her tapestry masterpiece.

"She's ours," she said.

"But isn't that just our bad luck?"

"There's more to her," Mama said. "But some things you have to figure out without being told. You'll understand more when you need to; when it's meant for you." Mama went on weaving the tapestry she'd never finish, and I went on wondering why she had to make things a mystery.

"You look like your mom in those braids," Dad says now, a little sad and a little happy, too.

What I don't understand about history is how to get away from it ever. Or why it attaches to you and shows up in the way you blink or smile or sing or how you look in braids.

Apple's hand finds mine again. Most of the bread is

uneaten, and I wonder if Dad will put it in the bread box or throw it away. Can you eat your dead mom's birthday bread after her actual birthday? What exactly are the rules about bread and death and families and love? Shouldn't the gods have figured this all out a little more tidily?

The rest of Our Hill is so obsessed with all the things we have to celebrate about the gods. But lately, I have some complaints. I lock them in my throat and tell them not to come out.

"I know the girls need to get to school," Heather says, "but I'm glad we could honor Penny like this. I don't know how the others out there do it." She gestures to the whole rest of the earthbound world. Everyone who doesn't live on Our Hill. Everyone not descended from the gods, everyone who has always been mortal and tied to right here until they are gone. Everyone who practices, over and over, saying goodbye forever.

We have been taught to find mortals a little bit silly and a little bit naive and very weak. We have been taught about the way they fail, the way they look to gods for guidance, the many mistakes they have made here on earth.

We roll our eyes. We sigh. We talk about how much better we would do, given the chance.

But there are things those mortal humans know that I can't seem to learn. There are ways they survive, go on in spite of terrible things, balance the limits of time, that we have never had to understand.

Until now.

Until Mama and me and Dad and our little family that broke the world on Our Hill.

3.

I have never walked to school with Apple before.

That's not entirely true. A long time ago when Apple and I were little, our moms walked us to school together, the two of them holding teacups, wearing matching gold sandals, taking slow steps while Apple and I raced, then stopped, then raced, then stopped. It was probably the closest we ever were, running to school in that stop-and-start way but never really talking.

But even back then it didn't take long for us to slide into our destined places—Apple at the top and me at the bottom and everyone else somewhere in the middle depending on which god they'd descended from and what mistakes or victories that god is known for. And pretty soon, Apple and

Heather stopped walking to school with us, a choice that would make Mama swallow and blush when I asked her why.

I knew why. Apple had other friends, better ones who were suited to her place in the school, her place here on Our Hill. Mama and Heather could be friends, because Mama was that special kind of beautiful and friendly and warm that helped people overlook who she came from.

I am not those things.

This walk today feels strange because of the history of us floating alongside it.

"Do you think she knew?" Apple asks. We were walking in silence, and now we're almost at the schoolhouse, and she says the words like they're no big deal, like I should have known they were coming.

"Knew what?" I ask. I walk a little faster and hope she asks something simple—like if my mom knew I wasn't popular, knew it would be an exceptionally chilly autumn, knew my dad would be good at baking bread in her absence.

"Do you think that at her last birthday she already knew she wasn't going to climb the ladder to Olympus? Because I remember that birthday and it was fun and she seemed happy and I don't know if that means that she knew or didn't know."

I look at Apple. She still sounds sort of breezy, but the look on her face is something else.

"I don't know."

"But she decided at some point, right? Like, she decided at some point before the actual day of solstice. When do you think it was?" There's a line between Apple's eyebrows that I've never seen before. Maybe this is the most deeply she's ever thought about anything.

"I guess," I say. There's a rushing noise in my head, like things are moving too quickly. I am still trying to understand that Mama is gone, and I haven't really gotten to *why* she's gone yet. In the distance, I can see the silver ladder. The sun glints against the highest rung. It is long and thin and looks delicate, leaning like it does against the clouds. "She decided not to climb the ladder," I say, because this is the one thing I do know, for sure, and don't have questions about, "but she thought she'd live to be old. She wanted time to be a human. She thought she'd have lots of time."

"Maybe they all think that," Apple says. She means all the humans, and I wonder if they do, or if they're used to the random heartbreak, the sudden change of everything they've ever known. Is that a thing you can get used to?

When we visit human towns to learn about human lives, we don't get to ask them questions about whether they think about dying, or how, exactly, they tolerate the way they have to get hurt over and over and over again.

We stay away from them, acting as sort of shadows so that they don't notice us. We buy things like toasters and watercolors of the ocean and paperclips and spicy salsa, and we try to say nothing at all.

Maybe it should be different.

"I don't know what they think," I say.

"I asked my mom why your mom would do that, and she said it has something to do with Pandora and your whole ancestry and destiny and I don't know, my mom is obsessed with that stuff so I guess she always thinks that's the reason for everything."

"Everyone's obsessed with that stuff," I say, because it is one of the biggest truths of our lives here. We learn the myths of our ancestors over and over again, weaving tapestries of the gods and writing poems about their lives and reciting the facts of each story until the words basically lose all meaning. We learn history, we make art about history, we talk about history, we promise that we understand it.

"That's true," Apple says. The sun shifts behind a cloud and it's suddenly a little colder. We pull our jackets more tightly around ourselves. I pull up my hood. Apple rubs her hands together.

"We need to go inside," I say, because it seems like Apple's forgotten what we're even doing. She's just standing there outside the door to the school, which is tiny and brick and golden and smelling of laurels. There is a statue of Athena out front, not the kind in museums in the human world, but one made by us at school, carved from a tree, a

41

little lopsided and strange, but beautiful, too. Every building in town has a statue of a god outside of it. Every home has something honoring them too. They are everywhere, reminding us of who we are.

As if we could ever forget. I sometimes feel magic in my fingertips or tingling along the curve of my ear, a feeling Mama called *the pull*, a reminder that we can change snow to sun or coffee to chocolate, a reminder that we will live forever, a reminder that we aren't human. The gods humming in our ears, calling us back to Olympus.

Pulling us toward the sky.

It startles the back of my neck now, and I strain to brush it away like it's a bug.

"Maybe we shouldn't," Apple says.

"Shouldn't go inside?"

"Shouldn't care so much about all the history." That deep line digs itself into Apple's forehead again.

"Don't let them hear you say that," I say with an almost-smile. It's the sort of thing Mama would have wanted to discuss, quietly, by the river, where she'd hope the rush of water was loud enough to cover up the sound. The gods up there don't mind us playing here on earth, as long as we don't lose sight of who we are. Apple knows that as well as I do, but maybe she's forgetting. Maybe she hasn't been sent a shiver of magic lately. Hasn't been pulled by the gods.

Missing my mother makes me forget things too, sometimes.

"I care about *our* history," Apple says, whispering so that either the gods or the girls she's best friends with, who are moving toward us fast, don't hear. "I care about our moms and all the things our families did together and your mom's birthday last year and that she's not here now. I care about that stuff, you know? I know it's been a while since she— since the car—but that stuff is real. And today just really made me—"

"Apple, oh my god, that dress is literally perfect, do you like mine? Come on," Dawn says, moving quickly from one side of the yard to the other. She wears her black hair in a long straight ponytail down her back and has light brown skin. Most people on Our Hill don't look too similar to the gods and muses that many humans think of today. Those days were long ago, and many generations have followed. We've seen humans in normal towns care so much about what everyone looks like. We've watched terrible things happen to all kinds of people down below who aren't white.

I don't fully know what it's like for Dawn, or Chloe, or any of the many other near-gods who aren't white to watch that. It's the sort of thing Mama would have asked about, but I don't know how to have conversations the way Mama did. It's always seemed that up here, on Our Hill, nothing matters but what god you've descended from.

Dawn is followed by ivory-skinned, towering-tall Reece, who has maybe never looked directly at me. They are Apple's best friends, and their ancestors are Poseidon and Ares, other powerful gods whose descendants here are given adoration and respect. Those of us descended of muses and minor gods and flawed humans, even, are never invited into their little world of picnics by the silver ladder and front-row seats in class and sleepover parties under the moon.

At least, I'm not.

"It's nice," Apple says. "You guys go in, I'm talking to Dorothy."

"Oh. Hi, Dorothy," Dawn says. She looks nervous at having to talk to me, but she stays pleasant in spite of herself.

"We don't hang out with Dorothy," Reece says. She speaks without any sorry in her voice, and it makes me confused—like maybe I'm wrong, for being hurt.

Apple's popularity makes sense—she is bubbly and composed and when Hera sees her up in Olympus, at the tree, she holds Apple's face in her hands and smiles at it. We all see that, and it matters. Reece's popularity is different. It's built on everyone being afraid of what she might say. It's built on her closeness to Apple and the ruthless way she doesn't let anyone else get near.

Dawn and Apple both roll their eyes. That one eye roll holds a novel-sized amount of shared history. This is the kind of thing Reece does, and this is how Apple and Dawn always respond.

Being known like that seems scary.

"It's not funny," Reece says. "Dorothy and her family are trying to ruin things here. My dad says so. He says there will be consequences, for what Penny did." Sometimes I get the feeling that people are waiting around for me to apologize for my mother, explain what she did and why she did it, and let them all know that I am appropriately ashamed of it or her or myself, even.

What no one here on Our Hill understands is that grief is so big that guilt can't even get in. I miss my mother so enormously that there's no room for all those other ugly feelings they want me to feel.

"What's changed for you, Reece?" I ask. "In the last ten months, what's different in your life?" I've maybe never asked her anything directly before, and she looks about as stunned as I'd imagine.

"I'm just saying they're angry. The gods. Because of your mom," Reece says. "No offense. We all miss her. But still."

Reece is the kind of person who says "no offense" instead of just saying something nicer to begin with. Mama always said there's something to like about everyone, but it's hard to find that something right now with Reece.

"You miss my mom a lot?" I go on, the words a freight train that I didn't mean to start up.

Reece looks at the ground. So does Dawn.

Apple sort of smiles—the sides of her mouth shuddering up, then relaxing.

"Sure," Reece says, tucking hair behind her ear, looking at the door to the building like she should have walked in it ages ago. "I mean, everyone loved— Your mom was nice. Of course I miss her."

I try to remember a single time when Reece and my mother might have spoken, but nothing comes to mind. I can't even think of a time *I've* spoken to Reece. Mostly, I don't speak to anyone, and that's the way I like it. If I have something to say I wait to go to the river and I tell the fish. I tell the birds. Or lately I tell Mama, wherever she is, hoping that she's somehow listening.

"Well, that's great," I say. "You missing her. So nice. I'm sure that would mean a lot to her."

Reece nods. Grimaces. I've made it awkward, which is fine by me but not okay for any of them. Dawn grabs her by the elbow and pulls her toward school. "We'll see you in there, Apple," she says, swallowing before she remembers to say, "and Dorothy. Both of you. We'll see you guys."

We watch them go, Apple and I. We have another minute or two before we'll have to run in, and it seems like Apple wants to stay out here with me for as long as possible. It does feel good. We don't have a whole novel of knowing each other, but we have something else—a book of poetry

46

maybe, that spans a whole life of tiny moments that exist outside of school and friends and whatever is going on up on Olympus. We have something.

"Sorry," I say, "I didn't mean to be rude to your friends."

Apple shakes her head. "You were great," she says. "They're sometimes— They're judgy. And sort of . . . I don't know. They're really fun, but I'm not sure they get me." She lowers her voice, a secret about to spill. "I've only ever said this stuff to your mom. She knew that I wasn't sure I really fit in with them, even though I'm supposed to. You know?"

I don't really know, but I want to be like Mama, so I nod.

"See? You get me," Apple says. She loops her elbow with mine, and we walk into school like that, hooked together in this way I've never been before. It's hard to move in exact right time with each other. I trip a little, on the steps. She doesn't let go, though. Only pulls me closer in. Only grips harder.

4.

Mr. Winters is writing today's lesson on the chalkboard. On the rest of earth, they've moved on from the scritch-scratch of chalk, the way it gets on everyone's sleeves, the way the words written on the board sometimes turn to clouds before you have a chance to copy them down onto paper. We've peered into classrooms, we've snuck around schools, we know how things are now. But Mr. Winters likes chalk. He says we're here to *understand* humans, not *be* them.

Everyone else is sitting down, pretty much, except for me and Apple lingering at the door. Apple's seat is open and so is mine, but they're far away from each other, which didn't matter one bit until just this second.

Apple's elbow doesn't untangle itself from mine, and she marches us right to Chloe, who is in the seat next to Apple's. Chloe is buttoned up with straight black hair and pale skin and an undeniable calmness that makes her easy to be around. Her blue dresses always travel all the way up her neck, practically to her chin, which is also right around where her hair hits. I like Chloe, who knows absolutely everything there is to know about history, whose ancestor, Clio, was a muse who loved history too, who doesn't get caught up in whether someone has new sneakers, or started wearing a bra, or has a crush, or got a bad grade. She reads every book about history—the gods' but the humans' too. She cares more about it than anyone else here, which is saying a lot. When she speaks about it, she beams.

Sometimes Chloe and I eat lunch together outside, away from most everyone else, and we don't talk, really, but we swap my apple for her orange or my yogurt for her cheese and we read books or stare at trees and are okay, in that quiet.

Today is different. "Dorothy needs this seat," Apple says. She doesn't say it loud or mean, but it's abrupt, a stomp of the foot when everyone else is tiptoeing.

"My seat?" Chloe asks. She looks at me, as if I have any answers, and it feels like she should already know that I don't, that I'm following Apple, waiting to see what happens, just like everyone else.

"We really need to sit next to each other," Apple says. "It's Dorothy's mom's birthday." She whispers that part, and my insides squeeze uncomfortably. My mom's birthday is special. Sacred. It isn't the sort of thing you bring up to get what you want from the quietest girl in school.

"It's okay," I try to interrupt, turning to my own open seat in the back.

"Please?" Apple asks. She isn't begging. It's simple, the way it comes out, like they both know the right thing to do and Chloe just needs to do it. It's how Apple talks— sure of herself and not worried about the response. It's how my mom talked too, and I've missed it so much that I don't argue or try to go back to my old seat again.

"Sorry about your mom's birthday," Chloe says, sort of wincing as the words come out, because they don't sound quite right. We've learned about mortals our whole lives— their books and their movies and TV shows and all the old myths about the ways the gods tried to help them, tried to understand them, tried to love them and marry them and all of that.

But still, they've always been way over there and we've been right here, taking our ladder to Olympus, knowing things would stay the same forever. So trying to figure out how to be now that things have changed is awkward and strange.

"Thanks," I say, but that doesn't sound like the right

response. "It's okay," I try, but that's not exactly true. It's not okay. What do mortals say? Do they try to tell the truth or make the other person feel better or something else entirely? Do mortals with dead mothers get to take people's seats in class and do people look away from them like mortality might be contagious? "I mean, it's not okay," I say. "But it's—"

"You can have my seat," Chloe says. "I get it." Chloe gathers her stuff and Apple gives her a smile—a genuine one. That's the thing about Apple. Dawn and Reece, when they smile, it seems put on, like something they know they have to do to get what they want.

Apple's smile is different. She looks Chloe in the eyes and thanks her and beams and means it. "I knew you'd understand," she says, and Chloe smiles back. I haven't seen Chloe smile much. At our lunches she's thoughtful and kind and nice to be around, but she's not smiley. And in history class she's focused and always says something I hadn't thought about, and she nods along with what the teacher says, but she doesn't smile much there, either.

But Apple can make anyone smile.

Even me, now, today, I realize, because I'm smiling as I sit down next to Apple in the seat that used to be Chloe's.

"Everyone's settled?" Mr. Winters asks. On the board is the word ECHO, all in capital letters, and nothing else. "Who can tell us about Echo?"

We all can but it's Chloe, of course, who raises her hand to give the answer first, reciting the facts of the past, her warm brown eyes lighting up with excitement. She has a way of making even a story of cruelty and pain and the way fate can be so brutal seem meaningful and fated. "Echo was a very chatty nymph," she says, "who Hera eventually punished by making it so she could only repeat back what others could say. She's around us now when we're in a cavernous space and our words bounce back from the walls. That's Echo, reminding us she's there." Mr. Winters's chalk has been scratching out the main points of the story onto the board, and he looks up every few moments to make sure we're scribbling it down too.

Echo's story makes me sad. I look around for Coco, one of Echo's descendants here. I wonder if she feels defensive, the way I do about Pandora, or if she's fine writing down the mistakes of her ancestors over and over and over, year after year. She catches me looking at her, and sneaks her arm around her paper, like there's something there I'm not allowed to see. She frowns.

I guess my past is worse than Coco's. After all, her parents are still here, and no one suffered from Echo's mistakes but Echo herself. That's the way the gods prefer things.

Next to me, Apple writes down all the old facts too, unbothered by Hera's role in what happened to Echo. I stare at the board, at the four letters that I guess are supposed to mean something very specific, the lesson you have to learn—be quieter, listen to the gods.

On human earth they learn other things, like long division and how to talk really smartly about books and music and the rules their government makes. On our few miles of the world, it's just this, all the time, relentless reminders of mistakes that have been made and who to honor and how to wear blue and what to feel when you look up at clouds and constellations.

"What are you doing?" Apple whispers, and I look at my paper, which is just a drawing of clouds and stars, and nothing at all about Echo. I shake my head and sort of smile like an apology I don't really need to make. Then I take a breath, ready to do what I'm actually supposed to do, when there is a crack of thunder and a shudder of lightning, and the whole classroom collectively gasps.

Mr. Winters grabs the desk like it's an earthquake, but it's not—the gods haven't sent one of those in a while.

It's something, though. Because the lightning practically hits the schoolhouse this time, the thunder so loud I cover my ears like I'm some little kid.

"A screed," Mr. Winters says, looking out the window.

"A screed?" Apple asks, the voice of all of us as usual. "Are you sure? Today?"

"It's there." Mr. Winters juts his chin to the lawn in front of the schoolhouse and we all get out of our seats to see what he's seeing. I can practically hear the new rhythm of everyone's hearts. Feel the change in temperature in the room.

Apple gets to the window first because Apple gets everywhere first. Always up the ladder before the rest of us, the first one to grow her hair long enough for braids when we were toddlers. She even kissed someone two years ago, before any of the rest of us even thought about it. It's okay, usually. It's almost nice to have Apple to tell us how to feel before we have to feel it.

For everything but losing your mom, at least. Maybe that's why I'm so confused. I've never had to figure something out without having seen her do it first.

"Oh. Wow," Apple says when she gets to the window, her voice deceptively soft. I stand back, letting Reece and Dawn and everyone else join Apple to see what she's seeing, but Apple notices and reaches her arm out for me. "Come here, Dorothy," she says. "Come see."

And like that I have the unlikely place next to Apple at the window, and there it is, a thing I've never seen before in real life but have heard of before, dozens of times. There is a bolt of Zeus's lightning stuck into the ground like a flag he's planted. It's smoking and brilliant. And pinned to the bottom of that, about to get rained on, is a rolled-up piece of paper. A screed from the gods. An order from above.

5.

"It's real," I say, unable to look away from the shock stuck into the earth. "They really do that."

"Of course they do," Mr. Winters says, even though I obviously wasn't talking to him, or to anyone really. "Last time was ten years ago or so." He doesn't say more, doesn't tell us what that screed was, but his voice shakes like it wasn't good news. And maybe nothing that flies down to earth on the tip of a lightning bolt can actually be good news. "Come on now. We have to read it right away. The gods aren't known for their patience, are they?"

They aren't, of course. They aren't patient. Or forgiving. Or very good at staying out of things. Sometimes late at night, the older generations can be heard reminding one another that that, too, is why they decided to leave Olympus. The drama and chaos and cruelty was too much. They wanted to be grounded, close to humans, remembering what it meant to be gods to begin with.

I swallow a dry bit of air and hope that it's somehow a coincidence, the gods sending down a screed on my mother's birthday. They've been silent about her, until today.

We follow Mr. Winters outside and circle around the bolt. It is sharp, a cartoonish zigzag, and so bright I squint looking at it. The thunder keeps rolling, and rain is moving from a drizzle to a drench.

Mr. Winters's hands shake. I wonder if anyone else notices. Outside the sky spirals, like the toddler has put their paintbrush in it to give it a whirl.

The gods don't talk to us much while we're down here, screed or otherwise. They're busy with other things—humans make messes that the gods try to clean up. The world, they tell us, is troubled and it takes all their time to untrouble it. It takes something big for them to get involved with our lives on Our Hill.

Today is big. My heart is thudding—I want to skip ahead to five minutes from now when I know what this is all about, but I try to make my face look neutral, like I'm feeling nothing at all. Apple grabs my hand again, like it's a thing we do all the time, just because we did it this morning.

"You don't have to," I say.

"Yeah, I do," she says. I try to make my mouth look like hers. Straight across with a tiny part between her lips. I match my shoulders to hers too. Pull them back, pull the rest of me up, like my whole body is saying *I'm fine I'm fine I'm fine, you can't hurt me.*

It feels okay, to take Apple's approximate shape. I'm a little sturdier like this, a little less scared.

Mr. Winters unfurls the scroll. The words are etched in gold. The air fills with the smell of flowers and the moon. Even the rowdiest kids, the ones descended from Titan gods, the ones whose ancestors were known for creating chaos, quiet. Still. The smell of the gods' screeds is beautiful but serious, just like we've been told for years. I can't stop breathing it in. We've been taught to look up to toward the sky when their words are read, so we do exactly that, all of us at the same time. It's like we're finally getting to do a thing we've practiced for our entire lives.

Mr. Winters clears his throat. I don't think he's ever been in charge of reading a screed out loud, and the whole of his body seems to be screaming *Get me out of here,* but he does it anyway.

"'For generations, the earthbound near-gods have beautifully existed on this hill, straddling two worlds, two selves. But the mortal world is not meant for forevers. We have learned that this year,'" Mr. Winters reads. His eyes flicker to me and I want to be invisible, to be unattached to this world so that I don't have to be at the center of this awful moment. He clears his throat again. I'm starting to hate the sound. Around me, wind blows and rain splatters. Fingers scratch, tongues click, hair is pushed aside, rain comes down harder, louder this time. People struggle to keep their gaze focused upward. I do too. My knees feel shaky, my body swaying from being in the wrong position. Apple holds my hand tightly and whispers so quietly that it almost gets lost, "It's okay. It's okay." It's so kind, it hurts.

Mr. Winters pauses. And continues on after another loud rush of thunder. All over Our Hill, lightning bolts are hitting the ground, and we feel each hit with a shudder-shift-shake. On every street, scrolls are being unscrolled, these same words are being read. "'There is a line between gods and humans. We have always known this, and though we struggle to keep that line firm, it must be present. Earth-bound gods—it is a beautiful idea that no longer works. Gods are meant to be up above. Humans down below. It is time for you to make a choice. To know who you are, and to live with that decision. This winter solstice will be the final climb up the ladder. In one month and two days, those who come up will stay with us, resume their positions in Olympus. And those left behind will live human lives on earth. Die human deaths. There is Olympus. And there is earth. There are gods. And there are mortals. This is how it must be.'"

My fingers squeeze Apple's hard. Hers squeeze back harder. I'm breathing, but just barely.

Mr. Winters drops the scroll back to the ground, where the rain soaks it. The words start to bleed, turning into blurs. Finally it rolls back into itself and we watch the tube of it move back and forth and back and forth on the ground until it settles. There's a stillness, all of us watching the scroll, listening to the rain. Then a shuffle of bodies trying to find themselves. Another stillness, then Reece speaking first. "This is because of Penny," she says. She isn't wise, exactly, not a descendant of Athena, that's for sure, but she's confident, which can feel the same. She stiffens her chin, darting her eyes to the braid that my fingers have made with Apple's. "It always is."

"What does that mean?" Apple asks. Even her perfect hair is wet, pieces of it escaping her braid, sticking to her face. "This has never happened before. I mean, unless I'm wrong. Has this happened before, Chloe?" We've all asked Chloe questions over the years about who we are and where we came from and what happened before. For a moment, I wonder if it feels exhausting to her, having to explain everything to us all the time.

"Pandora opening the box," Chloe mumbles, like she wants to answer without answering, like she wants to protect me but also protect the truth of history. I'm suddenly aware of the wetness of rain. The way it's made its way through my socks, all the way to my toes. The way it makes my blue dress heavy. A few steps away, Eric stands with his arms crossed and a half-smile on his face, like he always does when someone cries, when someone gets hurt, when an argument breaks out and blows up in class. He stands and smirks, a strange boy descended of the god of darkness, who likes when things go wrong.

He is loving this.

"This isn't the same as Pandora," Apple says, but maybe Reece is right, and I come from something bad; something cursed and wrong and fated to ruin. "Penny didn't open a box. She didn't disobey the gods. She, you know, she made a choice, and it—"

"She let her own curiosity, her own feelings, get the best of her, and she ruined things for everyone else. Just like Pandora. Obviously," Reece says, as if she's now the keeper of our histories; as if she knows everything there is to know about our ancestors. "Bringing misery to earth again."

"Okay, all right," Mr. Winters says, but he doesn't seem to know what words to say after that. "Let's not assign . . . This is a difficult . . . I know we all have a lot to take in." His voice is thin, not believing itself, and I don't believe it either. The wind wants to blow it away.

This is our hillside home. None of us have ever lived on Mount Olympus. The earthbound near-gods have been here for ages, this is where we belong. We wear our blue dresses to remember the sky, we climb the silver ladder on solstice to renew our magic, we go through our human years and then choose the age at which we want to stay forever, we learn our history over and over and over, but we aren't gods on Olympus.

I have always thought I'll like twenty-seven. It seems like an age where you get to just be yourself and no one says much about it. Dad talks about wanting to return to thirty-nine one day. We are supposed to have all the time in the world to decide.

I look around. There's anger and confusion and a few kids sure they must have misunderstood. "We don't have to leave, right? I mean, we can just do what we've always done, right?" someone says. Someone else tells them to shut up. And there's Reece setting them straight, repeating what the screed just told us in her loud, sure voice—we have to leave. We can stay gods and live forever, going up the ladder to Olympus and never returning to Our Hill. Or we can choose to be humans on earth. And die eventually.

Like Mom.

"It was not meant to be an eternal home here on earth," Mr. Winters says, but I'm not sure if he believes that exactly. I'm not sure anyone does.

"I'm sorry," I say. Most people don't hear me, but the few that do don't seem to care. I don't know what I'm apologizing for, exactly. My mother dying? It being her birthday today? That I am also a descendant of Pandora? Existing at all? It's hard to say.

Mr. Winters's face is a shade of gray. He keeps swallowing like maybe he's going to be sick.

"I think we should all go home," he finally says, "be with our families. Process on our own. Yes. Yes, I think that might be what's best for everyone. It's a bit . . . I think we all need to . . . yes. I think it's best for everyone."

"We just got here," Apple says.

Mr. Winters's face is so grim. There's a thin line of sweat gathering on his forehead. Or maybe it's just rainwater. It's hard to really know what's what anymore.

"We will be back tomorrow," he says, his voice's steady calm in sharp contrast with his body, which seems to be pressing him in other directions, to dangerous thoughts and impossible decisions. "A month is a very short— We don't have much time to make a decision that is quite . . . Well. We should process. With our loved ones. We have to act quickly."

"Maybe they don't really mean—" Apple begins, but Mr. Winters shakes his head.

"Olympus has spoken," he says.

And above us, there is another crack of thunder. Another—bigger, brighter—bolt of lightning. Our hands fly up to cover our heads, our knees buckle to bring us to the ground, like this bolt might hit us, might strike us all down, right here, before we have to decide anything at all.

The earth smokes. It smells burnt and bad. This second bolt a jagged spike in the ground, reminding us of who the gods are, what they want, and what they are willing to do to get it.

Mr. Winters doesn't wait for us to leave. He doesn't go back to the classroom to retrieve his backpack, his glasses, the thermos of coffee he has on his desk all day every day. He just turns around and leaves us there, in between two lightning bolts, our brains worrying over questions that we don't even know how to ask about what comes next.

6.

Dad's not home when I get back. He's probably been at work, where he teaches music to babies with their parents. Dad's ancestor, Orpheus, the son of a muse, had a supernatural gift with music. Dad has that same gift, and maybe it doesn't mean much to some people here, who whisper, sometimes, about why it is that the descendants of muses are allowed on Our Hill and not just those descended of gods, but Mama always said music is just as magical as anything the other near-gods can do anyway. And those same people don't complain when they bring their babies to Dad's classes and he lulls them all into smiley, sleepy bundles. Besides, gods married muses all the time, so most of us are the descendants of both.

We learn the myth of Orpheus and Eurydice in school, and I squirm in my seat when it comes up, because it's about love and music and trust and sorrow and it's kind of awkward, the way the past and the present get all intertwined. Now more than ever, Dad looks the way the paintings of Orpheus looked, after he lost his love to the underworld.

Maybe he's wandering around with his guitar right now, singing sad songs. Or maybe he'll be home any minute. Sometimes I wish I'd gotten his gift too, but I mostly take after Mama. I don't have any songs to tell people how I feel. I can barely carry a tune.

It's raining hard, the thunder continuing to grumble at us, the lightning a shock in the swirling sky every few minutes. I can still smell the ashy earth from in front of the schoolhouse. My knees haven't straightened, haven't unwobbled themselves.

I pace the house looking for someone. Mama, really. She's who I want to be here, and I can't ever seem to fill the empty space she left behind, but I do try. I grab another piece of bread and take it up to the attic, where her loom is set up, the tapestry asking me to finish it, even though I've barely done anything with it so far except stare at it and try to see what it was that Mama wanted it to be. She wanted to make a different kind of Pandora, a different vision of the way things were. Or are. Or could be.

I sit down on her little wooden stool and smooth out the

threads. People on Our Hill love to weave. Some are descendants of the Fates, and they take their weaving very seriously, honoring some grand family tradition, like maybe they are contributing to destiny too, just like the Fates themselves. But we all learn the ancient art, and Mama was especially good at it. Our home is filled with her rugs—always pinks and purples and ivories—beautiful, sweet colors and patterns that make our home feel different from the rest of the houses on Our Hill. In other homes, the tapestries hang on walls. But Mama loved that the art was functional, that it made our feet cozy and our home bright and more like the mortal humans' homes we'd peeked into over the years. Other homes on Our Hill are filled with Olympian heirlooms in beige and gold. But Mama made our rugs and sewed our curtains in bright patterns and we built our kitchen table together, sanding wood, staining it, trying our best to make the legs even, the whole thing looked like we'd done it on purpose, even the mistakes.

People thought Mom's way of doing things was strange. Even people like Heather, who called my mom *cute* and our house *filled with character,* but once I heard her say something to one of the other moms in the park: "She's my best friend, but she's a strange one. Have you ever been in their home?"

Moments after she said it, she saw me nearby. Smiled like she was checking to see if I'd heard. I smiled back and tried to believe I hadn't. Apple was so close to my mom, but I was never very close to hers.

I don't know if anyone's really close to Heather now that Mama's gone. Maybe that's how she likes it, though. Hera doesn't have a million friends either—everyone is too scared of the way she likes to take revenge, how unstoppable her power seems to be.

I shake my head. I don't want to think about Heather, because if I do I'll think of her hearing the screed read aloud. When Heather is upset she blinks too fast and makes her mouth into this mean pucker. She'll dart her eyes around, making sure everyone else feels the same way she does, shares her bad feelings. I know that's what she's doing right now. Scanning everyone in town to see how they all feel about the order from the gods. Tightening her mouth until it's a knot in the middle of her face.

No, I don't want to think about Heather. So I think about the tapestry, something solid and as close to Mama as I can get. I'm not a very good weaver, but Mama's loom is a little bit magical, and it guides my hands so they don't have to make decisions on their own. They start to move in familiar patterns, a little bit like a dance learned a hundred years ago. It feels good.

"Dorothy?" Dad calls up when he's home a few minutes later. I barely did anything, a line or two of color added onto the weaving. I want to see the whole thing, but I won't know what it is until I make it.

"I'm up here," I call back and Dad thumps up the stairs. He doesn't speak when he arrives, just sits next to me and pulls me close. "You heard," I say.

"I heard." Dad's voice is cracked and crooked. He's absolutely drenched, from getting caught in the rain. We're quiet for a while. I start a hundred sentences in my head and I can tell by Dad's twitching fingers and heavy sighs that he's doing the same thing. "One month," he says. "One. That's— It's nothing."

The attic creaks sometimes, the whole house makes noises that don't have reasons attached to them. Heather always pointed them out: "You're the only family who doesn't fix the things that need fixing," she said once. She was smiling when she said it, but it was pointed. She meant that we don't summon our godly powers to fix floor squeaks or cracks in the paint or a certain room being too cold when another is too hot.

"We're the only family who thinks not everything needs fixing," Mama replied. She smiled bigger than Heather. Mama's smile made you feel like she had a secret treasure that no one else could see, that she knew something special about the world that the rest of us didn't.

Heather shook her head and rolled her eyes, but the moment stayed with me. The memory sort of lives in my chest, I think, and it pounds there now, making it hard to think about anything else.

I want Mama here, telling us why this is okay or at least what we're going to do about it. Are we going to stay on earth, or climb up to the sky forever, or something else entirely? Mama always seemed to have a way of making choices that no one knew existed until she made them.

Dad shifts his body and the floor creaks again. "There are bolts everywhere," he says. "Stuck out of the ground. Don't touch them, okay, Dorothy? There are dozens. They aren't safe."

That's why I still smell the smoke from school, I guess. Because actually it's everywhere.

"Happy and Sad?" I say. Dad and I have never done Happy and Sad. It's something I only ever did with Mama, a private ritual between us that seemed a little sacred. And until right this second I guess I thought that meant it should stay between us forever.

But she's gone. So if I keep it between her and me, it will be gone too.

A feeling I try never to feel rises up: *Why make a ritual with me, why make me love this tiny thing so much, if you were going to leave me?* I push the feeling, the questions, back down.

She did it for a good reason. She must have. She *must* have.

"Oh, Dorothy, I don't know," Dad says. He's heard

Mama and I do Happy and Sad more times than we could count. Once in a while she'd ask him if he wanted to join in, but he'd always tell us he didn't want to intrude.

That was good, back then. But I need him here now.

"My happy was walking to school with Apple," I say. "It was nice. Familiar and new at the same time, which is sort of weird but sort of cool. She wants to be friends I think."

Dad doesn't say anything. He looks out the skylight, through which you can really only see a cloud and a branch's shadow. The leaves are almost all the way off the trees.

"My sad was the way everyone looked at me after Mr. Winters read from the scroll," I go on. "It was like I wasn't even supposed to be there, like it was my fault or something. I don't know. It sucked."

I look to Dad. This is the part of the routine where he should tell me that he gets it. No matter how small my sad was, Mama always nodded seriously, like it mattered a great deal to her. It didn't take away the sadness of the day, exactly, but it changed its shape and texture into something softer, smaller, less pointy.

Today's sadness is jagged and hard—it's sandpaper and square and doesn't fit anywhere. It needs smoothing and softening. It needs my mom.

Dad's hands find his eyes and he rubs and rubs, like maybe if he presses hard enough the way things are will change. "I can't, Dorothy. There was nothing happy. It's been an awful day. It's— I'm sorry. You're okay. It's okay. We'll—I don't know."

"When Mama and I did Happy and Sad she always—" The sadness is even pointier.

"I'm not Mama," Dad says in a sort of gray tone of voice that sinks and sputters and leaves no room for me to say anything else. He kisses me on the head and tells me he loves me and I know he wants that to do something, to be enough, and it's not but I guess it also has to be.

Outside, I can hear people walking by, talking, their voices high and panicked and frantic.

Inside, the house squeaks one more time.

It rains even harder. I guess the gods are sad too.

APPLE

7.

Mom rushes out when she sees me, flying out of the house all dramatic and too much. Somehow Mom always makes big things even bigger. "Apple, baby girl doll, what are we going to do?" Her arms wrap around me and she pulls me close. Sometimes I wish she'd find someone to marry. Someone descended from a really shy muse or nymph or something, someone who could take moments like this and remind Mom to breathe. Mom says she's not interested in all that love stuff, that if you study the myths, you see that love only makes everything more confusing. She's never thought it very becoming.

Most kids come from two parents, but like Athena, I come from one. Athena came from Zeus's head, no mother needed, and maybe because Mom is his descendant, she was able to have me on her own too. I asked her why, once, and she said it was because of where we came from, and how close to the most powerful gods we are. She said it like it was a prize, but it feels, sometimes, especially maybe right now, more like a heavy thing we carry around, something that is wearing us out.

The thing about Mom's whole *love is bad* theory is that loving Penny, even just in the friend way, was good. Made her better. Calmer. Penny made her do things like sit by the river and listen to its little laps, and drink green tea, and talk about her dreams. Without her, Mom is unwound and too much.

"We need a plan," Mom says. "People look to us for guidance. We need to be strong and solid with all of this, Apple. Okay? Okay, you understand?" She's still hugging me, and every time she finishes a sentence she squeezes a little more. I feel like an orange being wrung out for juice, but there's nothing in me, she's already gotten everything I have.

"I understand."

"How did you respond? When they read it out loud? Did you keep your composure? People need you to keep your composure." *Composure* is one of Mom's favorite words. She's been saying it to me since I was too young to even know how to pronounce it.

"Yeah, I think so."

"This is a big moment, so you need to *know*. Not think. You can break down here, okay, but at school, out there, you need to be a leader. You need to be solid and strong and beautiful for them. Okay?"

"Yep."

Mom strangles one hand with the other. We're on the front lawn still, which is surprising, like maybe she's forgotten that we can be seen here by anyone who passes by.

"It's an awful day," she whispers. "Everything about it." Mom wears a golden choker around her neck, something passed down from Hera that looks a little ridiculous on Our Hill, even with all our godly traditions. When she's stressed out, I always watch the choker, the way it bulges and bounces as she swallows and strains. "Absolutely awful," she says again.

I nod. I don't entirely agree, though. I liked walking with Dorothy and eating breakfast in her home and remembering that once upon a time I told Penny that I'd look out for her. It was right after Penny skipped the climb up the ladder. I saw her down by the river. She was always there, painting trees and floating leaves in the water, and talking at odd hours with my mother. So anytime I went there, it was maybe at least a little in the hopes of seeing her. And that time I had questions. And thoughts. And feelings. A lot of feelings. She must have seen them on my face or in the way I walked toward her, because she sat right up, her back straight instead of sloped.

"I'm sorry," she said, which was weird because there were probably like a hundred people she needed to apologize to for doing something so absurd, so unreal, but I wasn't one of them. I don't think a grown-up had ever apologized to me before.

"I don't understand," I said, which I'd never say in front of anyone else, because I'm Apple Montgomery and I'm supposed to understand everything.

"I think that's okay," Penny said. "To not understand." She smiled this sad sort of smile, and no one in the world, or at least no one on Our Hill, was anything like her. Not then and not ever. "I know how important these rituals are to your family," she went on. "To your mom. But I don't think I was ever supposed to be a god. I've always felt I'm a human. That's who I'm supposed to be, even if it doesn't make much sense. It won't really change so much. I'm just not a god anymore. But everything else is the same. Really."

"But someday you'll—"

Penny waved her hand, like it was nothing to worry about. "In years and years and years and years. We'll all be ready for it."

She sounded so sure. Death was impossible for either of us to imagine, a thing that no one we'd known had ever done, something that seemed so far away, so far into the future it wasn't even real. Maybe, when the time came, it would be fine, we'd be ready, just like she said. Maybe that's how it was, for humans.

"Apple?" Penny said, looking at the river and not at me. "Look out for my girl, okay? At school and everything. In town. People will talk and they'll make her feel bad and if anyone's doing that, you send them my way. Dorothy shouldn't have to pay any consequences for this. You'll look out for her at school while we all figure this out?"

"Of course," I said. "I promise. I'll make sure she's okay." I figured the job would mostly be about telling Reece to shut up when she said something mean, or asking a lot of distracting questions in class if Mr. Winters started talking about Penny's choice as some kind of lesson.

Maybe, if she'd known about the car, if she'd known she wouldn't be there to take care of Dorothy in all the bigger, more important ways, she would have chosen someone else to look out for her. But she didn't. We didn't.

So now it's just me and the promise I made Penny and have mostly done a terrible job of keeping. But I'm finally ready to be who I promised Penny I'd be. It's something I'm good at—being the person grown-ups ask me to be. I've been doing it my whole life.

"Want to go down to the river?" I ask Mom now, because the one thing we both want is to remember Penny today. That I'm sure of. The rain is starting to let up, and anyway

Penny would have told us not to think too much about the rain, not to let it tell us what to do. Penny always made sure Mom and I had rain boots and colorful raincoats even though Mom insisted an umbrella was more than enough.

"Oh, Apple, that is the sweetest. You are just the most thoughtful girl. Yes. Let's go to the river. I would love that. It's a day—it's still Penny's birthday, in spite of . . . everything else." She gestures up, up, up to our ancestors and their ultimatum and the attention they have turned to us, after all this time.

We go to the closet and get our rain gear—it's all squeaky yellow and oversized—Penny had erred on the side of caution, getting us jackets a little too big, boots with room for thick wool socks, and now even the way the sleeves hang too long reminds us of her.

Maybe she should have given us blue jackets. Maybe that would have better honored the gods. But at the time it seemed like a silly sort of slight, almost accidental. Too small to worry about.

The walk to the river is short but feels long, with rain still coming down and the streets filled with our neighbors, talking about the orders that have been delivered. They are huddled under umbrellas—clear ones, where you can see every rain drop hit and slide. Humans have clear sometimes, but they can have purple and blue and red umbrellas too. Black, I've heard, in droves. But here we have to confront it, have to watch and honor every drop, especially when it's from the gods above.

Mom and I must look strange in our yellow jackets, our boots built for jumping in puddles, our umbrella-less hands, our hoods pulled snug over our heads.

In spite of the rain, smoke still billows out from the lightning bolts all around us. Occasionally one or another flashes, reminding us they are still alive, still thrumming with energy and rage.

"We didn't think," Mom whispers. "Yellow, what a mistake. We shouldn't be wearing—well. Maybe they'd understand if they knew she gave us— But then I suppose they could think we think what she did was right." Mom almost never talks about Penny and what Penny did. I catch her crying sometimes, when she eats certain foods or hears certain songs, and other times that I can't pinpoint—maybe a color shading the sky or the way the house feels at the times of day she used to be with her friend. It's like we made some agreement for me to leave the room whenever it happens, so that's what I do. I leave the room and she cries into a dish towel and we both look out the window at the ladder and wonder what would have happened if Penny would have just climbed it like she was supposed to, if we could have gone on with the way it was forever.

"Smile, Apple," she says now, waving tightly to whoever looks our way. Then she clears her throat and starts talking too loudly, a volume that isn't actually meant for me at all. "We'll join the gods, of course. It's sad to leave, but Olympus is beautiful." I think I'm supposed to say something in the pause that heaves itself at me. But I don't know what to say. I didn't know we were definitely going to leave. I barely understand that this whole situation is real, that today actually happened.

"Mom, can we talk about this in private maybe?" I start, but Mom squeezes my elbow and keeps us walking at this brisk, straight-backed pace. She unbuttons the raincoat so that everyone can see her perfect blue dress underneath. The exact shade of the sky when it's at its bluest. The shade of the place we came from, the place we are being asked to return to.

"They had to do it. The gods. It had to be done." She stares straight ahead and talks like she's giving a speech and people passing by stop to listen. Some of them nod their heads. They make eye contact with us, lift their hands in greeting, make sure we know they are with us, they are on our side. They will climb the ladder. They will leave this place.

"Mom," I say, keeping my voice low but still firm, still needing her to hear it. "We can't just decide without even—"

"We'll be lucky to live there," she interrupts. She sounds absurd, trying too hard, the way she's always told me not to be. Her hand moves from my elbow to my shoulder, a tap that reminds me to straighten my back a bit. Hera is majestic, that's the word my mom always uses to remind me of what we're meant to be, too. Majestic. Elegant. Composed. She taps again, and I finally give in.

"Yes," I say, my mouth making words my heart is saying no to. "I've always wanted to live there. Alongside Hera and Zeus and, um, everyone."

Mom's whole body relaxes. She starts walking more slowly, her arms swinging a little more loosely. I said the right thing, but it feels all kinds of wrong.

The river feels wrong too. Mom and I have never really come here together. Our traditions aren't wet and barefoot and sunny. We do things like read history books to each other at night and water the cherry blossom tree, even though magic will keep it alive, and try different hairstyles on each other—a swirly bun for Mom, a thick braid for me, loose curls and three barrettes for Mom, a very high, very bouncy ponytail for me.

We talk about clothes and shoes and which blue dresses go best with which gold sandals and sometimes, even though we'd never tell anyone, we sit on our front porch and watch our neighbors walk by, and we try to pin down who they descended from and why they are here. We whisper their histories to each other, and sometimes Mom says something that isn't mean, exactly, but isn't kind either, about their hair or their house or the sound of their voice.

And I nod and nod and nod. My job is to agree. But not today.

"You should have talked to me first," I say. Away from other people, I can say things to Mom that I'm not supposed to say in public.

"There's nothing to talk about." Mom picks up a fallen leaf. It's the perfect shade of orange. I wish we could bring it home and keep it exactly the way it is, but I know from experience that leaves turn brown and crumble. They don't last.

"I don't want to live up there."

"Apple. Come on." I think Mom wants to sound strong, but her voice is as crumbly as a leaf, dry and brittle and breaking. "We saw what happened." She doesn't say Penny's name. I wonder if she can feel her here the way I can, in the chill of the breeze and the low sounds of ducks and bugs and lapping water.

"Why didn't she climb the ladder? Why did she feel like she was human and not one of us? How would she know something like that? Do you ever feel that way? Does everyone?" It's a risk to ask these things. I'm not supposed to. But I swear Penny is right here next to us, practically begging me to talk about her.

For a moment, Mom's body is in the shape it used to take when Penny was around: relaxed shoulders, tilted head, legs splayed out instead of knit together. I inch closer to her. I miss Penny, but I miss Mom too, the Mom she could be when Penny was there making her laugh, insisting they go barefoot, making sure their slices of lemon cake were over-sized and heavily glazed, forgetting about gods and what it means that we come from them.

In all the books I read about humans, I didn't hear anything about missing the versions of the other people we used to be when someone dies. It's awful.

I wait for Mom, the hanging-out-with-Penny version of her, to answer me, but before she does, the other version, the proud-descendant-of-Hera Mom, snaps back to attention, her body becoming taut, wound up. She touches the choker around her neck like it's a touchstone, an anchor to who we have to be. "Penny was fated to make terrible decisions. To let curiosity get the best of her. To open up boxes that were meant to stay closed. I thought maybe she could get beyond all that but . . . well. Well. Here we are."

When Penny was alive, Mom let Penny go on and on about how misunderstood Pandora was, how lovely and sweet and good curiosity could be. But Pandora opened a box filled with misery. The earth could have been perfect without her. What is there to understand?

I should have asked her. I should have made her spell it out, tell it to me plainly. Instead, I felt uncomfortable, like she was telling me a secret we might get in trouble for knowing, like she was asking me to be part of something I didn't exactly want to be a part of.

Penny never tapped Dorothy on the shoulder to remind her who to be.

She never made sure her hair was perfectly braided, her dress draped the right way.

She bought yellow raincoats instead of blue and ripped out pages of history books that she didn't like.

It felt a little frightening, sometimes, to be around someone who had so many questions about the way things were. Sometimes, Mom tried to keep me away, giving me a list of chores to do before visiting Penny at the river, or making a plan for me to go to Dawn's house on the same day she was going to have dinner with Penny. Once, at a cookout in our own backyard, Mom slipped between me and Penny, putting an arm around me to remind everyone I was hers.

It feels like forever ago.

The rain lets up, and Mom takes off her coat so fast you'd think she was allergic to it or something. "Let's go," she says. "I don't want to be here anymore. It's over. You know? It's just over."

I don't know if she means our time on Our Hill, or this moment right now, or the love we're still churning through for Penny, or just life, the way we thought it would be. But she gets up and holds out a hand to help me get up too.

"People like Penny—things could have stayed the same forever. But some people just . . ." her voice drifts off like the wind, and I don't think she knows what the end of the sentence is at all. "We were supposed to be best friends forever."

My mom sounds so young when she says it. People like Reece and Dawn and me talk about best friends. Not people like my mom. She's supposed to be more serious and measured.

She shakes her head, and we both watch the clouds part, the sun shine through, Apollo, up above, giving us the gift of light, whether we want it, or not.

8.

School is quiet the next day. Heads are bowed and even Reece moves gingerly from outside to in, not commenting on who is wearing what or what she thinks we should be saying or doing now that everything's changed.

I should have stopped by Dorothy's on the way to school, walked here with her, talked about what it all means and if she's okay. Penny would have wanted me to do that. And I sort of want to do it for myself. I've only talked to Mom so far. Reece and Dawn each stopped by last night, but both times I shook my head when Mom came upstairs to tell me I had a visitor. Mom said they sounded upset, and I should talk them through the hard situation, and in my head I screamed, *Who's going to help ME???* But in reality I shrugged and told her I would tomorrow.

Even Mr. Winters looks lost. He's paper-clipping a sheet of paper to itself. He picks up and puts down a piece of chalk. He stuffs his hands in his pockets and looks out the window. He doesn't start class.

Chloe's sitting in the back, in Dorothy's old chair, so the one next to me is empty. Dorothy's never this late.

"Well," Mr. Winters says. "Well. Our work here is quite important now, isn't it?"

We all stare back. School seems tragically unimportant, in fact. Sort of like a thing we're doing to pretend everything's fine when actually nothing is. I wonder if he can read that in the way we're all sort of slumped over, looking at the sky like it's going to give us more impossible news.

He clears his throat. "What I mean is, it's now very important that you understand Olympus. That you really know the world you'll be . . . or you may be . . . the place we have to consider going." He says it carefully but it lands hard. Some of us will go to Olympus. And maybe some won't. And both options seem too big for this tiny classroom on this rocky hillside in the middle of this little town that we built and thought was really ours.

Someone in the back of the room is sniffing, the way you do when you want people to think you have a cold but actually you're crying. Dawn's arms are crossed over her chest. Reece's chin juts out like it wants to start a fight.

"The winter solstice is in a month," Mr. Winters says. "That's not very long. Not very long at all. It's pressing down on us, time, isn't it? But I'd like our focus to be on what the gods' responsibilities are, and when that has gone awry in the past, as well as refreshing your understandings of what gods control what aspects of life. And the gods' triumphs too. Of course. And my hope is that, for those of you who climb the ladder in December, you'll feel prepared to join that world, you'll know what you need to know."

Mr. Winters's voice is shaky and thin and even he doesn't believe what he's saying. He's speaking mostly to his desk, where he shuffles some papers around and moves his stapler from one side to the other and back again. He doesn't know how to do this any more than we do. His gaze finds me, and his eyebrows do this thing where they pop up, asking a question, and I think the question is basically *Can you do something to help, Apple?* And it seems obvious that the answer is *No, I'm literally twelve, I can't help at all*, but I picture Mom's face if she knew I was called to be a leader and did nothing, so I clear my throat and try.

"That's a good plan," I say. "We need to be prepared. And to learn, um, what we can." The words do nothing, just sit in the air, all pointless and flat. Mr. Winters shakes his head like he's disappointed I can't somehow take control of the class, inspire us—and him—into action. And everyone else doodles and shifts and sighs and looks out the window, to check for the hundredth and thousandth time that yes, the twin lightning bolts are still there, and no, nothing has gone back to the way it was.

It's on the stapler's third journey across Mr. Winters's desk that Dorothy comes in. Her blue dress is buttoned all wrong—she missed one near the top and it's made the whole thing lopsided and strained. She's got yesterday's braids in her hair, all frizzy and undone, and she's flushed.

She looks in the back to the seat that used to be hers and winces at seeing it full before sort of slinking in next to me. Mr. Winters hands out some reading: *Zeus: Protecting Through Strength* and *Transformations: Ten Humans That Turned into Other Things*. He asks us to read on our own, and that we will have a classroom discussion later, I guess about whether it's okay to turn a human being into a rock or tree or a cow.

"Hey," I whisper.

"Hey."

"Are you okay?" I ask. What I mean is, *You look like a sort of big mess and you should have brushed your hair and today is a day you needed to get here on time and not let everyone look at you all extra long like they're doing right this second.* I think she hears the words under the words, because she blushes.

"I'm pretty sure I'm not okay at all," Dorothy says, which seems like a really weird way to say no, but it also sounds a lot like Penny, so it makes me half smile.

We read but don't really discuss the handouts, and then we read and don't really discuss some more stuff, about Hades and Athena, and none of it is new information, but it all sounds so different when you have to picture joining their world, living up in the sky for real. And soon the tension in the air is itchy and weird. Before we get up to head to the cafeteria for lunch, Reece raises her hand. She sort of flutters her fingers, a thing she's always doing that I've never really liked. It makes her hand look like a really demanding butterfly.

"Mr. Winters? I want to read about Pandora," she says. Her voice singsongs like it's some casual curiosity, but Reece is a terrible actress and isn't fooling anyone, most of all Dorothy.

"We'll get to her," Mr. Winters mumbles.

"I just think she's the biggest mistake, so we really should spend the most time reading about her and talking about her and figuring out how to not be anything like her." Reece crosses her arms over her chest. Next to me, Dorothy goes statue-still.

"Noted," Mr. Winters says. I wait for him to tell Reece that we don't speak that way about any parts of our history, that we don't speak ill of people's ancestors. We've had whole assemblies about how we are supposed to talk about the past, and how to honor the mistakes made over these centuries of time. Our principal, Ms. Starster, paced back and forth on stage and read a poem that the older students had written about the way we all live together on Our Hill, accepting the mistakes of the past and approaching each day with understanding and appreciation or whatever.

I don't know. I don't love poetry, not the way we're all supposed to. I get lost in words and rhymes and not-rhymes and why some people think it's better to tell something in a complicated way instead of a simple way. But I know that poem meant we weren't supposed to call even someone as complicated as Pandora a mistake.

And especially not in front of Dorothy.

But all Mr. Winters does is rub his hands together like they're going to start a fire right here in the classroom. And in the absence of Mr. Winters telling Reece to stop, she goes on. "I think we all know that history, like, repeats itself. I mean, it's written on the front of this actual building and is like the number one thing you guys tell us, and history is literally repeating right this second, so it seems like we should focus on that. On Pandora and people who can't leave things be and why they feel the need to ruin things for everyone else."

I'd thought Reece's voice was cruel, cutting, but actually underneath the sharpness there's something else. A warble, a blubbery sort of shake like she used to have when we were seven and things weren't going her way. Dawn and I used to tease her for it—the way she could go from tough to trembling in five seconds, the way her chin used to quaver, how she'd sound like a baby way past the age we thought that was okay.

It's been a few years since that side of her has come out, and even now it's hidden underneath her narrow-eyed stare at Dorothy, the sharp consonants of her words and how very tightly her arms make armor over her ribs. But it's there. She's upset.

"We don't need to keep walking on eggshells around Dorothy because of what her mom did. Our life's ruined because of her, so why do we keep having to pretend—"

"It sounds like you need to cry," I interrupt, because it's clear Mr. Winters isn't going to be interrupting. "It seems like you're really upset and need to cry and you should go do that somewhere else."

I am careful to make my voice sound soft and a little bit bored.

Dorothy un-statues next to me. Her head turns all the way to the side to look my way, and she looks startled, and I'm sort of startled too—Reece is my best friend and I am a descendant of Hera and am supposed to be royal and coldly kind and not get embroiled in this sort of thing, but the thing about being a descendant of Hera is that sometimes that isn't quite as big as the bigness of having loved Penny and missing Penny and wanting to make Penny proud.

"It's fine," Dorothy mumbles, to me or the whole class, I'm not really sure. And Reece just sits there stunned and even shakier and Mr. Winters won't stop organizing his pencils in order of most to least sharpened. Maybe I need to grab Ms. Starster and have her be in charge for a few minutes while Mr. Winters does whatever he's doing.

But I imagine the whole of Our Hill is this way right now, uneasy and unsure and unable to find even the simplest words. I think of the oldest people in town—the ones who have been around for generations but have decided to stay at twenty-two or fifty-four forever. Maybe one of them needs to take over this classroom, this moment. But even they haven't been through this before.

Everyone in the room is sort of twisting and tapping and some of them are even closing their eyes to get away from the situation. But I'm Apple Montgomery and I am supposed to be a little bit in charge, and I'm also supposed to be protecting someone and I don't understand anything that Penny Hardy did, but I know that she didn't do it to hurt Reece or Mr. Winters or anyone in a blue dress who loves things the way they are.

"Penny Hardy loved Our Hill," I say. "And she loved everyone here. The gods sent down the screed. Not Penny."

"*Apple,*" Mr. Winters says, as if what I'm saying is more shocking than the jabs of cruelty that Reece directed at Dorothy and her family, as if the horrible thing is me pointing out the truth and not the truth itself.

"Mr. Winters," I repeat back, a sentence all on its own. I'm ready to stare him down for all eternity if I have to—I think it might even feel good to stand up and not move an inch until Reece and Mr. Winters and maybe everyone else in our whole town apologizes. I imagine a crown on my head, a scepter in my hand, Hera's own throne at Olympus beneath me.

"I can't," a small voice next to me says, though. And Dorothy scurries out the door, taking her leather satchel with the *History of Our Gods* book inside.

We all pause in the space she's left behind. Most days on Our Hill are regimented and familiar and a cozy sort of boring. But since yesterday, it is only mess and anger and this feeling, here, of trying to do the right thing but not knowing what the right thing is or if there even is one at all.

So I pick up my satchel too, and try my best to make my exit from the classroom a sort of glide-slide-float away.

And I follow Dorothy right out the door and all the way to the river.

9.

"You don't have to be here," Dorothy says. "And you shouldn't be here. Just go back there and talk about my mom and whatever else, it's fine. I'm fine." Her back is to me, but even just from the hang of her head and the skew of her legs—feet in, knees knocking—I can tell that it is not fine.

"Reece is really weird about stuff sometimes," I start. "There was this time last year that I wore this whole dress that was blue, it was totally blue but Reece thought it was purple and she—"

"This isn't about a dress," Dorothy says. "It's my *mom*."

"I know, I just mean that Reece gets like this."

Dorothy turns to face me. She's wiping tears away with

the backs of her hands and she's looking at something just beyond my shoulders, something behind me. I look back to see what it is, and of course it's the silver ladder and its climb into the sky.

"I know Reece, too," Dorothy says, still squinting at the ladder's lean. "I know Reece and Dawn and you and Mr. Winters and this whole place. I've lived here as long as you have."

"I know."

We're quiet. Everyone in our life has lived here forever. No one moves to Our Hill. No one moves away. We can't. Generations ago, our families chose to build the ladder and climb down and claim this land as ours, as a way to get closer to humans, as a way to understand the world better, as a way to get some space from the chaotic fighting and anger and mess of Olympus. We stay and live and choose ages and more of us are born, and it's perfect, mostly. But we don't talk much in school about the first part, about what we left behind and why. Dorothy and I used to listen in when our moms were deep in conversation and forgetting we were there. At breakfast picnics and nighttime swims in the river and the few attempts they made at having us all go shopping in town. For a minute, we'd talk as a group—*how's school, who is your favorite muse, do you like poetry or sculpture better*—but quickly our moms would fold into each other and talk about everything else—who my mom might go on a date with and what Dorothy's dad did that made her mom mad, and always, eventually, what new bit of tension was running through Olympus, which gods wanted what to happen down here, and how none of them understood anything real about this delicate and beautiful earth and the strange, brave, smart, naive humans running around it.

I wonder what the ladder looks like to Dorothy now—a threat? A promise? A haunting? I think of it as this reminder of everything I'm supposed to be. Of destiny.

Maybe that's what me and Dorothy are. The way our moms were. Maybe we are destiny.

"I didn't know she was going to do it. Or, I didn't know that she was going to not do it," Dorothy says. She's quiet, and maybe it's because the gods can hear us, if they're listening, which they sometimes are. I step closer to her so she knows I want to hear, I'm ready to hear.

"Oh."

"It was sort of like her, I guess."

"Yeah."

"I think she thought she could be human and not change much. She didn't know there'd be some fast-driving car at the edge of town. She didn't know she wouldn't have fifty years to be human. And she definitely didn't know that the gods would get so mad. I know that sounds weird, because when your mom does things it's all thought out and stuff but my mom isn't—wasn't—like that. We were planning my birthday party. She was making her tapestry of Pandora. She wanted to try a new bread recipe. She wanted to be old and here on Our Hill with the rest of us. She didn't know this would all— This wasn't supposed to happen this way."

"I know she wanted to live," I say, because that's the easy part, that's the one thing we all know for sure about Penny Hardy. She loved being alive. "But maybe she wanted Our Hill to change. Maybe she wanted things to be all mixed up, for there to be some upheaval. Maybe she knew the gods would get mad and would make us choose." I don't know why I say it exactly, except that I can't stop thinking it and there's no one else to talk to about it. Penny talked about change, sometimes, in a way that no one else ever dared to. And all the talk about Pandora. She didn't always believe what the rest of us did.

"She wouldn't do that," Dorothy says, but she doesn't sound as sure as she sounded about her mom wanting to grow old and make bread. One of her hands makes a bracelet around the other and twists and twists and twists.

"You're sure?" As soon as it comes out I realize it's the question that's been pounding in the background of every morning of these last months. It's why my mom sometimes stays up all night long drinking tea on the back porch and I find her asleep in one of the wooden chairs out there in the morning, and she looks confused and alone in that early morning light. It's why I've started looking away from the ladder, even when I'm sitting directly underneath it with my friends. It's why I'm here now, I think, trying to understand what Penny wanted when she did what she did. And if what she wanted was this. The end of Our Hill.

Dorothy doesn't answer that question, so I guess she's not so sure either, about what it all means. "I miss her," she says instead. Penny should have left an instruction manual. She should have told us what she wanted us to understand.

She should be here.

A heat that feels a little like anger flames in me, and maybe in Dorothy too. Her jaw is tight. "I miss her," she says again, the words harder and faster.

"Me too," I say. "I mean, not like how you do obviously, but still."

"It's okay. You can miss her too."

It is maybe the kindest thing anyone has ever said to me.

"One month," Dorothy says. "You guys will go up, right?" I like how she cuts to the heart of things.

"That's what my mom says. You guys too?" I want her to say yes, so that we're together up there. Even though we were never best friends, Dorothy is familiar in a way that Reece and even Dawn can't be. She's always wearing the same type of blue dress—sort of shapeless and knee-length—in the same shade—a navy blue that looks like the night sky. Her hair is the same unusual strawberry-blond color Penny's was, and she usually has grass stains on her knees, a leaf in her hair, she smells kind of like pine trees. And she says what she means.

She has to come to Olympus, to make it home there too.

"I don't know what Mom would have wanted. She loved it here."

"Well, you can't just stay on earth and be a human like—"

"Like she did?" Dorothy just keeps looking at that river, like maybe her mom is in there and can tell her what to do. But of course she isn't.

"I guess," I say. It's getting dark early these days, and the beginning of the moon is showing. Stars will prick their way through soon, too. There's so much I want to tell Dorothy—about the last time I talked to her mom, and the things I promised her and what it means to me that she's gone and we're here and how my mother can't be the person she was without Penny and how maybe actually none of us can. I want to talk about how little we actually understand about being human, even living on earth our whole lives, visiting their towns, buying things from their stores. How we may be near-gods, but that's still far, far away from being human, so we have to make our decisions carefully.

But I don't know how to say any of that, so I keep watching the sky, and so does she.

A few more stars alight, and I find myself looking for

Penny up there, alongside the constellations we know so well—Orion and Cassiopeia and Andromeda and all the others who the gods placed in the sky to punish or remember them. Last year we stayed overnight in the field by school to learn the placement and story behind each and every constellation. We stayed up all night counting stars, charting them onto large pieces of heavy paper, drawing wobbly lines to connect the dots and see what the gods intended for us to see.

"She should be up there," I say, before thinking it through, but once I say it the truth of it is heavy and real. "Ms. Callow talked about how she'd placed a star in the sky for her sixteenth birthday when she was a kid, remember?"

Dorothy nodded. She never says much, but I think she is curious to hear more.

"If she could do that, we could too. And what's a constellation but a bunch of stars, right? I mean, that's what they're for, the stars. To remember people who mattered. Right?" My heart is pounding from the thrill of a plan emerging.

"A constellation of my mom?" Dorothy asks. She tilts her head far back so she can see as much of the sky as possible. I do the same. We could do it. We could put Penny in the sky. We could make her last forever.

"Yes! I mean, I know it doesn't— It just would be nice. To know she's there. She deserves it, doesn't she?" I'm getting so excited, I'm already trying to imagine what it would feel like to take the silver ladder and lean it in a new direction and rearrange the night sky. We are near-gods, after all. We can do it. We are not mortal humans.

Not yet, anyway.

"She does," Dorothy says. I can tell she's thinking but she doesn't think out loud, which is hard. It makes my feet tap and my nose itch, waiting to find out what's going on in there.

"She loved stars," Dorothy says.

"I remember."

And for a moment I'm sure that even though Dorothy doesn't say it out loud, we are thinking the same thoughts, remembering the same things: The night when we saw a shooting star in the sky on my mom's birthday and Penny squealed so loudly, with such excitement, that she woke up the new baby who lived next door. The star-themed tapestry that Penny wove and laid out in their living room so that, she said, she could walk in the sky like a god and be here on earth with her family at the same time. The night that Penny and my mom woke us up because, they said, it was the perfect temperature, the perfect nighttime weather, and we needed to take advantage. We all lay on a thick white blanket Mom had made, and we watched the stars in the sky until the sun came up. Dorothy fell asleep and they thought I was asleep too, but I wasn't. I stayed up listening to them talking about everything I could have imagined—families and food and gossip and what bit of godly magic they liked best and which they could live without, and what they hoped for me and Dorothy, when we got older.

"I hope they're friends," Penny had said. "I know right now . . . But someday, you know? They could be like us."

"They have to be," Mom had said, and she leaned her head against Penny's shoulder, something I never saw her do with anyone else, and at the time I thought it was silly, but now it feels like a wish I have to make come true. "They're meant to be."

"They're good for each other, if they'd just see it," Penny said, her smile a little faraway but also right there.

"Okay," Dorothy says now. "Okay. A constellation. We could do that I guess."

"We'll have to climb the ladder," I say, remembering what our teacher said last year, when she told the story about the star she placed in the sky. "Obviously not all the way up to, you know, Olympus and stuff. But up past the clouds a little."

Dorothy looks at the ladder so I do too. "And we'll have to gather stars," she says. "Do you know how?"

I shake my head, but how hard can it be? I'm from Hera, after all. From Zeus. I'm the only near-god born without the help of a father. I can do almost anything.

Dorothy smiles. "I know how," she says. "I've done it before."

"Caught stars?"

"With Mom." Dorothy's smile grows. When it's that big, it looks the way it did when we were little and she was happy and things were easy. "Why do you think she liked the river so much?"

And then I watch as Dorothy glances up at the sky, squints, then kneels down to the river. There's the reflection of a star right there on the surface of the water. She plunges her hand in and grabs it.

And just like that, there's a star in her hand, ready to be pinned to the sky.

"This is my Happy today," she says. She looks at me, waiting for me to remember something, and I do, of course I do.

"Mine too," I say. "My Sad was you walking out of school today. Or I guess my Sad was Reece. The things she said. The way Mr. Winters didn't stop it." I look at her, gauging her response to this. She nods. She takes it seriously, Happy and Sad, and so did Penny. "What's your Sad?" I ask.

"Right now," she says. "I mean, it's my Happy. But my Sad, too. Because Mama would love it. You and me here. Getting stars. Planning a constellation the way gods do. My Sad is her missing it."

It's my turn to nod.

And I do, and do, and do.

10.

"Let's do it tonight." I almost grab the star right from Dorothy's hand, but I catch myself before snatching it.

"Tonight? Like, right now?" Dorothy laughs, and I sort of want to shake her, because she's taking her time when we don't have any. She's thinking things through, but Our Hill is falling apart right this instant, a little more every day.

"The gods probably won't love us putting up a constellation of Penny, you know? So we shouldn't do too much at once, so they don't do anything to stop us." I'm talking fast, which I know I do when something matters to me, and Mom's always telling me to slow down, that people listen more when you are slow and steady.

I try, I really do, to be that person who gives calm

107

smiles and happy half-shrugs when things are going well. But I mostly fail at being that way, at waiting and thinking and looking calm and elegant when my mind is sparking with ideas. Sometimes almost everything feels like an emergency—choosing what to wear and who to sit with, deciding where to have a birthday party and what god to choose to do a report on, how to talk to a teacher and whether to take piano or flute lessons.

And now, this. An actual emergency. A choice so big, my brain can barely think it.

"One by one," Dorothy says. She's gripping the star in her hand tightly.

"What should your mom be doing, in the constellation? Or holding? They're always holding stuff and doing stuff." I'm getting excited, at the idea of seeing Penny again, making her real. And even more than that. Of having something with Dorothy that is just ours.

A secret.

Our moms always had secrets. Dawn and Reece and I share bangle-y bracelets and clementines at lunch, and sometimes a shiny swipe of lip gloss before a party.

We share a lot. But not secrets.

Dorothy isn't saying anything. She's just looking back and forth from the sky to the star in her hand, like she can't quite figure out how they'll work together.

"Bread?" I ask. "Your mom baking bread in the sky? She loved that."

"She did," Dorothy says, but she doesn't sound enthusiastic, so I guess it's not the best idea. "But bread is sort of . . . I mean, my mom was more than bread."

"Of course," I say, blushing. I want her to know I understand, I get it, I care about her mom in a big and unbreakable way too. "Yeah, bread is silly. It's like, nothing. Your mom was a lot more than that."

"She's the one who didn't climb the ladder," Dorothy says. Her eyes squint, and I think she's searching for the perfect place for her mom. I have to be careful with what I say, but my heart is racing.

"Well. Yeah. But that was sort of— I guess that isn't quite exactly how we want everyone to remember her, maybe?" I need my heart to slow down so I can think better, so I can think of something better than bread, but also better than the worst mistake Penny ever made, the reason the world is breaking right now.

Dorothy shrugs. "Yeah," she says. "I guess it's a bad idea."

"She liked weaving," I say, and I don't think it's any better than bread, but it's definitely better than a constellation of Penny and the ladder, Penny messing up everything we've ever known.

"Yeah. I mean, bread was a good idea," Dorothy says. "She's the only one here who baked bread. That's something I guess."

"Really good bread," I say, but it sounds sort of small and sad, and I wish I could think of a way to capture all that Penny was—funny and bighearted and so at ease that she made even my mother calm down. I don't think any of that can be captured in the stars, though. "And bread is warm and sweet, like her."

Dorothy laughs, and I think she's thinking the same things I'm thinking, that the ways Penny was special aren't easy to draw. "Sure," she says.

I found Penny at the river once, after a fight with my mother. Reece was playing at my house and had said something about the weirdness of Athena being born from Zeus's head, and how maybe that's what made her make some of the mistakes she'd made. We had just learned about how when Athena was little she accidentally killed her friend Pallas, then was later filled with regret and made a statue of her, and our teacher insisted that that long-ago mistake made Athena even wiser, even more worthy of worship, but Reece disagreed.

I'd started to cry, knowing I was born from just my mother, like Athena was just from her father, and that even though for my whole life everyone had said that was special, maybe it was all a lie and it actually made me weird, wrong.

I tried to explain it all to Mom, but she couldn't get over the crying. The messiness of it. How I was crying and Reece was straight-backed and sure, and how disappointing that was. How I wasn't being very elegant, very godlike. How I wasn't honoring Hera with all of my silliness.

So I went to the river and told Penny the whole story.

"I'm not enough like Hera," I said.

"Of course not," Penny said, and it stung at first, but she kept going. "You can't be Hera. You're Apple."

She said it so simply, like it was the most obvious thing in the world, like we weren't all destined to take after our godly ancestors, like the myths weren't the stories guiding our lives.

"I'm Hera's descendant," I said.

"Sure," Penny said. "And I'm Pandora's. But we're also just us, right?" She smiled, like it was really simple. It was windy and she'd brought a blanket, so she pulled it around the both of us, and we stayed like that for a while. And under that blanket with Penny, it felt simple.

Maybe this is what she meant. Maybe this is just me being me and Dorothy being Dorothy.

Kids are heading home for dinner and grown-ups are thinking of ways to talk to us about the new world we're living in, and we have a pocket of time now, maybe, before people remember to care that we ran away from school, before Mom calls Reece's mom or Dorothy's dad worries that she's been at the river too long.

Now is the moment. When the sky is gray and the night hasn't really officially begun, but almost, and the ladder is empty with no one next to it.

"This is her dimple," Dorothy says, lifting the star so I can see whatever it is she's seeing. "You remember her dimple, right? She just had one. Left cheek. But deep. I always wished I had one too, but I didn't."

Constellations don't usually get so detailed as to include dimples, but I don't say that.

"I don't know how to do it," I say instead. I don't think I've ever said that to anyone. No one has ever asked me to do something I wasn't fated to do, no one has ever been better at something than I am. I'm Apple Montgomery, descendant of Hera and Zeus, fatherless daughter of Heather Montgomery, born from her like Athena from Zeus, heir to the apple tree of immortality, honored family of Our Hill. Most popular girl in school.

"I'll show you," Dorothy says, and she points to a star just now budding in the sky. She traces a line from the sky to the river, where the star's reflection is wavy and slight, barely a trace. "Just scoop it up," she says. "Focus. Believe. And reach in."

I look back and forth—sky to river to sky to river. For eleven whole years everything in my life was the same every day. If something went wrong, we could change it. Smooth it out with magic. Make a piece of cake sweeter or a hot day cooler. We could fix everything that needed fixing, which wasn't very much, actually, because Mom and I were the head of Our Hill, immortal near-gods floating through life.

And now I'm here, doing something brand new. Lightning bolts in the ground flicker their warnings. Maybe the gods see us, even. Maybe they'll punish us. I don't know. I don't know much of anything anymore.

"Come on," Dorothy says. "You can do it."

And I don't know what else to believe anymore, so I believe her. I lean over the river, and my hands dip in, and I scoop.

And there it is. A tiny baby star. The start of something big.

It doesn't take long to walk to the ladder with stars in our hands, but once we're there it's like we have no idea what to do.

"I think we just . . . do it?" I say. I lean my head back to look at the ladder. It's tall and thin and delicate as always. "We climb up partway and then we just, like, let go of the star I guess?"

"There's a good spot, over here," Dorothy says, pointing at an empty bit of sky.

"Pretty."

And I guess one of us should actually do something, but we don't—we just stand there, squeezing our stars and looking at the place in the sky where I guess Penny might belong.

"Hey," Dorothy says, interrupting the silence. "This was a good idea. Thank you."

"You're welcome."

"You're sure you want to do it? We might get in trouble."

"Dorothy?" I say. "We're already in kind of a lot of trouble."

The sky darkens. The lightning bolts stand there, all straight and sharp. Time just ticks away, every second one second closer to having to decide to be god or human, here or up there. I reach for Dorothy as I've been doing the last few days. Her hand is always right there, something good and solid in the midst of everything terrifying and new, and I squeeze for reassurance, but I guess harder than I mean to, because she sort of winces. "Sorry."

She squeezes back, not as hard, then lets go. "We have to tilt the ladder the other way," she says. I nod like it's nothing, like it's easy. We grab the bottom and lean and it leans with us, until it leads to the spot in the sky we've chosen for Penny. My hands are sweaty and my mouth is dry, but we're doing it. We aren't saying much, we aren't holding hands anymore, but it doesn't matter. I feel so close to Dorothy,

I almost feel like I *am* Dorothy. We've crossed from some sort of awkward family friends to something else, just from moving the ladder.

"Wow," I say, about the ladder and also about us.

"Come on," she says, and I guess Dorothy is the leader and I'm the follower and even that feels sort of good, in its new, weird way. She steps on the first rung. And the second. "You're coming, right?" she says, and there's a shake in her voice, which I think is the memory of being on the ladder all those months ago with Penny staying behind, and I have to be strong for Dorothy, I have to be clear-headed and ready.

"Of course," I say, and get on the first rung, behind her. And we climb.

And we climb.

We pass through a cloud. There are still dozens above us, more miles before actual Olympus, but we stop in the same moment, right above that first cloud. "Here," I say. I think she needs me to be the one to decide.

"Yeah?" Dorothy looks around. I've never seen the sky from quite this angle, not really, and neither has Dorothy.

"It's good to have her low. So we can always reach her. This will take a while, probably."

"Right. A while." Dorothy nods and reaches her hand with the star out and over the sky. It hovers there for a moment, like she doesn't know where in the graying expanse it should go.

"It's going to be perfect," I say, and I guess that's the right thing to say, because she lets go of the star, placing it the way we used to glue plastic jewels onto paper crowns, once again turning something plain into something spectacular. She pulls herself back squarely onto the ladder. "See?" I say. "That's great. Her dimple."

"Thank you for doing this with me," Dorothy says, touching the place on her own face where she wishes she had her own matching dimple. Her voice is small, and my heart is surging with the sureness that I am doing something right for her.

"Okay. How about her hand," I say, and I try to chart the constellation of Penny in my mind's eye. We'll need a few dozen stars, maybe, to make the outline of her holding a loaf of bread. She can't be a huge constellation—there isn't room for that—but her bright dimple-star will make her a visible one. I linger above a certain spot, a half a foot below the dimple. "This looks about right, right?" I ask Dorothy. She nods and holds her breath as I place my star too.

Right now they're not the kind of thing anyone would ever notice. Just two stars among millions in the sky. But someday soon, they will be our memory of Penny.

We climb back down the ladder and Dorothy seems sadder and happier at the same time, the whole night heavier and harder and more ours. She keeps her eyes skyward, barely blinking.

"You're really going to live up there, aren't you? You're going to be happy up there?" she says. My stomach drops even though I've already told her what Mom told me. That yes, we will go up there. That it has been decided already. But I want to sit on the ground with Dorothy and look at a constellation of her mother and I want to be her best friend and to make Penny proud and to be someone more than Hera's great-great-great-great-great-great-granddaughter. I want a best friend, the way Mom and Penny were best friends.

I am doing what Penny asked. I am doing what our moms both hoped for, that long-ago day when they whispered about it. And I want to hold on to it more tightly than I've ever held on to anything.

"You'll come too," I say.

Dorothy shrugs.

"Let's walk to school together again," I say. "That was really fun. We could even get ready at your place together. And people will be nicer tomorrow. I'll make sure."

Dorothy shrugs again, but then she nods her head so it's a yes, but not a very enthusiastic one. It's okay. It is. We're both tired and it's getting late and it has been a long few days.

"Sounds okay to me," Dorothy says before walking off on her own. She doesn't say goodbye, so I do, kind of loudly. "See ya," she calls back, just like Penny used to do, a sort of singsong of a goodbye, a promise that it was just temporary, the parting.

I look back at the sky one more time. Penny's dimple-star is the brightest one up there.

At home, I wait for Mom to yell at me for leaving school. I assume Mr. Winters has called or will call any moment now to tell her what happened, to express his concern. He is always expressing concern about kids who do things he doesn't understand.

But Mom doesn't yell and the questions don't come.

Instead, Mom is building tiny statues out of clay, of the thrones on Olympus. A reminder, she says, of where we belong, where the best of us must go, of the duty we have to our ancestors. She barely says hello. Her nails are caked with gray, there's glaze on her forehead, she looks focused, as if what she's doing matters a great deal.

I don't know if it does. Mom is here, making tiny statues. But Dorothy and I are changing the sky,

Dorothy and I, in our friendship, which is both old and new at the same time, are maybe changing everything.

11.

I show up at Dorothy's house first thing the next morning and knock on the door, loud and sure the way Mom always does. But I don't like the sound it makes, it's too much, so I try again, softer, three quiet knocks that aren't regal and strong but feel better for the moment.

"Oh!" Dorothy's dad answers the door with a start. "Gosh, Apple, what are you doing here?"

"I told Dorothy we could get ready for school together," I say, and peer around him, assuming I'll find Dorothy waiting for me, but she's at her kitchen counter, looking just as confused as him.

"Well, come on in," George says. He half sings everything he says, and it's impossible not to smile at him.

Dorothy isn't smiling. She looks tired and confused and like we didn't make this whole plan already. I have a dress for her over my shoulder and I brought thread to weave matching bracelets and I need to braid her hair for her again so that it looks like mine. We've watched our moms braid each other's hair before. They stuck flowers in the weaves. They looked more like nymphs than near-gods by the river. And Penny made Mom a scarf that matched her own once. It was silky and three shades of blue and Mom wore it with everything for a while, except I haven't seen it in months upon months.

Dorothy should be excited, but she's just sitting there, munching on bread with butter and blinking like I have to explain what's happening here.

"I have two of these dresses, so this should be perfect," I say, holding out a light blue toga that is the twin of the one I'm wearing. It doesn't look at all like the sort of thing Dorothy usually wears, but that's the whole point. It has tiny crystal beads on the straps and it's long and swingy and the color the sky used to be, before the gods sent down the screed and darkened it with the never-ending soot and smoke from the lightning bolts.

"Oh," Dorothy says. "Wow. That's fancy."

"We can't let anyone say anything else to you, you know? This will help."

"What are people saying to you?" George asks, his brow

furrowing. George is the sort of dad who cares about stuff like bullying and who is friends with who and all sorts of drama that happens in sixth grade. I don't know much about dads, but I know not all of them are like that. Not all moms, either. Mine asks about the ins and outs of classes and friendship and what everyone's talking about at school, but sometimes she forgets to listen to the answers. I'll try to tell her about how Reece said something sort of rude to Chloe, and she'll interrupt and start giving a speech about how I can't concern myself with everyone else's minutia, that's not what leaders do.

By the time she's done, I've forgotten what I was trying to tell her in the first place. But she'll have this contented look on her face like we've had some great conversation, like we've bonded.

She was never like that with Penny. With Penny she could lean back and listen.

"Nothing, Dad," Dorothy says. "They're just being all whatever about Mama and the screed and Olympus and whose fault it all is and stuff. It's nothing. I ignore them."

"We're ignoring them," I correct her, because we're in it together and I want George to know that too. "Don't worry, I won't let anyone say anything to her."

Dorothy looks like she wants to say something—thank me? Agree? I don't know—but she doesn't. She just sort of shrugs and finishes her bread and reaches for the dress. "So you think I should wear this?"

"That?" George asks, even though I don't think she was asking her dad for fashion advice. He looks confused.

"It'll be fun. Reece and Dawn do matching all the time, for holidays and stuff."

"Okay."

"Do you remember when our moms did matching dresses for the last Panathenaia? Matching laurels, too, gold ones? And they tried to get us to match with them too, but I wanted to wear something short because everyone was wearing short stuff then and you just wanted to wear what you always wear, so they just matched each other? Remember?"

George's confusion slides into something else—that happy-sadness or sad-happiness that means he's remembering.

"I remember," Dorothy says, and she looks up at me with these achey eyes, and then I feel it too—the moment we missed, the way we should have dressed up with them, the memory that isn't there, which would have been even better than the one that is.

The fact that we can't fix it now.

"Let's do it," Dorothy says, and finally she smiles at me, her shoulders a little looser than they were moments before. "It's a good idea. Mama would have loved it."

When I'm done with her, Dorothy looks a little unfamiliar in this new-to-her shade of blue and with perfectly combed braids and the shine of crystals reflecting in the early morning light. She looks like me, but not; like her mom, but not; like herself, but also not quite that either.

We weave bracelets for each other on the way to school. The rhythm of weaving something is so familiar we can do it while we walk, we can do it anytime, anywhere. I choose silver and blue thread for ours. I keep sneaking glances at Dorothy's, which is a very simple braid, different from the one I'm doing, which is a twisty-turny type of pattern that Penny herself taught me.

"You don't have to be a god to make something beautiful from something simple," she'd said, helping my fingers make the patterns. She was always saying things like that.

We don't talk much on the way to school, but when we pass the ladder we both pause to look at it, to make sure we left it where we found it, leaning the right way, looking untouched and unremarkable.

And right outside school, we tie the bracelets around one another's wrists and I take Dorothy's hand to walk in together.

"Don't do this," Dawn whispers when she passes us by. "Your mom is worried about you, and Reece is . . . Reece. And people are talking and this is serious, Apple." Her eyes keep darting in Dorothy's direction. I wonder if she notices, too, the awkward way Dorothy holds her body in her new clothes, how her arms are looking for a place to be.

"I know it's serious," I say. "What do you think I'm doing?"

"I honestly don't know. Being really weird mostly. You know this is all sort of happening because Dorothy's mom—"

I see Dorothy's shoulders twitch and I wonder what it's like, to be the sort of person that no one really notices, even when they're right there, even when they're talking about her dead mother.

Everyone on Our Hill is talking about what's next, even my mom, but I can't seem to get past what used to be— eating Penny-made donuts in the front yard, naming cloud shapes in the sky, and the laugh my mom had when we were around her— and when I'm with Dorothy, that's fine because that's where she is too.

"I'm not going to let what happened to Penny happen to Dorothy," I say.

Dorothy clears her throat.

"I just mean we're in it together," I say, turning to her now. She nods and looks at the bracelet I made for her. "And we'll go up there together. And figure it out together. Right?"

Dorothy and Dawn look at one another. They both look a little sad and a little something else, like they know something I don't know, which isn't even possible. I know them both and they barely know each other at all.

"Mama always said our hearts know best," Dorothy says,

and the sentence stops me, because my mom always says the gods have told us everything we need to know about who we need to be, and it feels like the things our moms have told us don't quite line up, and that maybe there's not room for both.

"There's a month before we have to decide," Dawn says to us both. "God or human. You know? One month. You're Apple Montgomery. She's Dorothy Hardy. This is a really bad time to get confused about who is who."

Dawn turns away from us before I can respond, but I don't have a response anyway. I know who we are. And what it means. I reach for Dorothy's hand and look at the way we match. Two near-gods in blue, entering our last month on earth together. Changing the stars in the sky.

Nothing could be clearer. Nothing could be less confusing.

I squeeze Dorothy's hand, and wait for the heartbeat thump of her squeezing back.

DOROTHY

Two Weeks Later

DECEMBER 5

12.

"Something is different in the sky," Dad says. Two weeks have passed since Apple and I started placing stars in the sky in the shape of Mama and her bread and I've been waiting for someone to notice.

I didn't think the someone would be Dad. He has been saying less and less lately, going a little quiet at strange times, walking us every few nights to the ladder, just to look at it, to talk about what is up there and what's down here and what it means. We don't conclude anything. Mama would have made a decision by now, with time pressing down on us, the gods reminding us with weekly thunderstorms about the decision we have to make.

Sometimes Apple says I'm quiet too, so maybe that's just who I am, more like Dad than Mama. Or maybe that's who we are without Mama. Quiet people, looking up at a ladder, stuck.

Tonight, though, Dad lifts one long arm and points to the half-made constellation.

"Oh. Huh. I don't know," I say. The shape of Mama is unmistakable to me. We've placed over two dozen stars and somehow I can make out the flyaway hairs she sometimes frowned at, the strong thickness of her legs, the delicate way she used to handle bread. It's all there, it's her.

"Constellations are for people we want to remember," Dad says.

"Right. Or people that the gods are punishing."

"Or both, I guess," Dad says. He raises his eyebrows. He wiggles them. He smiles. "It's both, isn't it?"

"What do you mean?" I ask, but I know he knows and he knows that I know that he knows, so the question comes with a giggle, and then we are surprised into silence because Dad and I don't laugh together, not anymore.

"It's beautiful," Dad says. "You know, constellations are for remembering, but stars are for wishing. Mama said to be careful when you've got a star in your hands. They're powerful. Okay, Dorothy?"

I nod. It's not something Mama ever mentioned to me,

and I wonder how long the list is, of things I needed to learn and understand that she just never got around to telling me.

"What kind of wish—" I start, but I don't finish the sentence because the bell in the center of the town rings. That bell only rings when a meeting is being called with all of us on Our Hill, something that happens a few times a year. To commemorate Athena's birthday. To send prayers up to Zeus by offering cakes and fruits. To plan a trip to a mortal town, to watch them celebrate their holidays or talk about their heartbreaks or just play one of their big sports games, where they all cheer and yell and eat melted cheese.

The bell hasn't rung in a while, but now it's insistent that we all gather down at the bottom of the hill, where the mountain meets the rest of earth, where we are farther away from the gods. Our meetings are meant to be ours without them, and of course they could still visit, they can go anywhere on earth, but there was something good about being away from the ladder and the sky and our past.

"Town meeting?" Dad asks, like I know anything at all.

"I guess."

Dad runs his hands through his hair and hums a few lines of a song I think he's been writing since Mama died, about ladders and fate and blue dresses and sunsets. It sounds like the sort of song Orpheus would have sung about his lost love, and I hear him singing it outside some nights while I'm trying to sleep. It sounds heavy now, like a warning or a worry.

Everything Dad does and says lately sounds like a worry-song, a worry-tune, a thing sung or said when your heart is twisty-turning and your breath is slow and shallow and waiting.

"I'm sure everyone knows it's Mama," he says, nodding up at the sky.

"That's okay," I say. Everyone knows I miss her. That I want to remember her. That I am looking for ways to hold on to her.

"It might not be," he says. "You know how people are now." He gets up. Holds his hand in my direction to help me up too, and we walk down the hill together hand in hand, forgetting to let go.

Apple's already there. Of course she is. She's pacing the outer edge of the meeting circle and when she sees me she flies at me, crushing me in a hug I'm not sure I want right now. "Mom's having a moment," she says. "She says it's time to know who's where."

"We're all right here," I say. *Except Mama*, I don't say.

"She wants people to commit. To up there or down here. To our side or, you know, the other side."

"Our side?"

"Mom's side."

"Oh."

"She's— This has been hard for her," Apple says. She wants me to understand something from the words, but I don't know what, exactly.

"Yeah, it's a weird time."

"She really loved your mom." I don't know why Apple's saying the things she's saying but every sentence is making me nervous. She's telling me things I know, but in this tone of voice like whatever is about to happen might make me question these always-known things.

"They were best friends," I say, trying to speak in the same code as Apple, but failing because I don't really know how.

"When Mom loves someone it comes out all weird sometimes. Like Hera. She did all kinds of weird stuff for love, you know?" I think through the list of things Hera did out of love and jealousy and rage and passion. Curses and killings and transforming people into cows and making decisions that lasted forever because of a single terrible moment.

Whatever Apple was telling me was bad.

"Sure."

"Okay. Yeah. I knew you'd understand."

I don't really, of course, but I don't say that because the meeting is starting and I don't know that Apple would really hear me anyway. My voice is quiet or too fast or not the sort of voice people listen to, I think. And mostly that's okay.

Mostly.

The meeting circle is lit by lanterns made by magic. I know, because lanterns lit by magic glow silver and warm. And because we always light our meetings with magic, the thing that brings us together. It's cold today, so there are thick sweaters around people's shoulders, mostly blue, or an occasional gray that could be blue, in the right light.

"We don't need to be in the cold," Heather says, her voice poking through the dark. She's in the center of the circle, standing on a crystal box to give her height above us. The box looks elegant and official and I have no idea where it's come from. Usually we stand on equal footing, here. Usually we are all on one single level. "We are gods," she goes on. "We can change the weather." She raises a hand up to Olympus, and this is when Mama would usually interject, reminding everyone about everything we love about winter. Snow and hot chocolate and the way ice makes trees look like fairy forests. How good it feels to wear thick socks and step into a warm home after a cold walk.

There's a pause, like Heather's waiting for her too.

The words stick in my own throat, the things Mama loved about the world, the reasons she wanted to stay here, the way she asked us all to be more human than god, to try to understand them and figure out what they liked about being here. "We chose this," Mama would remind us. She wouldn't have stood on a crystal box, but her voice would have been loud and sure.

I'm not strong and certain like Mama. I'm not brave and in love with the world like her.

Most days, I don't really know who I am anymore. A little bit Dorothy and a little bit Apple, and a little bit a shadow of a person who used to be fuller and happier and easier in the world.

The pause ends, and Heather's hand whips the air and the temperature spikes. "There we go," Heather says. "Much better. I'll change it back after the meeting."

But it isn't better. Sweaters slip off bodies and the crisp air turns muggy, and it's almost November: it is not supposed to feel this way.

We are not in the habit, on Our Hill, of changing the weather back and forth at whim. Every once in a while, sure, as a treat for kids on winter break or in the middle of the summer heat wave, someone may make a perfect snow day. Those bits of magic feel different from this. Heather looks proud of herself and Dad is rubbing his forehead and Apple's hands grip around my arm and squeeze.

"She's excited to be a god," Apple whispers, a secret that isn't really a very well-kept one, because I think all of Our

Hill can tell. My stomach turns and I look up in the sky to see Mama's constellation and it's the only thing that makes sense right now.

"The solstice is coming," Heather says. "And we need to decide what we are doing. We're a community. And this community is born of gods and goddesses. Born of power and magic and history and fate. And I urge us all to hang on tight to that destiny. To make this decision together."

The crowd is still. I wonder if everyone else feels the hole where Mama once was, the things she would be saying if she were here.

"A terrible decision was made, and it's put us here, in this moment. It's clear what we have to do. We can't let ourselves sink to the level of human. We can't give up our exceptional destiny. We can't let one person's mistakes bring us down the wrong path. We have to rise above."

She isn't saying Mama's name, but she's talking about her plain as day and everyone knows it. Everyone here watched Mama and Heather walk around town with their elbows hooked like they needed to be physically attached at all times. They saw them barefoot with their feet in the water and lying on their backs looking up at the ladder on clear nights. We all know they were best friends.

It was a couple weeks ago that Heather sat in our kitchen celebrating Mama's birthday, wiping away tears at the memory of her, at all the beautiful memories of who she was and why we loved her.

"We are better than someone who would choose that path," Heather continues, and I want Dad to speak up and defend Mama, but instead I watch him walk away from the meeting, something no one ever does. His sweater—a little too green to be blue, another one of Mama's creations that weren't quite in line with the way things were supposed to be—is in one hand and the other hand is stuffed in a pocket and his whole body is slumped a little, the way it's been since Mama died.

"Generations ago, Pandora made the world miserable. We will not allow one of her ancestors to ruin things for us, too." Heather's so angry, she's shaking a little, and I finally see myself in her a little bit—the way anger and grief can get all mixed up together, the way missing Mama hurts so much that sometimes, late at night when no one's looking, it makes me hate her a little too, for making me love her, for giving me this new and awful feeling in my heart.

Heather's anger is turning to tears, I can tell from the flutter of her eyelashes, like frantic butterflies trying to get away, and how her voice is starting to gravel and grump in her throat.

"Okay, all right, Heather," Chloe's father says. He is tall with hair as straight and black as Chloe's. Like Chloe, he cares about every part of history—from his own godly and Japanese ancestries, elaborate family trees he works on for himself, and also for everyone else on Our Hill. The family trees he crafts are beautiful, with details about human countries and godly alliances and even tiny stories of who each of the humans and gods in the trees really were, what they did and who they loved and how it all fits together. But also like Chloe, he doesn't speak much, so when he does people listen. "That's enough. We understand. We hear you." His gaze finds me and then quickly flicks away. There are hung heads and eyes that are looking anywhere but at me. There are kids from class sort of laughing and sort of staring and sort of rolling their eyes, like they've known all along who I am and what that means.

There is Heather, who doesn't look over at me and Apple, but speaks so loudly and so quickly that I almost hope maybe she hasn't heard herself, that she's lost track of what she's saying altogether.

Because she can't be saying that Mama is nothing but a person who ruined the world.

She can't be saying that she rejects the whole huge history of their friendship.

Except I guess she is. And all the angry grief in the world can't make it okay.

Maybe she won't even want me to come up to Olympus. Maybe she thinks Dad and I should stay down here, in the mess that she thinks Mama made.

Maybe she wants to be able to forget all about Mama

and us and the life we had before, and I understand and don't understand in the exact same amount. No one told me that so many feelings were possible at one time, ones that don't fit together, don't match at all.

I guess this is being human, too. The part we've been avoiding for all these generations.

"It's okay," Apple says in this whisper that is so strained, I can practically feel the tightness of her throat. "This will be okay."

"Apple. No, it won't," I say. It is almost always true that Apple knows exactly what is happening on Our Hill and exactly what it means for us. Some humans passed through our town once. It had never happened before. We visit their towns but they never stumble upon ours. It's out of the way and hidden behind other hills and other towns. The one time they found us, Apple knew before the rest of us that our plan was to vanish from sight until they passed, which we did, temporarily letting Apple's mom and a few other ancestors of the most powerful gods transform us into flowers that scattered the hillside. Blue flowers, of course. Sturdy ones.

The humans passed through over the course of a day, and then we were able to shift back into ourselves. I still dream sometimes about being stuck in the earth—the smell of dirt and how scary it was, to watch shoes stomp around us, to be unable to speak or move except for if the wind wanted you to.

I didn't like being a flower.

But that was something Apple knew about. She promised it would be okay, and it was.

This is not that.

"We'll live up on Olympus," Apple says. "It's pretty up there. My mom will chill out. The gods will calm down. And you and me will be together. Okay? I mean, we're best friends now. We'll live up there and eat cake and walk in the clouds and maybe we'll come down to earth to do something nice for humans once a year. Like make spring come early or something. I don't know, we'll figure it out—that's what gods do, right?"

I look up at the clouds. They're hard to see at night, but there are a few gray patches of them visible. Heather is yelling some more stuff about fate and obligation and duty and all kinds of words that sound huge but also mean nothing when they're said all at once like that, so loud, one rolling on top of the other so fast you can't even take them in, like a storm I wasn't expecting but should have been.

"I don't know," I say.

"I do," Apple replies. She rubs my back and I know I'm supposed to lean into it a little, but I can't—my body decides to shift the smallest bit away. I want Dad. I want Mama. I don't want Apple right now.

Heather calls a vote, trying to grasp who has decided and who has not, and of the two hundred people living on

Our Hill, one hundred and forty-three have decided to go up to Olympus.

The rest aren't sure.

No one has decided to stay. Or at least no one will admit to it.

Heather smiles, pleased with the numbers and herself, and I miss her—not this Heather here, but the one she was with Mama, laughing and adding too much cinnamon to a loaf of Mama's bread, and listening to Mama talk about Pandora and what no one understands about her. I miss that quiet nod of her head and the way she'd say, "I never thought of it that way before," like she was really listening and thinking and considering. I even miss the prickly way she used to get when Apple scooched next to Mama at a party, how she'd try to chat with me when the two of them were whispering or laughing about something or other, and how it never felt right.

The meeting starts to break up and Heather steps off the crystal box.

"Want me to walk you home?" Apple asks, and it's nice but I am not feeling nice. I am feeling something else that I've never really felt before—something shaky and sudden and swirling.

Heather strides toward us. When her gaze meets mine she looks like she has something to say, but I don't let her say it.

"Mama would be so disappointed," I say right to her straight-backed, smug-faced self.

And I turn to go before I can see the words register on her face.

I hope they do. I really hope they do.

13.

Apple is over the next morning like she's been every morning since the screed. She has apple scones and matching blue bracelets, one with her name and one with mine.

"More bracelets?" I ask. The ones we wove on the way to school are still on our wrists, but I guess they aren't sturdy enough, aren't doing quite what she wants them to do.

"I made these last night," she says. "They have our names on them. Mine has yours, yours has mine. Like how I have Hera's name on my necklace, you know? It means we're together. It means we're like family."

She didn't make these, though. Not the way we made the little bracelets we have now, not the way Mama made bread, not the way I am trying to make the tapestry Mama left behind in the attic, the thread showing me a single hand of Pandora's.

"What did they used to be?" I ask.

We can't make things from thin air. Gods don't work like that. We can only transform what we have in front of us. Gods have always done this, shifting the people and things in the world into whatever they want. Mama said it was the most impulsive gods who did this, the ones who didn't respect life on earth. "But don't all gods do it?" I had asked.

"Exactly," Mama had said, winking like she used to do when there was something important I was supposed to understand but maybe never really quite did. Mama had secrets about what she knew about the earth and the sky and the space in between that we sort of occupied. She never really spelled out what all those secrets were, but she left little clues, so I could try to figure it out myself. But it's hard, without her around to give more clues, to answer more questions in her airy, dreamy voice.

"Oh, these were blades of grass," Apple says. "They came out really cool, right? I haven't done much transforming, but Mom said I should practice, to be ready. You know. For Olympus." Apple raises her eyebrows like she needs me to nod my head in agreement, to commit to also going to Olympus with her. The bracelets are maybe supposed to be some sort of promise, but I don't want to promise anything to anyone right now.

"They're nice," I say, and I'm trying to think of how I can explain that I don't want it, that the one braided bracelet is enough, when she starts tying it to my wrist, and I just let her. She ties it tight, so tight I should say something, but I don't, because anyone who Apple wants to be best friends with should do whatever she says. She makes a triple knot in the bracelet, and I'll never be able to figure out how to undo it.

"Put mine on me," she says, holding her wrist out to me, so I do. "There. Perfect. Best friends forever."

Apple braids my hair and adjusts my dress, tying a sash around the middle because "it looks better that way, prettier," and I keep not saying no.

Dad finally bumbles into the kitchen. His hair is messy and he's got on his favorite thick red pajamas again. Apple hasn't asked about them after the last time, but I can see her wondering what he's doing in them. A few years ago, Mama started getting tired of blue, and she said we could have some cozy clothes in other colors—just for in the house, just when no one could see. I'm glad he's wearing them all the time now.

"Oh!" she says.

Dad's surprised too, though, so he says his own "Oh!" at the same time. "Apple, I didn't know you were here."

"Dorothy and I always go to school together. We love it,"

she says. "And look, we have matching bracelets now."

"Oh, well, very nice," Dad says. Even in the early morning, even when he's craggy-throated and confused, his voice still sounds like music.

"Don't you think she'd look nice with dark hair?" Apple says, as if she's been thinking about it for days and finally feels able to say it. I reach my hand up to my hair. We've never talked about my hair before. I like it strawberry-blond like Mama's was.

Dad tilts his head, then shakes it like he's trying to escape a dream. "Darker? Gosh, I don't know. What do you think, Dorothy?" He knits his eyebrows and looks worried. The last thing Dad needs is something else to be worried about, and besides, this is fine, this is no big deal, this is, I'm pretty sure, just the sort of things friends talk about and do.

"Maybe," I say. "Apple probably knows best, right?"

"Apple's very stylish," Dad says, but he still looks worried. "But I love your hair. And your mama—"

"She can always change it back!" Apple says. "I kind of think we'd look like sisters if we both had dark hair. Mom always said she and Penny were like sisters, you know? So we're sort of like sisters too. I bet Penny would have loved it."

"Penny loved Dorothy's hair," Dad says, then catches the sharpness in his tone. "But she loved your mom too, of course. What do I know? You do what you'd like, Dorothy, okay?" His voice sounds a little heavy, like I'm supposed to understand something very specific from the way he says the words. They sound a little like a warning that he's too tired to fully give.

"Well, now your mom thinks my mom—" I start, but Apple doesn't let me finish.

"I thought of something to add to our constellation," she interrupts. "A few stars for her smile. Your mom had that sweet smile when she was baking bread, you know? She was so *nice*, and I want that to be part of the constellation."

"Okay." Mama was nice. Of course she was. But she was so many other things too.

"It's going to be a really amazing constellation. Really detailed. I want people to remember her the way we do, you know? Baking bread and smiling and making my mom happy and teaching me how to knead dough and stuff."

I wait for Apple to realize she hasn't mentioned me in her description of Mama, but she doesn't. She's busy holding her braid up to my hair, seeing how I'd look with her dark strands. We were both there yesterday, and now we're here, both of us trying, I guess, to smooth something over, but things are so wrinkled, I don't know that it's possible.

But Apple's eyes are wide and needing me to be okay, so I try to be okay.

"You don't have to go to school today, bug," Dad says. "I know things are a little . . ." He trails off. There's no point in coming up with the words for how things are. I mean, they're awful. The lightning bolts in the ground are still, somehow, smoking. Mama is gone. The screeds have been read. In the distance, the ladder shifts and sways in the wind.

"Of course you do!" Apple says. "I need you there. And we're doing our Goodbye Project."

"Goodbye Project?"

"Yeah, Mom told me. In school we're going to start saying goodbye to Our Hill. Photographing our favorite places. Gathering things—grass and stuff I guess—that we'll put in a glass box to bring with us to Olympus—it's a whole thing."

"Like the box your mom stood on last night," I say. The words are heavy but I don't know how to not say them.

"Things will be better when we're up there," Apple says, not quite looking at me. "We'll be able to start over together and Mom won't be so . . . She'll be better. It's beautiful up there."

"The Goodbye Project," I repeat, instead of agreeing that life in Olympus would somehow magically be wonderful. My voice hitches on the word *goodbye*.

"That's what they're calling it," Apple says, shrugging. "Anyway, everyone gets to choose something to put in the glass. So you have to come and make sure your favorite part of Our Hill gets in."

"My favorite part was Mama," I say.

Apple bows her head. She is a hundred miles an hour until you say something really true, and then she knows how to pause, and that keeps me loving her.

"I don't think I want to go," I say in the silence that follows. "I'll stay home. I don't need to do a whole Goodbye Project thing. I don't have anything left to put in."

Apple's head jerks back up. "But you have to come," she says. "We'll find something. Something from the river? Or one of your mom's rings or something? Her apron? Something she used to wear, one of her not-blue things that drove my mom crazy? That would be perfect."

"I don't want to put those things in a box," I say.

"Okay then, something else. Or nothing. I mean, you don't have to participate, but I think you'll be sad up there without anything of yours in the box, you know?"

"I think maybe you should stay home, sweetheart," Dad says. Even his voice is small next to Apple's, but he's trying. Only Mama knew how to say something that Apple would agree with, would stop her own plans for. "It sounds like you might not be ready to do all of that . . . goodbye-ing."

His hand finds my shoulder, and for a moment that gap between right now and life before Mama died closes. I give the tiniest nod of agreement.

"Oh," Apple says. She licks her lip and her chin does something—tightens, trembles. She looks down at her bracelet, like she's disappointed in what it was able to do.

"Maybe it would be a good day for me to stay home," I say, but it doesn't help.

"Please come, Dorothy," Apple says, and I think she just means to school, I hope she just means to school. "You're my best friend and after everything my mom did and said last night and stuff—I just . . . Let's go do it together, okay? With our bracelets. As a team. Like your mom always wanted us to be."

School is not Olympus. And Mama did want me to have a best friend, a person I could count on no matter what. I can give Apple this one thing, so I do.

But that's it, I say to myself. That's the most I can do.

14.

At school, Apple's chin does not tremble. She hooks elbows with me and tells me to slow down so that we can walk at the same pace. Left leg. Right leg. Left leg. Right leg. It feels more like marching than friendship, but I don't know how to say that or really anything, anymore.

The glass box is at the front of the classroom when we get there, and everyone is gathered around it looking inside, touching its smooth surface.

"Wow," Apple says. "It's perfect."

It's empty. And really is only exactly what she said it would be—a glass box. It doesn't feel like something magical, but I guess it must be, since it's traveling to Olympus.

Mr. Winters stands behind his desk with his arms

crossed, watching us watch the box.

"Wow, right, Dorothy?" Apple says. She nudges me with her hip so I guess I'm supposed to say *wow* when she says it. I guess maybe friendship has something to do with it not mattering what you feel as long as you do and say the same things as your best friend.

It's not exactly what I remember from watching Mama and Heather, but I do remember the way they'd crack up when they'd say the same thing at the same time, the easy way Mama could finish Heather's sentences, how they both loved to watch birds splash in puddles, loved the sound of a roaring fire, both said the smell of fresh-cut grass was the absolute best, lying out in it sometimes right after Dad cut it, making him roll his eyes and smile at their silliness.

"Yeah. Wow," I say. "Glass." I don't think Apple hears the little rip in my voice. She only smiles at the way I sound like her. I look around the room. Most kids are holding something in their hands, things I guess they assume won't be up on Olympus. Things I guess they care about. A leaf. A stuffed giraffe. An umbrella. A candy bar.

Mr. Winters takes a breath and holds up what's in his hands, a copper teakettle. It looks burned in some spots, like flames from the stove got to it, like it's been used every day for years and years. "Won't need this up there," he says, which is maybe the same as saying he's decided to live on Mount Olympus and leave behind Our Hill. I guess everyone with an object in their hands has decided. I try to take stock. Chloe isn't holding anything but her hands are closing and opening like she sort of wishes she'd brought something, maybe one of her father's beautiful family trees or some piece of history she wants to preserve. And Eric, who has very pale skin and wears the darkest blues and sits alone at lunch, is empty-handed and sitting next to me. No one really talks to Eric, so it might not mean he wants to stay here—it might just mean there's nothing he really wants to remember. He's descended of Erebus, the god of shadows and darkness, a god of the underworld. Eric is the only descendant of such a god living here on Our Hill, and no one likes to talk about the underworld, so no one really wants to be friends with him.

Mama always tried to say hi to him the same way she'd say to hi to anyone, and he'd mostly just laugh at the gesture, like it was all so ridiculous—kindness, politeness, Mama and me.

Still, I know what it's like to be at the bottom of things, to be someone everyone wants to avoid, and I've only been this way for a little while. Eric has been this way forever, always sitting in the back, always the kind of person who you go out of your way to avoid. I try to make eye contact with him now—I want to show him my also-empty hands, or let him know it will be okay if we both stay down here while the rest of them head up the ladder forever. He raises his eyebrows and smirks. "Wish I could thank your mom for the chaos," he whispers, leaning in close. I don't know what he means by it—if he's sincere or sarcastic, if it's supposed to help or hurt, and I guess that's why no one talks to him. The things he says are too strange to parse.

"Hey, Mr. Winters is putting his object in and then he said everyone else can, so pay attention, okay?" Apple interrupts, loudly. Speaking with Eric is unbecoming of her best friend, maybe.

"Sure," I say. Apple keeps touching something in her pocket, and I guess that something is whatever she wants to hold on to from here.

Mr. Winters puts the teakettle in the box. I guess on Olympus we don't make our own tea. Or maybe magic makes it. I really don't know—I haven't been paying much attention in prep-for-Olympus classes. Which are now all our classes. He looks sad that it's out of his hands. He sort of swallows and his nose does a funny little movement like it wants to tell the rest of his face to be still, to look okay with everything that's happening.

The umbrella goes in—I guess it must not rain up there. Or if it does, maybe gods don't get wet. The stuffed giraffe goes in too, with a sniffle that could be the beginning of a cry. Someone puts in the novel *Little Women*, a book real humans love that we are always trying to figure out. Someone dies in it, and I wonder if I'd understand it more if I read it now. Someone else puts in a set of watercolors—are we not allowed to paint up there? My heart is beating at the idea of all the things we are apparently saying goodbye to, things Mama never would have said goodbye to, like a jar of cinnamon and a pair of sparkly shoes. On Olympus, they go barefoot.

"My turn," Apple says. She's been waiting patiently, which isn't really her thing, but she's beaming now and looking from me, to the box, to her pocket, and back to me again. "I picked something sort of unusual. I think it's allowed. I mean, we'd see it up there, but not the same way. It means something different down here."

I am trying to think of what in the world Apple is talking about. She's speaking in riddles, which isn't very much like her, and it makes me nervous.

"Actually, it's really from me *and* Dorothy," she goes on, which isn't right, isn't true at all. I don't want to put anything in the box and I don't know if I'm leaving Our Hill and I definitely don't know what's in Apple's pocket, what's making her shoulders shimmy and her mouth twitch up and up and up.

"No, it's—" I start, but Apple puts her other hand on my arm and squeezes.

"It is," she says. "Dorothy's shy. But it's ours together. And it's perfect." I don't feel shy but I also don't feel like talking, which is maybe not so different from being shy, if

155

you're not paying attention.

Apple finally takes her hand from her pocket. It is a fist that opens up to reveal her object for the Goodbye Project.

A star. A single, sparkling, perfect star she must have grabbed from the river.

My heart grips and my toes curl.

"No," I say, but it comes out too tiny to really hear.

"Isn't it cool?" Apple says, and the room nods and leans closer to look, to touch.

"Oh, well, hmm, yes," Mr. Winters says, tapping his left foot and circling his right wrist around and around and around. "It is cool, that's for sure. Very cool. But not quite what we had in mind."

"It's what I'll miss," Apple says without skipping a beat. She's never been afraid of teachers, Apple Montgomery. Not afraid of teachers or bullies or older kids or stars or ladders or leaving earth forever. She's not afraid of anything I guess, except me disagreeing with her. So I don't.

"I understand that," Mr. Winters says. He looks out the window like maybe another lightning bolt will come down and tell him what to do, but it doesn't. "I guess, I guess it's fine. It's a star, it's not anything— Gods like stars."

"And constellations," Apple says, with a quick glance my way, a smile that holds our secret. But she's making it into a joke, all of it. The constellation of Mama, the saying goodbye, the way we sit by the river and pluck stars from

156

the water—our whole delicate friendship is all something silly and cute to show off to everyone. I am something silly and cute to show off to everyone.

"Well, okay," Mr. Winters says, as if it is Apple and not he who is in charge of the class, of the day, of everything really, just like her mother. "Anyone else? No one can top a star I guess, but there's still room!"

A few people add in their objects sheepishly, apologizing to Apple about how their thing isn't as cool as her thing. They apologize to me too, like I'm a part of her now, her sidekick or something else that I never quite signed up for. A jar of bubble bath goes in. A recipe for pear pie. A pair of brown slippers with worn-out toes. A fistful of grass from someone's backyard.

I don't understand what they want to remember, or why those things are enough. There's so much that can't go into a glass box—like the way the closet still smells a little like Mama, or how good it feels to walk to school on a really crisp day in a really thick sweater.

"Ours was the best," Apple says when class is over and we head to eat lunch outside—peanut butter and jelly sandwiches—a combination we learned from humans on earth, the sort of thing it's impossible to hear or even care about up on Olympus.

"It wasn't ours," I say. I can barely look at her, barely eat the sticky-sweet sandwich, barely tolerate being here at all.

"Sure it was—they're all ours together. It's our thing."

"It was Mama's thing." I try to make my voice sound like a brick wall, like I'm saying something that she can't possibly break apart or rearrange.

"Right," Apple says. I guess she's waiting for me to say something more, to be able to explain better why any of this matters, but I can't, I don't know how.

"Right," I say, before listening to Apple talk about brace-lets and boxes and how we should cut our hair (chin length), and what sort of new dress we should get (fitted and the palest blue), and what we should do for my birthday (have a party).

I wait for her to hear my silence, or see the way I sort of turn my shoulders away from her and this, but she doesn't.

"We'll get another couple stars tonight," she says, ready-ing herself to throw her paper bag in the garbage, return to class. "We're almost done with the constellation. More than enough time to finish before we go."

"Before we go," I say, like I'm Echo, fated to only repeat what my beloved says, forever.

Apple smiles, like she's thinking the same thought. But I get the feeling it sounds sort of nice, to her. Like maybe the myth of Echo means something else to her than it ever did to me.

Like maybe all the myths we've spent our lives learning don't mean to her what I thought they might.

And maybe I don't mean the right thing either.

"The bracelet's itchy," I say, handing her the gift she'd tied around my wrist before we go in. "Sorry. It's just—it's itchy. I don't like itchy."

Apple tilts her head. "We'll figure out something else then," she says.

And I'm worried that she won't stop until she does.

15.

"My place, then the river," Apple says when school's out and all I want in the world is to be alone, to go to my attic, to work on Mama's tapestry, to be able to sit and think and wonder for long enough to make a decision about what I want to do. There's this chill in the air that isn't really chill anymore. It's downright cold, the moment when you realize you have to move from one kind of jacket to another, the sort of cold we rarely feel here, because people like Heather say if our winters can be mild, why not make them mild.

Mama used to always insist on letting the weather do its thing at least for a few days a winter, and sometimes that meant ice and snow and sometimes that meant nothing at all—just the luck of the draw.

I always hoped for snow.

This year, though, it seems like everyone's agreed to let the last winter on earth be a real one, without magic, without influence of near-gods, and it feels a little bit good and a little bit scary on my skin right now. Even my bones feel the cold, my neck aching for a scarf, my fingers curling into themselves for warmth. Winter won't officially happen until the day we have to climb the ladder or not, but weather, when it's untouched by gods, is unpredictable and December can feel like May or like January, without ever answering why.

"I sort of want to go home," I say in a quiet voice that I never used to use and now seems to pop up all the time.

"There's nothing to do at home," Apple says. "And I can't be alone with my mom. She's out of control right now. All she does is go on and on about Hera and lightning bolts and how powerful we'll feel, living in the clouds. It's gross."

"You want to go up there though," I say. She put the star in the box. She won't even talk about other options. She's going.

"Everyone's going," she says. "I'm not all obsessed with it like my mom, but it's just what we'll all do and then not much will change."

"But everything will change," I say. Apple looks a little frantic, like she can't let that happen, but it will. No matter what I choose. No matter what anyone chooses. It's changing. We can't stop that.

Apple shakes her head. "You know what I mean. It will be you and me up there and we'll be best friends and we'll talk and have fun and we'll sit somewhere else—not a river, but somewhere—and we'll remember everything from before and there will be new things I guess, but we'll like them. And if we're sad we'll visit. Gods visit all the time. They come down and talk to humans or turn goats into rocks or whatever, and we'll do that and it will feel good and we'll live forever like we were always supposed to."

"We'll turn goats into rocks?" I ask. My head rushes with all these ideas of what's next when I'm not even really sure what's happening right now. I never said yes to going to Apple's house, but that's where we're going anyway, our steps just heading in that direction, like the force of Apple is too strong for me to possibly resist. I meant to go home but somehow I'm at Apple's door, climbing Apple's thickly carpeted stairs, even though it's not what I wanted at all.

My heart quickens and I want to point it out to her, but she wouldn't understand. She's just happy I'm here.

"I think you'd look good with brown hair, like me," she says for what feels like the millionth time when we're in her room. Her mom must be somewhere convincing someone to do something, and for once, I want Heather here, monitoring us.

"I have strawberry-blond hair. Like Mama."

162

"And Pandora," Apple says with this thick sort of warning in her voice, this raise of her eyebrows like I should know better.

"Yeah," I say, and I try to make the tone of my voice carry the same seriousness, the same certainty about who I am and what it means to look like Pandora, but it doesn't work. I'm shaking from the cold or something else and so is my voice.

"You said you can't do the bracelet, it's itchy or whatever, so let's do this." Apple reaches out and takes a lock of my hair between her fingers, near the crown of my head. She smooths it between her thumb and forefinger all the way to the bottom. She grins—"Oh it's perfect"—and I don't want to see what she's done, but she turns me to the mirror and I look anyway because I just cannot say no to Apple Montgomery.

That lock of my hair is brown now, the same brown as Apple's—dark and nutty and warm. A really pretty color.

I hate it.

"No," I say, but I think I only say it in my head, because Apple runs her hands through more of my hair, more of it turning brown.

"People are going to freak out!" Apple says. "This is so much better than bracelets. You look amazing. *We* look amazing!" She puts her arm around my shoulders and we look in the mirror. I'm still me—my face is mine, it's nothing like Apple's, and I'm the right height and size, but it's all wrong. Apple beams next to me, though, so I smile too.

"Cool," I say, even though I don't know why I'm saying it. I need to be alone, in the attic or by the river, I need to catch my breath and figure out what I feel and think and want. I like being Apple's best friend—I like the constellation and the way she is familiar and comfortable and knows so much about me and Mama. But there's all these little things I don't like—my hair and the star and the way she is so *big*—not her actual size but the size of the things she wants and the way she tells me. Her whole self is so big, I can't figure out how to make me fit.

"Okay. More stars, right? That's what we should do next?" Apple keeps touching my hair, keeps looking at us in the mirror.

"Sure, yeah," I say. I do want to work on the constellation. It's taking shape—a few more stars and I think it will be easy to point out, easy for almost anyone to recognize it as Mama. But more than stars, I need space. It's been weeks since I've sat in the kitchen with Dad, eating grilled cheese or burgers or the kind of pasta he's good at—oily and garlicky and cheesy. I'm flooded with a certain kind of missing that is especially tender around my heart and ribs and throat.

Apple threads her elbow with mine, and locked in that

way, we walk to the river. People wave to Apple and tilt their heads at me, not recognizing me as Dorothy until they've already passed us. I feel them turning back around, saying my name, shaking their heads.

We pass Chloe, who is walking alone, getting sort of lost in the cracks in the sidewalk. It's me who says hi to her, a little too enthusiastically maybe. "Chloe! Hi!" Like I'm some whole new friendly type of person.

It's just that Chloe reminds me of quiet lunches and being hidden and un-thought-about. We were two people who liked to be mostly silent together, who liked to be ourselves in a way that we hoped no one else would really notice. After Mama died, Chloe handed me this little note. It wasn't a condolence note, the kind of thing people here heard about humans doing so they attempted it too. Those notes were sweet and awkward and they all sort of blended together. Chloe's note was different. It was a list of things I might not know about Pandora, a list of ways Mama was like her. "Don't show anyone," she'd said, because the things she'd listed about Pandora were nice things, and we weren't really supposed to have nice things to say about her. We weren't supposed to want to be like her.

I don't remember where I put that list. I want it now, though, to see how I line up against it, to check if I'm still even really here.

"Dorothy?" Chloe says, a question instead of a statement.

And then, "Your hair." That one is a statement, and not a good one.

"Hey, yeah, it's me."

"And me," Apple says pulling me a little closer with a jerk of her elbow.

"You look— Wow."

"Yeah," I say. "Wow." Maybe I'm trying to tell Chloe something with the way I say the word, the way I lean into the weight of it. "We're going to the river," I say, even though I'm pretty sure Apple won't like that.

And she doesn't. She sort of hiccups in response, a funny sound that doesn't fit her very well.

"You should come," I say. Apple clears her throat like I've forgotten she's there, but I don't think anyone has ever forgotten she's anywhere.

"It's yours, isn't it?" Chloe asks. She has a way of starting a conversation in the middle, like we all just have to catch up to where she's at. Maybe some people would find it annoying, but I like it.

"What's ours?" Apple says. She keeps pulling me tighter. Our bodies are touching, we're turning into one being, but it's still not close enough for her.

I remember when Mama first died, I needed to be by the river as much as possible. I practically lived there, begging Dad to let us bring blankets and sleep on its shore. I would have drunk from it, if it weren't for all the fish and mud. I would have swum in it every day if it weren't so cold. It was the thing I wanted to hang on to, the thing that made me feel safe, in all that change and sorrow.

I realize, with a start, that I am Apple's river. I am the safe thing she wants to hang on to while the world breaks.

I'm not a river, though.

I don't know what I am.

"Up there," Chloe says, pointing at the sky. "I've been watching it. And then you brought the star in. So I'm pretty sure it's yours. What is it?" She's looking right at the constellation, at Mama, and I move quickly from nervous that she knows, to sad that she can't tell who it is.

"It's a secret," Apple says. But it's not a secret. The point of putting Mama in the sky is for everyone to remember her. A constellation is the opposite of a secret. It's the opposite of the way things have been lately, all low voices and trying not to say the obvious things, and trying not to ask the big questions and trying to pretend a woman with strawberry-blond hair and a huge smile and delicious homemade bread and a tapestry of the wicked Pandora up in her attic never existed.

"It's not a secret," I say. "It's Mama. It's my mom. Can't you tell? She's making bread. We need to put up another five or ten stars maybe. Then it will be done."

Apple says something under her breath about being quiet and best friends and the weird mood I'm clearly in, but Chloe just looks up at the sky. She adjusts her glasses.

She has been wearing wire-framed glasses that make big circles around her eyes since she was a little kid.

"It doesn't look like Penny," she says. "I mean, bread? No offense, but history is not going to remember Penny Hardy for making bread."

"That's what we love about her, right, Dorothy?" Apple says. "That's who she was."

Chloe shrugs, looks at the stars again, and I try to see what she's seeing, understand what she understands.

"She was the woman who changed everything," Chloe says. She pushes her hair back, adjusts her glasses. "Pandora, too. I mean, I know it's—it's sort of complicated I guess, but Penny Hardy didn't climb up the ladder. I don't know much about stars or bread or whatever. But I know about history. And that's history."

If it were Reece or Dawn saying something about Mama, saying even these same things about Mama, I wouldn't like it. It would come out cutting and cruel and it would make me feel that sticky red-faced shame that I feel whenever someone takes a big, disappointed inhale at all the awful things Pandora brought to earth and all the ways I have to apologize for those mistakes. But when Chloe says that Mama changed history when she didn't climb the ladder, she says it the way she says every other fact about history—dates and names and big wars and tiny battles and little details that no one else ever remembers, but Chloe does.

She says it like it's okay. Like it just *is*.

Apple shakes her head. "You don't get it," she says. "You didn't know her like we did. Right, Dorothy?"

"I don't know," I say, mumbling, because I can't disagree with Apple and I also can't agree with her. "I knew her really well." It feels like a true statement that I can say without saying any of the other maybe-true things—that Apple didn't know Mama so well after all, that Apple decided what she should be doing in the constellation and I let it happen, that Apple and I believe different things entirely—about Mama, about Our Hill, about stars and friends and rivers and what to do on the solstice.

"Right. We knew her really well," Apple says. Chloe raises her eyebrows, because Chloe is exactly the sort of person who knows the difference between my sentence and Apple's.

"Well," Chloe says. "There you go."

And she leaves. And I wish more than anything in the world that I were leaving too.

16.

We put two more stars in the sky, but neither of them look exactly right. We dip hands into water; I let Apple climb the ladder first while I hold it down below, and then we switch, but we're quiet.

"That's enough for today," Apple says after the second star—a pale one she added to Mama's left hand. The constellation is just Mama's face and arms and the bread, the rest of her just an imagined form, and I like that blank space in the sky better than the constellation today. I can picture her legs doing any number of things they used to do—tap dancing even, though she didn't actually know how to tap dance, climbing the stairs to the attic, tangling themselves up with Dad's legs on the couch when we were all lazy after a big dinner, bending down to sit next to me on the ground on days when I felt too sad to straighten my body all the way up.

"Okay," I say. Apple looks at me like she's waiting for me to say something more, and I almost tell her about Mama's legs—how they were strong and how they always seemed to know what to do and where they were going. But I don't. Maybe Apple would be thinking the other thing I think about, when I think about Mama's legs. That she could have used them to climb the ladder.

"We're doing this for you," Apple says when she realizes, I guess, that I'm not saying anything.

"What?"

"If you don't want to do this we don't have to. I was trying to help you. That's all I want to do. Help you. Be your friend. Be your best friend and take care of you like I promised your mom I would."

"You promised my mom what?"

"She didn't want you to be all alone. She knew after she didn't climb that people might be mean to you, and she wanted me to look out for you. So I do. I look out for you. I know you don't care, but I do." Apple's not looking at me. She's not really looking anywhere, and it almost sounds like she might cry, which makes no sense. Apple Montgomery doesn't cry.

"She knew people would be mean to me?" The words

are spiky and sour in my mouth. I try not to think about what Mama knew. I try, so hard, to not let my mind wander into the place where it has to wonder if she knew that not climbing the ladder would change not just life on Our Hill but also my life—the way it used to be quiet and still and easy and all mine.

I try not to think about the ways Mama made a decision that hurt me.

I try not to think about the pocket of anger that sits somewhere deep down, underneath all the sadness and missing.

Now Apple is making me sit in this place, this very place I didn't want to visit at all.

"Of course. Your mom knows what it's like here. And you can't stay here all alone. Your mom didn't want that. She wanted you with me. She wanted us to be like her and my mom. She wanted this." Apple is actually crying now and talking with this desperate sort of voice—all fast and whisper-loud and I wish the river would swallow the sound up, I don't like it. I don't like any of this—the things she's saying or the way she's saying them or how I feel hearing them.

"I don't know what Mama wanted. She loved it here." The anger in me rises, making my throat dry and tight. I have a thousand questions and she's the only one who can answer them, but she left. Left us. Left this. Left me.

"My friends don't even want to be my friends anymore," Apple says. She grips my hand. "And my mom— I don't know how to be when I'm around my mom. You're the only person who makes me feel like me. You can't leave me and us and everyone you've ever known. You can't. You're not a human, Dorothy. I mean, I know, your mom became one, but we're supposed to be gods. We've always been gods."

When Apple says stuff, it sounds so sturdy and real. Even while she cries, it sounds like a life raft. Like I'm drowning or the world is drowning and her words are right there, ready to save me.

I guess I just can't tell if I want to be saved.

"I'm a descendant of Pandora," I say. I try to say it with pride, the way Mama used to do, and not all embarrassed and awkward the way everyone else does when they bring up our family's history.

"And Orpheus. And gods," Apple says.

"I don't know how to make this decision." She's not wrong, about who I am and where I've come from. I'm both. I'm from gods and muses and mistakes. I'm from Our Hill and Olympus. "Mama knew how to decide things and I don't know how and I'm still trying to understand every-thing that happened and I can't decide with you watching my every move and telling me how to feel!" I'm yelling, and it leaves me breathless because I never yell. It's a whole new feeling.

"Why don't you want to be my best friend?" Apple whispers. The tears speed up, rushing down her face, flooding the moment. I look away, down to the river, and catch sight of myself. In one of our most famous myths, Narcissus looks down at himself in a river and is captivated by the way he looks. He falls so in love with his beautiful reflection that he stays there forever. The story is so familiar, I know it like the alphabet, like my name, like the way I know to climb the ladder at solstice.

But things that you know that well can change, can look different or mean something different from what you thought they did.

My reflection now doesn't look like the one I know by heart. My newly brown hair makes no sense on my head, and I'm wearing one of Apple's lacy blue dresses, and my shoulders have a new slump.

"I want to be your best friend," I say, quietly, carefully. "But I also want to be me."

"I want to be us," Apple says. "Like Penny and my mom. They were always an *us*. A together thing. A unit."

It's not exactly how I remember our mothers and their friendship. I remember the way they fit together oddly, how it seemed kind of wrong but still somehow right. I remember how Mama moved slowly and Heather moved fast and they were always trying to slow down and speed up on their walks, creating this impossible rhythm.

"Please," Apple says. She sounds little, the way she sounded when we were five and I overheard her asking her mother if she could cut her hair or skip Reece's birthday party. The answer was always no, and Apple's voice always sounded like she already knew that but wanted it to be different.

"We're best friends," I say, which isn't a yes or a no but is the truth, the new and strange and bewildering truth that I don't totally understand. It happened so fast that maybe we were always best friends without even knowing it, like all those hours sleeping next to each other, eating the same batch of pancakes, listening to our mothers, living our parallel lives added up, accidentally, to something big.

Apple hears a yes and not what I actually said, so she hooks her arm through mine again and smiles, walking us away from the river and back to her home. "Sleepover?" she asks at her front door, but I shake my head.

"My dad will start getting worried. I'm never home."

"We're each other's homes," Apple says. "That's why we both have to go to Olympus."

"Okay," I say, even though I shouldn't, even though it sounds a lot like I'm agreeing to something I don't mean to be.

Apple grins again and goes inside. My brown hair and I start to walk home but veer at the path that leads back to the river. It's late to be going there alone, I'm not really supposed to be there in the dark by myself, but it will be quick. If I can just be at that river for one minute alone, maybe I'll remember something important about who I am that I can't seem to remember when Apple's around.

It's quiet at the river, of course. Quiet and beautiful, the stars reflecting in the water, the crickets chirping, the moon all huge and round and kind above. I don't plan to do it or anything, but the stars are right there, and some of them blink in the little river-ripples like they're saying *Dorothy, come on, grab us, use us, fix Mama.*

I can only look at a blinking river-star for so long before I have to scoop it up and out of the cold water, so I do.

My heart thumps. There is only really one thing I want to do with a star like this, and that's add it to Mama. Not her hands or her smile or the loaf of bread she's meant to be holding. This star deserves to be something bigger than any of that.

The ladder is right there. It sways. It shakes. It leads up to Olympus, where I don't want to go, not now, and I'm realizing maybe not ever, and anyway we aren't allowed to go to the ladder when it isn't solstice. But Apple made me brave enough to go with her, and maybe I am brave enough to go without her, too. I put my hands on first, then a foot, to see how it feels. It shakes, of course.

Gods could do anything, to get us up there: They could build a golden staircase or an elevator or an airplane. They could send down an enormous dove that we could all fly up to Olympus, or drift a cloud down to earth that we climb onto to be carried there.

They could do anything. They *do* do anything. This ladder, made generations ago by the ones who came down, is what they wanted for us. They let it get wet in the rain, they let it lose rungs from age or weather or maybe their own mischievous ideas. We've asked them to strengthen it, to make it larger, to give us something new and sturdy. But they don't respond to those prayers we've sent up, those favors we've asked for.

I put my other foot on, just to see if I can do it alone, just to see how it feels.

The ladder shakes and so do I, but the star tells me to keep going.

So I do. Hands, then feet. Hands, then feet. All the way to the constellation, while the ladder shivers below me, threatening me to get back down. Maybe the gods can see me now, maybe they're watching Our Hill right this moment. We don't know when they're looking our way and when they're worrying themselves with human matters or when a fight has broken out in the sky that has them concerned only with themselves.

We don't know them at all, really.

Mama's constellation is where we left it, of course, nearly done, getting there, and Chloe's words pound in my ears—she doesn't look like Mama. This isn't what Mama will be known for.

She was Penny Hardy and she was mysterious and brave and once upon a time, she was here. With me.

The next few stars are supposed to fill in the vague shape of Mama's arms, but I put the star somewhere there aren't any stars, a part of her we weren't planning on placing in the sky.

I put it below the lifted left arm holding the bread. In the space where her heart would be.

It's not the brightest star in the constellation. It doesn't need to be. It's just cozy warm and all the things Mama was. It is perfect.

And I know I need to do more. Not now, not today, but soon.

I need to make a constellation of Mama that is really Mama.

17.

Back on ground, I'm as wobbly as the silver ladder to the sky. Doing something bad with Apple felt safe. Because Apple is safe. She's the descendant of Hera, her family protects the apples of immortality, she is beloved in ways that I don't even really understand. But doing something bad alone feels scary. I practically feel Zeus looking at me, readying a lightning bolt.

I walk home and Dad's outside, waiting for me, like he knows what I've done.

"You can't do this," he says. I think he's talking about the constellation, my trip up the ladder without Apple at the bottom holding me steady, without permission from the gods to change the sky.

"I'm sorry," I say. "I don't know what came over me. It's just that Apple is so . . . she's so . . . like, big. Forceful. Like wind, you know?"

"You're saying Apple's keeping you out late? Not letting you call home and check in?" I notice Dad's eyes, which are a little pinked, and his hands, which he's rubbing as if to calm them down. A few years ago, we went to a human city and picked up phones. It was meant to be a learning experience, a way to get to know humans better, to understand the hunch in their shoulders and the way they almost never looked away from their little hand devices. But somehow we adopted them as our own and began to use them to communicate when we could just have easily used magic or the descendants of Hermes and Iris to carry our messages for us.

"It's late," Dad goes on. "It's past dinner. I don't want to hear you blaming Apple. I called her home an hour ago and she was there and thought you were here. This isn't like you. This isn't like my girl."

It's not like Dad either, to talk so much and so deliberately. To be shaky-voiced and outside without a coat on, without shoes.

"I'm sorry," I say. "I lost track—I—I can't explain it."

When Mama first died, Dad and I both did a lot of inexplicable things. I didn't ask him why he was only eating toast. He didn't ask me why I woke up before the sunrise and walked to the river. The answers were obvious, I guess.

I thought it might be the same now. The deadline is coming so fast, solstice two weeks away now, and I don't know how to be. "What are we going to do?" I say at last, a question I haven't been asking him but definitely should have been.

"Tonight? Go to bed. I'm probably supposed to punish you. Ground you or something? But can you just try harder, Dorothy? At least call me if you're not going to be home."

"I'm not talking about tonight, Dad." I can tell how tired he is. Too tired to understand what I'm saying even though it feels so obvious to me. Too tired to make a decision, probably. "I meant what are we going to *do*? About Olympus? About here? Are we going? Are we staying? We don't talk about it. And Apple just assumes we're going up and I—I don't know what I assume. I don't know what we're doing."

We should move inside. It's cold out here, and Dad's all underdressed and maybe the gods are listening in on our conversations, maybe they're looking for houses lit up after dinner, and they are turning themselves into birds so they can hear what we late-night renegades are talking about.

"I miss your mom," Dad says. "She'd know what to do." Dad looks at me, and our eyes say the things our mouths don't say. Of course Mama knew what to do. She did it.

I didn't know that something could be obvious and impossible at the same time.

"She wanted to stay," I say. "She wanted to be human. Just regular human."

Dad looks up at the sky, so I do too. Not long before Mama died, after she refused the climb, Heather and Apple came over for dinner. It was a sad dinner, everyone stressed and not saying the things they were thinking. Until Heather spoke up.

"Fate's funny, isn't it?" she'd said.

"Not particularly," Mama had said. There was tension between them that was new and uncomfortable.

"I mean the two of you. Fate, right? The descendant of Orpheus falling in love with someone he'll lose. Just like Orpheus and Eurydice."

"Heather," Mama had said, half surprised and half something else.

"We all know the same history," Heather said, and she was caught somewhere between angry and grieving. I know the place now too. My heart beat, and I wondered if this was what everyone thought of my dad, my mom, their love story.

"I'm not history," Mama said. "I'm me, right now. I'm not a myth."

The words or the way Mama said them quieted Heather, and we ate dinner quickly and said goodbye and it felt like the end of something, maybe because it was. That night, Dad stayed up late playing sad songs on his guitar and Mama didn't complain, didn't say a word about it, just let him play all night, practically.

I don't know if Dad's thinking of that night or something else entirely when he says now, "You and your mom. So alike, aren't you?"

I shake my head. Mama was a lot of things—pretty and confident and reckless and mysterious—and I don't think I'm any of them.

"Brave," Dad says. "Curious and brave."

I turn the words around in my mind. Dad says them like they are good things, but when people talk about Pandora and curiosity they say it a different way, like it's a terrible impulse, a thing to be avoided.

"Do you want to stay down here?" Dad asks.

"Maybe," I say, so quiet I can barely even hear it.

"Maybe I do too," Dad says. I sit next to him and we look at the sky, at the stars, at the ladder in the distance and the clouds that roll around even at night, even after dark. It's a nice place to be, Our Hill, especially right now, when it's quiet and Dad and I are breathing the same air, feeling the same things.

Dad goes to bed and I say I'm going to bed too, but instead I visit the tapestry in the attic. It's been a while since I've been up here, I don't know why exactly. Maybe I've been avoiding Mama's work or just too distracted by the force that is Apple and the change that is coming.

But now I put my feet on the pedal and my hands on the loom and I press and press and press. The threads weave themselves together and it feels good, to be weaving, to be doing the ancient art that ties us to Olympus. I wish I hated everything about being a near-god. I wish I really hated the ladder and the clouds and Zeus's beard and Hera's apples and nymphs in the water and Athena's blue, blue eyes. But I don't. I am a little like this tapestry—a mix of colors and shades, a collection of threads that make up a whole, a picture I can't yet see.

Pandora's face is appearing, so I press my foot harder, faster, wanting so badly to see whatever Mama wanted to say.

In most images of Pandora, she is bereft, watching the world's miseries fly out of the box. She is wide-eyed and confused; she is shocked at what she has done. I can already tell, just from the way her left eye is coming in, that she will not look that way here. Her eye looks pleased, the left side of her mouth reaching up into a small smile.

I've never seen Pandora smiling. The loom is loud. A *clunk-clack* every time I press and release the pedal. It shouldn't be a surprise that the sound brings Dad upstairs.

"Bug. You should go to bed," Dad says. He's in a green robe that Mama got him, terry cloth and cozy, like his pajamas, a color we only wear inside.

"Pandora is smiling," I say. I don't want to go to bed,

and I need someone to talk to about everything.

Dad leans in close and squints. "Huh. Guess so," he says.

"Mama loved her." It's true. Mama was quick to defend Pandora when people spoke about her awfulness. *You don't understand*, she'd say. *You're missing the point.* But when anyone asked her what she meant, she'd say they needed to figure it out themselves. Not everything about Mama was perfect. That part of her was annoying. She didn't like to explain herself. She would give hints, but never the whole picture.

The memory of that part of Mama starts winding itself up in me, and turns from thought to rage, the way colors mixed together turn from red and green and blue to muck, to a gray-brown mess.

"Mama loved her but never told us why, and then she left. She just *left* and didn't tell us anything about that choice, either. Why was she like that? Why couldn't she just say what she needed us to know? Why couldn't she just tell us what to do and how to think about things? She obviously knew all kinds of stuff. And had all these opinions. Why couldn't she just *say* them?" I'm pressing the loom harder and harder, faster and faster, my feet and hands flying around in a controlled fury. The anger feels good and bad in equal measure, and I watch as it passes over Dad's face too.

"It's not fair," he says. "It's really not fair, her leaving us with all this." I think Dad is supposed to say something neutral or nice about Mama and the mess she left behind. I think he's supposed to tell me it's okay that we are left with all these questions. But he just shakes his head. "She had all these big thoughts we were supposed to somehow figure out, but she left before we had a chance to figure it all out. Just—left." Dad sounds mad too. Not the loom-stomping, tears-poking-through anger that I'm feeling, but his own kind, which is rumbly and low and makes his arms cross tight tight tight over his chest.

"Why was she like that?" I ask. "Why would she do this to us?" I shove the loom out of my way a little, making room for me and my feelings and the way things aren't the way they were supposed to be. And I hated everything Heather said at the meeting, but maybe some of it was true. Maybe Mama, in all her Mama-ness, ruined something important and essential.

"I wish I knew," Dad says. "She was always— That's who she was."

I hate that we use the past tense for her. I hate that she liked to keep things mysterious. I hate that she's gone and I hate that she didn't have to be gone and I hate that this tapestry is unfinished and I hate that I am here, trying to finish it for her.

"I hate it," I whisper, even though it feels like a secret I

186

shouldn't be sharing, all that hate and madness and upset isn't what missing Mama is supposed to feel like. We've peeked in on human funerals and read human books about people dying, and I don't remember anyone being mad. Just teary and tired, frowning and hugging. I am a hundred kinds of wrong.

"Dorothy?" Dad says in his own gravelly whisper. "I hate it too."

We look back at the tapestry, which I want to rip up and I want to finish and I want to throw out the window and I want to keep forever and ever.

It's nearly finished now, and the image of Pandora is so clear. She isn't looking into a box, but a jar, and I remember Mama telling me that the story of the box was wrong, that it was a jar she opened, and I'm glad to see that bit of truth here. Above Pandora is a swirl of misery: shadows and dreariness and a sense of terrible things to come. It looks the way I feel right now, gray and spiraling and angry. But Pandora's not looking at all that. She's looking in the jar, and she's smiling at what she sees at the bottom. Her hand is reaching in to get it.

"What's in there?" I ask. "More misery or whatever?" I look over at Dad. He's got a smile that matches Pandora's. A little sweet, a little sad, a little knowing. The anger is still there too—I can see it in the fists his hands are making, the grimace under the smile. But tears are forming in his eyes now too, missing-Mama tears, which have their own particular shape and size.

"The thing Mama always said everyone forgets to mention," he says. "The thing I always forget was in there. They don't teach it in school here. But it's the truth. It was there. At the bottom. It always is. It's always right there, beneath all the most awful things, if you have the time to look."

Dad wipes the tears with the back of his hand. He's talking in one of Mama's riddles, and it makes me miss her and hate her and love him and miss the way things used to be. He hears it too and laughs. "I sound like her," he says. "Impossible Mama."

"What is it?" I ask, hoping he has an answer.

"It's hope."

I squint, as if it's something I can see, but there's just Pandora, the jar, and the promise that something worthwhile is down, down, down underneath all the awfulness.

I'm not convinced.

If Mama cared about hope so much, I don't know why she'd leave me without any. I can stay here or go up there. Either way, she's gone.

Dad's eyes are bright, like the image of Pandora and the reminder of hope is really helping him, but my heart just sinks. "Mama believed in the hope, here. On Our Hill. And I do too."

He doesn't say we're staying but I think it might mean we're staying.

More than the ladder, more than staying here, I want to vanish for a bit, into the sadness of it all, into the way the heartbreak goes and goes and goes.

And goes.

APPLE

Two Weeks Later

DECEMBER 19

18.

Dorothy's hair is still brown, but the rest of her is somewhere else entirely on this walk to school. She's been this way since the last time we put stars in the sky, which feels like forever ago, but I guess was only two weeks ago. But two weeks is sort of forever when you're about to leave the world behind.

A week is forever when the climb up the ladder is in two days. I feel like I'm supposed to remind her of how close it is, but I don't know how to say it exactly. *Hey, Dorothy? You're acting weird. You know we have to go become gods in two days, right? You're doing it, right?*

"We're going to find out where we're all living today," I say instead. Mom's been giving me the inside scoop on every

193

detail of our move to Olympus, and how the school is preparing us for it, and with each new layer of information I
get more excited. Not to leave here exactly, but to do something big and new. To be someone a little bit new, too.

"Oh," Dorothy says. She doesn't look at me or at the sky.
Just sort of keeps staring straight ahead like she's been doing
whenever I bring up Olympus.

"We're gonna be in palaces. Like princesses." Mom
showed me a painting of some of the residences and I folded
it up and put it in my pocket to show Dorothy. The gods'
palaces are all made of marble and gold, filled with fancy
vases and huge staircases and beds so big they take up entire
rooms. "Look," I say, unfolding the paper, trying to hold
it right in front of her face so that she has no choice but to
really take it in. "Isn't it incredible? We'll get to live in one
of these. Maybe even the same one. Some families will be
together because these palaces are so huge. And I bet my
mom can request you guys with us. It would make sense
since we both just have one parent anyway."

I watch Dorothy's eyes blink blink blink. I'm waiting for
a smile, which has to come eventually, it just has to. "That
looks . . . cold," she says. It isn't what she's supposed to say.
Mom and Penny used to plan vacations together, to human
towns, small ones without many people living there, and
they'd ooh and ahh over photos of pretty hotel rooms and

ocean views and palm trees. They did not blink and blink and blink some more.

"It's not cold up there!" I say, pretty sure it's true. Gods aren't ever cold or hot or uncomfortable in any way really. "It's beautiful. Come on, look. We'll actually get to live there. In a palace. A god's palace. That can't be so bad."

I watch Dorothy's face for signs of something like happiness. She has to understand how this is a good thing, a great thing even. To live in a palace together. To be best friends and gods and together forever, like I promised her mother we'd be.

But Dorothy's face is pinchy and wincing and wrong.

"I like my home," she says at last, in a voice so small I can barely tell it's there.

"I mean sure, your home is pretty. And, like, cute. But it's not a palace! In the sky! Can you please just get a little excited about this? It's what's happening and there are things about it that are actually sort of—"

"I'm not going." This is the first thing Dorothy has said at a normal volume in ages. I don't even know. Maybe I've never heard Dorothy's voice so solid and loud.

"Yes, you are," I say, because Mom said everyone would go. They'd realize it was the only choice and they'd climb up that ladder and live forever, like gods are meant to do.

"Our house was Mama's house. Our Hill is Mama's hill.

I never wanted to be a god. I—I'm meant to be here. We're staying here."

I'm sure I've misheard her. Except she's looking away from me with her arms crossed, and her face set in this straight line, like it doesn't even matter to her, leaving me behind, leaving *forever* behind. Things I try not to feel zoom through me—the screeching sadness of hearing that Penny was gone, the throbbing pulse of the thunder being sent to earth, the loneliness of wanting something so badly that she doesn't want at all. I shake my head. This is wrong. It's not what I promised Penny and it's not what Dorothy and I have been quietly promising each other, by making the constellation and walking to school and being best friends.

"We're supposed to be together," I say. "You're not meant to be here, you're meant to be with me." I feel like I'm going to cry. Then yell. Then cry again. Once, we took a school trip to watch mortal kids at an amusement park. They rode things called roller coasters, which dipped low and sped up high, jostling them around until they didn't know where they were anymore. I guess they think it's fun.

I feel like that.

"We don't have time for you to be like this," I say, trying to make my voice sound calm. "You want to come up with us. I know you do."

It has to be true. Penny said I was Dorothy's protector and we kept secrets and we have matching outfits and we have the same history, the same memories, the important ones that have to be protected by us being together, by our destiny.

We are gods. We believe in destiny.

"Apple. I can't," Dorothy says, and she doesn't even look sad, just calm and sure, like she's known this for months, like she never even considered being with me, like I mean nothing to her, like our friendship is over and she couldn't care less.

The story of me and Dorothy was so clear in my head. It was as simple as the myths I know by heart: Persephone visiting the Underworld and making the earth have seasons, Apollo turning Daphne into a tree because she didn't love him, Odysseus on his journeys, battling monsters to win wars and return to his beloved. Pandora and her box of misery. We were our own myth, weren't we? Our mothers were too. A myth about friendship passing down through generations, a myth about gods on earth returning home, a myth about losing someone you love and finding friendship through it.

But Dorothy is stony and cold. She is some other story than the one I thought we were writing.

"I can't go up there alone," I say to the impossible space between us. My heart squeezes in hurt and then anger. Then something even bigger than anger. "We're supposed to be like our moms were—inseparable. Until your mom ruined everything, and now you're ruining everything too. Which, fine, I guess you were always destined to do, right? Being so curious and *stupid* that you let misery out in the world, like Pandora and your mom and everyone who ruins everything." I'm crying now in this unhinged way that I'd like to make stop but I can't seem to get a handle on at all.

Dorothy steps away from me. She does something with her mouth, like there are words or feelings she needs to keep trapped in there.

"You don't understand," Dorothy says. "It doesn't matter if I go up there or stay here or whatever. It doesn't matter. The way this feels—you think the constellation was enough and mentioning her every once in a while is enough, but it's not. There is no enough. We're not in this together. You miss Penny Hardy, who baked bread and made you feel good about yourself or something. I miss my mom. I don't even miss her. It's so much bigger. I don't understand her and I am mad at her and I'm mad at Zeus and you want me to get excited about castles in the sky but I barely even want to brush my hair most mornings. I can't go up there for you. You're not— I love you but you're not enough."

I feel dizzy from the ridiculous things she's saying, the riddles she's winding up. "If we were really best friends you'd want to be with me!" I say, but I sound like some stupid kid, like some baby who doesn't get it and I guess I don't, not really, and there's a whole crowd of people around us now, too many to count, but I don't care. This is urgent, this is everything, this is the promise I made to Penny, and this is forever, and this is being someone else besides Apple Montgomery, Heather Montgomery's perfect daughter, Hera and Zeus's perfect heir. No one has ever seen me the way Dorothy does, no one else lets me be me, no one else teaches me how to put stars in the sky, how to sit still by the river, how to stop caring what other people think or need or how popular I am. I need her. I *need* her and she's leaving me and she can't, I won't let her. She doesn't even know what she wants, she's just sad, and that's not enough of a reason to do what she's doing. "You'll change your mind," I say. "You'll change your mind, and it will be too late. You can't do this. I won't let you."

"We have to go inside," Dorothy says. "I'm sorry. It's not that I don't want to be with you. It's that sometimes I don't want to be anywhere at all."

She reaches out to put a hand on my shoulder like I'm a child whose feelings aren't as big and real as hers, like I'm not Apple Montgomery, descendant of Hera and Zeus, daughter of Heather Montgomery, who practically runs this town. I jerk away from the touch and straighten my neck, my back, lift my head. I am Apple Montgomery. And this is not the end of the conversation, and I won't be babied by Dorothy Hardy, who a few months ago no one even cared about.

I walk into school without her, without my old friends, just on my own, which feels awful but also serves her right, and I take my place at my desk. Before Dorothy gets inside, Chloe walks in, and she heads to the back where she's been sitting, but I stop her.

"Sit here again," I say. I try to make it sound nice, but I think it mostly just comes out like a command. My head is swirling with how close and soon and urgent everything is, and how wrong Dorothy is and how I have to do something, now, to fix it, because if I don't, I will lose everything. "Sit!" I say, too loud and hard, but I can't help it—everyone is moving so slow when time is moving so fast and they need to catch up.

Chloe stiffens. She's quiet, but she's not a pushover, which is the sort of thing Reece would probably miss but is obvious to me. "No thanks," she says.

"Please," I ask. "I can't— And actually I need advice too—and just— Please?" It's the please that does it, I guess, because Chloe sighs and sits next to me.

"Advice?"

"History advice."

"That's not a thing." Chloe looks bored.

"Sure it is. You're always saying history matters and informs the present and gives us information about who we might be and what we could do and stuff, right? Aren't you always staying stuff like that?"

Chloe looks at me then. Behind her glasses her brown eyes are wide, but I don't know if that's the thickness of the lenses or just how her eyes are or if it's something more, if it's her really seeing me, really getting me.

"I do say stuff like that," she says.

"This is important," I say. "It's about Dorothy. And her mom and, you know, the ladder and everything. Can we have lunch together outside and talk?"

Dorothy walks into class at last. I watch her face and body react to Chloe sitting back in her old seat. "Sorry," Chloe says to Dorothy's confused face. "I— Is it okay that I— Apple asked me to—"

"Yep," Dorothy says, and she slides into the back and Chloe bites her lip and I try to figure out how I'm going to say what I need to say.

I need her to tell me how to keep my best friend with me.

I need her to tell me how to change the way things are.

We're gods. Almost. So there has to be a way.

19.

Dorothy watches me and Chloe move outside for lunch. Eating lunch outside was my thing with Dorothy, and I wonder if it hurts her, if she notices, if it matters.

I want it to matter.

Chloe has three apples and two pieces of bread and a slab of crumbly cheese for lunch. It's what most of us have every day. It's how the gods eat, Mom says, and who am I to argue. I have a bunch of cherries and a thick brown muffin and soft cheese. "Mix and match?" I say, and we do, sharing a little feast so we can each have a bit of everything. It's delicious. Maybe Chloe's family bakes bread by hand and not by magic, the same way Dorothy's family does. Maybe knowing the history of everything means you know which cheese goes best with apples or something.

"You wanted advice," Chloe says, interrupting me when I try to ask about the cheese and the bread and the shiny, shiny apples.

"About Dorothy," I say.

"She doesn't want to go to Olympus." Chloe says it like it's something we've known all along, a little nothing of a detail that we don't need to linger on or think much about. But I can't think of anything else.

"She has to though," I say.

"No one has to. The screed said everyone just has to choose by solstice."

That's the thing about Chloe. She is very literal. She doesn't seem to get that this is it, this is Dorothy's only chance to live in the sky, that otherwise Dorothy will be an actual human, like Penny. An actual human who dies.

My breath hitches.

Chloe doesn't get that saving Dorothy is a promise I have to keep. I don't know why we keep pretending there are two choices here, when there's only one choice that makes any sense at all.

"Gods fix things," I say. I try to sound certain, the way Hera is when she tells us which apples to pick and how many bites to take, and how to behave like the near-gods we are.

"They do."

"They use their powers and they fix things. And they

help humans, and they punish humans, and they show humans the way to be. Dorothy wants to be a human. We are about to be gods." I move my hair from one shoulder to the other and sit up as straight as I can. I sound like a god, I think, at least a little. Chloe taps her fingers like she's doing some sort of math, and she looks up at the ladder and down at the ground and over to the statue of Athena in front of the schoolhouse. She purses and unpurses her lips.

"They make mistakes, sometimes, when they fix things," Chloe says. She talks really slowly, like she's a teacher or a doctor or someone whose whole job it is to explain stuff to people who struggle to understand, and I guess in some ways she is exactly that. Like her dad, Chloe knows our godly history, but she knows a lot of human history too. Wars they've fought and reasons they hate one another and triumphs and victories and what it all means. I don't think I care about anything as much as Chloe cares about history. I can see from the way she talks about humans that she worries about them and wants us to worry about them too.

Still, she doesn't say that Dorothy would be better off on Olympus, in spite of all she knows about the injustices on earth.

"It's not a mistake to save someone from life on earth," I try. Chloe is unmoved. She shakes her head a little, purses her lips. "Psyche!" I say in a burst of urgency. "Psyche was a human saved from life on earth, turned into a god. So

204

there's, you know . . . it's a thing gods do." I don't have to say more. The story of Psyche is a love story about the goddess of beauty, Aphrodite, being jealous of the mortal human Psyche's exceptional beauty. She sends her son, Eros, to enact revenge on Psyche for drawing attention from Aphrodite's beauty, but he falls in love with her instead and they get married. Upon seeing how beautiful their love is, Zeus ends up granting Psyche immortality as a wedding gift. It's one of the happily-ever-after stories, so that must mean something.

Chloe closes her eyes and takes these huge, deep oceanic breaths, and when she opens her eyes she looks almost a little sad, like she's going to regret what happens next. "Transformation," she says. "It's the simplest and the most common, and this is exactly the type of situation that gods use transformation for."

"Perfect! Like what?" I am bouncing on my feet. I am ready to fly, practically, ready to do whatever she tells me.

"They often want humans to be with them, or they want to hold on to humans they love and don't know how. Zeus isn't usually turning humans into gods like he did with Psyche, so they transform them into something else, so that a piece of them can stay forever." Chloe's eyes flash with some sort of extra meaning that I don't want to know anything about. "It sometimes— It can get weird or not be what they expected, or—"

"She's my best friend," I say. My voice finally slows down to Chloe's pace, slow and real and sure. "She's the only person I feel like myself with. I know it's not a romantic love story, but it's— She and I are meant to be too. Penny said. My own mom even said so. It's worth it. I know it is."

Chloe nods. I don't think she has a best friend, but she seems to understand how important best friends are anyway. Maybe just from knowing everything about history. I bet there are a hundred amazing best friendships in our history, but me and Dorothy, ours is the best one, the strongest, the biggest. Getting her to Olympus will prove that.

"What about a tree?" she says. "Like Daphne. She was turned into a really beautiful tree. And Dorothy, she likes trees, right? Likes being outside. It could be by the river. And then you could visit her whenever you wanted. A tree that never dies. Something permanent and really sturdy."

I try to picture Dorothy as a tree. She'd be something unexpectedly hearty, not too flowery but really pretty anyway, and a little wild, with leaves all over the place and branches all askew, maybe some sort of twisty trunk.

But a tree on earth isn't what I want. Even one that lasts forever. "That would be—that's a nice idea. But she'd be down here and I'd be up there. I want her with me. With us. In Olympus."

Chloe nods. "Right. Okay." She sort of sighs. She liked the idea of the tree, I can tell. Maybe she wanted to visit tree-Dorothy herself. They aren't best friends like we are, but they're something. "So she'd have to turn into something small, I guess? Like, that you could fit in your pocket?"

"Yeah, maybe," I say. I'm trying to picture that and I want it to sound right, but I'm not sure it does.

"Eos turned Tithonus into a cicada. Maybe Dorothy could be a cicada and you could carry her up the ladder on the solstice? How would that be?"

"A cicada." I'm trying to recall the myth that Chloe is talking about. "I guess . . . She's not really . . . I don't even like bugs."

Chloe laughs. It's unexpected. She's usually so serious, with her thick glasses and five huge history books always lugged around in her backpack.

"We could trick her. Gods do a lot of tricking. Like maybe you could get some immortal apple and bake it into a pie or something and trick her into eating it?" Even Chloe doesn't sound very convinced by this idea.

"I don't think Hera lets those apples out of her sight."

"I don't know. Maybe there's just not a great solution, Apple." She's using her slow slow slow voice again.

"I want her with me. All the time. Not some bug or tree or whatever. But right here. You know?" I point to the space right next to me.

"Right here," Chloe repeats.

"Like with humans!" I'm remembering a group of

humans we saw one late afternoon last fall. They'd wandered onto Our Hill, a group of teenage friends who were laughing and loud and seemed so happy that I almost wondered, for a minute, what was so bad about being human after all. "They have those people attached to them! You know what I mean!" I can see it in my mind: They walked upright, but there was another set of humans, like echoes, walking beneath them, forms sliding across the sidewalk. I'd asked Mom what they were, those black figures trailing out of their toes. She'd laughed and explained that humans are like trees and houses and streetlights. They have shadows. It still seems so absurd to me—a person with a shadow, the kind of thing meant for an object—that I have to reach for the word. "Couldn't Dorothy be a shadow? My shadow? That's what I want. For her to be my best friend, always with me, walking with me, you know? Oh my gosh, it's perfect!"

Chloe's mouth tightens. "But what does Dorothy want?" she asks, as if we haven't been talking this whole time about what is best for Dorothy.

"Dorothy's confused," I say. "Everything with her mom confused her, and she could make a huge mistake that she can't take back." I straighten my back. This is right. This is the truth, even if Dorothy doesn't see it and even if all these other feelings and worries are strumming through me. Dorothy is confused. I can save her. And Chloe sees it too.

"A shadow," Chloe says. "That's never been done."

"It's like an echo, sort of," I say, because it is, isn't it? A shadow is an echo without sound. It's like a best friend who is always nearby. "And I'll live forever so she'll live forever, and that's better than being a human and dying." Chloe and I look each other in the eyes, both of us remembering Penny, the funeral, the sudden ending, the hurt that was so much worse than anything we'd felt before. For days and weeks Our Hill felt strange and slow and sorry, all of us shuffling instead of walking, trying on smiles that felt wrong, sure we were seeing Penny by the river, in the treetops, in our dreams. "Being her best friend's shadow forever is better than what happened with Penny," I say, making solid the thoughts we're both having. "Gods have turned people into echoes. This is like that. This way she doesn't have to be a gross bug or a tree or something—she can be sort of like a person, which is what she wants to be anyway."

Chloe looks like she wants to say something else, but there's really nothing else that needs to be said, nothing else I need to hear. We did it. We found a solution.

"Be careful," Chloe says, but she's the sort of person who's always telling people to be careful, always worrying about history and what it means about right now. "Do you even know how to do that kind of thing?"

I shake my head. "Do you?" I ask.

Chloe looks at the ground. She adjusts her glasses. "I

know history," she says. "That's it. We all have our own, you know, strengths and stuff."

She's saying something true, but it's not something we are supposed to ever discuss. On Our Hill, we are equals.

"Whose strength is shadows?" I say. There's a god for everything. That's something we learn when we're babies practically, memorizing long lists of gods and nymphs and muses and everyone in between, pairing their names with their interests and passions and accomplishments.

"I don't know, Apple," Chloe says. "This plan just seems—" Chloe takes her glasses off, rubs the lenses, and puts them back on. "I'd like to talk to Dorothy about it first. Can't we all sit down and—"

"We don't have time. She's being stubborn. This is too important. This is forever."

As if the gods themselves hear me—and maybe they do—there's a grumble of thunder in the clear blue sky. Chloe hears it too, a warning or an agreement or a reminder of the bigness of the moment we are in. She looks up at the sky, worried.

"Who knows about shadows?" I say. There's another grumble. Chloe rubs her forehead and takes off her glasses again. All the history in the world can't tell us what it means. The gods are listening and they're approving or they're mad or they're worried or they're frustrated—it's impossible to say. I take Chloe's hand the way I've taken Dorothy's. I want her to know I'm scared too. Of everything. Chloe looks startled by the gesture, but she doesn't move away.

"I mean, I guess I was thinking of Erebus," she says. "He's the god of darkness and shadows and stuff, but it's not like, you know, totally safe. He's connected to, um, Hades and stuff, and you probably don't want to get involved with all that."

"Erebus," I repeat, knowing what that means.

"Looking back at history," Chloe says, "we know what was a good idea and what wasn't. But when we're in it we can't really know—"

"I promised Penny," I say. "This is my destiny. I'm positive."

Chloe nods. "Eric," she says, the name I already knew.

"Eric," I say, like I need to test the idea out in my mouth first.

There's nothing intrinsically wrong with Eric outside of who he is related to down below in Hades. He wears blue like the rest of us. He raises his hand in class. He's fine. Surly and a little weird, but fine. And it would be fine, to get his help.

Chloe sort of cringes, still not sure about what I'm doing, but I don't need her to be sure. I'm sure. Chloe can know everything in the world about history, but that doesn't mean she knows about right now or the future or what you can and can't do to save your best friend and save yourself.

Her ancestor, Clio, the muse of history, isn't exactly the most powerful person in Olympus.

Zeus is. Hera is.

"Don't worry. I'll talk to him. This is— You really helped me, thank you. But I've got this now."

"Right now?" Chloe is clasping her hands together in worry. "Maybe she'd listen to me if I talked to her. We're friends too, and Dorothy likes history and getting Eric involved seems—"

"She won't listen," I say, and I think even Chloe knows it's true. This is the right thing. It's what Penny would have wanted. For me to look out for Dorothy no matter what. For me to make sure she won't ever be alone. Left behind.

Dorothy is so unlucky to lose her mom. But she's so so lucky to have had her at all.

And now she has me. And she won't be left behind.

Neither of us will be.

20.

As usual, Eric is sitting on his own after lunch. Mr. Winters is late coming back, and the rest of us are doing what we do when we have unexpected flashes of free time—gossiping about who is going to do what on Olympus, weaving complicated friendship bracelets, quizzing each other on gods and what they like to eat and how to make them like you.

Lately, we are just looking forward and thinking about how things will be and no one cares anymore about how things are. Even Mom has let the house get sort of sloppy. I guess I have too. My room is just piles of blue dresses and photos of me and Mom and Penny and Dorothy that I've taken out of frames and photo albums to look at more closely, to try to make those moments real again. There are crumbs on the counter and Mom's bed is never made and there's a haze to all the windows that shouts out, *No one is wiping us down! No one cares anymore! Soon, you will live with the gods!*

Here in the classroom, too, there's something unkempt. The desks aren't lined up. The trash cans seem too full. Lessons from yesterday and the day before aren't fully erased from the chalkboard, little ghost-words haunting the background.

Dorothy herself doesn't look any different from normal, but her normal is a little undone—hair slipping out of braids and dresses that hang all wrong. Eric, though, looks very put together. It's funny, and I wouldn't have noticed because I never notice Eric, but he's the only person who looks all ironed and combed and cleaned. Fresh. Like he lives here and will be living here and he isn't waiting for something else, he is just *here.*

I must be looking too hard at him while trying to figure it out, because he's glaring back at me suddenly, all elbows and eyebrows and irritation.

"Sorry. Hi. You look nice," I say, which is all wrong. I am not used to saying all wrong things, especially not to someone like Eric. "I mean, sorry. I like your shirt. And I wanted to talk to you." This sounds weird too, but I'm worried if I try a third time, something even more awkward might come out.

"To me?" Eric says. He has a half-smile on his face that I don't like very much.

"Yeah. I have a— I need help with something that I thought you might be able to help with. Chloe suggested— we both thought of you." I don't know why I bring Chloe into it, except that she makes things feel stable and grounded and good. I want my plan to sound logical and measured. I mean, it *is* logical and measured, but I want to make sure he hears it that way too.

"Oh boy," Eric says, almost laughing, but then just *not*. "Can't wait to hear what this is."

We've probably never really spoken before, even though we've been in a small classroom together our entire lives. Maybe it's a mistake, bringing someone like him into this.

But then I catch sight of Dorothy out of the corner of my eye. She's writing something in a notebook—she's holding her pen the same way Penny used to hold her pens—hard and tight and not the way we were taught in school. When we were little, we learned how to write letters together. Mom adjusted my fingers around the pen until I got it just right, but Penny never cared how Dorothy did it, just kissed her cheek and called her brilliant every time she got even close to forming a familiar alphabet shape.

I don't think I've ever been jealous of anyone except Dorothy, and I don't think I even knew that, really, until right now, watching her hand and the pen and the easy way she knows who she is.

Without Dorothy and the way she holds her pen I'm just my mom, part two. I'm just some heir to Hera's apple tree, some person who is already decided and figured out and boring.

Without Dorothy, I'm just alone.

And she'd be alone too. I straighten my shoulders. This is for her.

She needs me.

She *needs* me.

"Can you make someone into a shadow?" I ask. I could beat around the bush I guess, but Eric doesn't seem like the sort of person who would like that very much. His smile deepens. He has dimples, something I've never noticed before, and they are deep, like Penny's.

"Sure," he says. "Sure, I can do that."

"Okay," I say.

"Who?"

"Oh. Well. Dorothy."

"Dorothy. Wow. Okay. I thought you guys were close these days. Isn't she your new lackey?"

"She's my best friend," I say, crossing my arms and fighting a flush.

"Huh. Weird," Eric says. "And you want to turn her into a shadow? Like, permanently?"

I think I'm supposed to explain it all, but the bemused look on his face stops me. He makes me nervous, the opposite of how it felt talking to Chloe about all of this.

"I don't need to know," he says, noticing whatever is happening to my face, I guess. "You want her to be a shadow. Sure. Today?"

Maybe this is how Eric always is. Maybe this is how anyone related to Erebus, tied to Hades, is. Casual about big things. Not caring about the whys. Just doing whatever pops into their heads.

I guess I shouldn't complain.

"You think today would be good?" I ask, not even really knowing what the question means.

Eric shrugs. Smiles. Looks at Dorothy and tilts his head like he's trying to imagine what she'll look like as a shadow.

"If you're sure you want to do it," he says.

"I want to do it."

"Well, all right. Then keep her outside after school. I'll be right nearby."

"You've done it before?" This should have been my first question, maybe. "It's safe?" That one too. My heart is pounding. I'm a little breathless trying to catch up with myself.

"Not with a person, but I've played with shadows my

whole life. It's—you know, it's like any transformation. Gods do them. Things happen." He shrugs again. I am starting to hate his shrugs and how they say nothing and everything at the same time.

"Things happen," I repeat.

"You know that," he says, like we have some secret together about the way the world works. "Anyway. This afternoon. I'll be there. It'll be fun."

I nod. It doesn't sound like the right word to describe what this will be, but I can't find any other words. This is the choice I have to make. This is what Dorothy is making me do.

"She likes the river," I say. "Can you follow us to the river?"

"Sure."

"Wait for me to nod at you, okay? She and I have to talk first. So let us talk and then when it's time, I'll nod. Like this. Okay?" I nod my head, not in any particularly magical way, but I want to make sure he gets it. I have to say things to her first, I have to try to make her understand and maybe give her one more chance to just climb the ladder and do what we're all meant to do.

"A nod. By the river. Sure." Eric looks bored now, almost, like I've worn out my welcome. I'd think that for someone who never talks to anyone, he'd be happy for every moment I give him, but I guess not.

"I'm saving her," I say, even though I know he wants me to stop talking, even though he doesn't seem to care what I'm doing or why.

He shrugs.

I *am*. No matter what he says or doesn't say. I'm saving her.

She cannot stay on earth and be a human and live without me and then die, like her mom. She can't. Tears gather in my eyes just thinking of it. She *can't*.

21.

Eric's words stick in my head like a song I can't seem to shake. *It will be fun*, he said. I see his dimples, his amusement, how it didn't matter at all to him. *It will be fun. It will be fun.*

I stop Chloe on the way out of school and repeat the same phrase to her. "He said *It will be fun*. That's weird right?"

She sighs. She doesn't want to be involved, but I can't stop involving her. There's no one else I trust who I can talk to about this.

"It's not weird for Eric," she says. "That's how primordial gods are. That's how he is. He's from chaos. He's like . . .

your opposite. You are destined to be strong and together and stuff. He's destined to love chaos."

"And making Dorothy a shadow is chaos?"

Chloe looks at me like I should already know the answer to the question. And maybe I do. I rub my eyes like that might clear up how things are and what needs to be done. So many things are true at the same time, and I've never felt that traffic jam of truth before. That's chaos too, I guess.

"He just seemed to really like the idea," I say.

"I'm sure he did." Chloe's feet point away from me. Her whole body does. No one has ever wanted to leave me more.

"That's making it seem like not the best idea."

Chloe takes a big breath and turns back to me, but I can tell she means it to be quick. She'll say this last thing, and then she'll be gone. "Not everything has a solution," she says. "We try to fix things, and the gods work to make it right, to make it beautiful and perfect and then, you know, Pandora opens a box and perfect is gone and even the gods have to live with that."

"Even the gods," I repeat. It's a sad sentence about giving up or giving in or not ever really getting the thing you thought you were promised because maybe that thing doesn't actually exist.

"I want her to come up too," Chloe says. "And maybe your way is the only way. I don't know. Just . . . think, okay?"

"There's not time to think."

"Think quickly. I gotta go, Apple." And like that, Chloe leaves, her shoulders relaxing the second she's away from me.

Like clockwork, Eric taps me on the shoulder. "We going?" he asks. "River time?" He rubs his hands together, a gesture that puts me even more on edge. He looks too excited to do this. His excitement is some kind of alarm bell screaming at me to stop. Hera would never involve herself with Erebus. I look up at the sky and wish that she would say something to me from up there, give me a sign of what I should do. But they're too busy preparing Olympus for us. They haven't even noticed the constellation we've been making, or if they have, they've decided not to care. Right now, Hera can't help me beyond what I know of her from myths, from history, from the things Mom has told me about who she is and what she expects of us.

"No," I say to Eric at last. "Never mind. I decided it's not a good idea. I'll figure something else out."

"You're sure?" Eric asks. He looks vaguely disappointed, but mostly already uninterested.

I nod. He shrugs in response and I think of saying something more—apologizing, telling him his enthusiasm is what made me pull back on the plan—but Dorothy passes by, walking quickly, and I have to race to catch up.

We've avoided one another all day, which has been easy

222

because she hasn't participated in anything. Not sewing new togas for the trip up, not making gifts for Zeus and Hera, not practicing songs written to honor our ancestors when we arrive.

She has sat in the back and watched. She has looked out the window, where there are still lightning bolts stuck in the ground, smoking and sparking after all this time, the power of the gods never weakening. She has doodled in a notebook. She has gripped her pen the way she always does, like there are no rules at all, for someone like her. And she has asked if she can go home approximately ten times.

And now that she's finally on her way there, she probably doesn't want me to stop her, but I do. We have to talk.

"I'm sorry," I say, a little breathless when I catch up with her at last.

"For what?" she asks. She doesn't stop walking, but she slows a little and soon we're walking side by side.

"For whatever, for everything," I say, because it doesn't matter, really. I'm sorry that she sat in the back, I'm sorry that we haven't finished the constellation, I'm sorry things are weird.

"We're different," she says. "We've always been different." Her voice is edgy. Unlike her.

"I can't let you stay," I say when we reach the river. She kneels down and picks up a star. "I don't want to do the constellation right now. I want to talk."

"I know you do," Dorothy says, so tired that I almost wonder if she's going to fall asleep right here, right now. "I don't want to keep talking about it. Grab a star. We have more to do."

"Okay," I say, squinting at the river ripples and pulling one out. "It's just—your mom wanted us together. I know she did. She told me she did. And we can't do that if you stay here. The choice is forever. And you deserve to be up there with us. And I'm scared for you if you stay here. Remember when we visited that one town and there was a whole wing of the hospital with sick kids in it? That's the world. It's scary. It's cars that crash and things that go wrong and it's endings and heartbreak. Why would you want that? I know you miss your mom, and I do too, but she wouldn't want that for you."

"She's not here," Dorothy says. "She can't tell anyone what she wants. Even you. Maybe we'll go down the hill, meet other people, do things that people do, like have barbecues and go to dance class and, I don't know, take planes to other countries for no real reason. Or we'll figure out what the reason is, I guess. We'll just be people. It will be okay."

"No. It's not okay," I say, talking too loudly now, so loudly that birds flutter away, Dorothy takes a step back.

"You're not a person! You're a god!"

"I have a dead mom," Dorothy says, her voice getting quieter with anger instead of louder. "Maybe that makes me a person. A person who just wants to disappear for a while. I don't want power and glory and some castle. I want— Most days I want to fade away. I want to do anything, to stop feeling the way this feels. I'm so tired of thinking and feeling and making decisions and then explaining them to people like you."

She squeezes the star in her hand, and I squeeze the one in mine.

I want you with me, I think. *We both want the same thing. You have to come up with me. You have to, you have to, you have to.*

My thoughts feel loud and the star burns a little. The palm of my hand stings and I let it go at the same time Dorothy lets hers go. They both splash back into the water. We aren't climbing the ladder today. We aren't finishing the constellation. We aren't becoming what we were meant to be at all.

"So that's just it?" I ask. "You're just going to leave me with my mom and my friends who don't even know me and you're going to let the whole past be nothing, be forgotten?"

"I'll be right here," she says.

"Until you're not."

Dorothy kneels by the river again, like she's going to recapture her star, but instead something else entirely happens.

Her hand, then her knees, then her shoulders, then her hair shift from ivory and brown that used to be blond to a gray-black that at first seems strange because of it being a new color, and then seems stranger because the color itself isn't solid, isn't sure of itself. It is a little transparent. She is a little transparent. Her feet, her torso, her face, her back— the whole of her takes on the new shade, and then, slowly, a new shape.

"What's happening?" I ask.

Dorothy's eyes are wide. She doesn't speak.

She flattens. There's no other way to say it. She flattens and her toes meet mine, and the shape that was Dorothy becomes a different shape that is more like me but also nothing at all like me.

There is no more brown hair that she maybe wishes was strawberry-blond again, no more silly smile and freckles and the way her body moves sort of slowly and like it wishes it were climbing a tree instead of just walking. That is all gone, so fast I didn't have time to say goodbye, even though I'm the person who made it happen.

I must be.

I don't know how—Eric's nowhere to be seen, and I didn't think I knew how to do it. But I wanted it. And I thought it. And I held a star, which are known for wishes. And I am a descendant of Hera. Mom has always said I am powerful and special and closer to the gods, maybe, than the rest of Our Hill. So it must have been me.

My stomach lurches like I might have to throw up, but I don't, I just move like I'm going to. *Gods make mistakes too*, Penny said once, when she was fighting with my mom about why she should be able to celebrate Pandora the same way everyone celebrates Athena and Aphrodite and Apollo and Poseidon.

The exact shape and sound and piney smell of Dorothy is gone. And in its place, in her place, is a shadow. My very own shadow, which is me but not, which is Dorothy but not, which is dark and strange and knit to my shoes. I am not meant to have a shadow, but now I do, I do, and it is Dorothy and she can't leave me, she can't stay here while I go there, I won't have to be alone, not now and not ever again.

It's what I wanted.

It's a mistake.

It's—it's something.

Time passes with me looking at Dorothy and the sky and the sky and Dorothy. The sun lowers a bit and her shape changes a little. Lengthens. I don't know what to do about it. And she is even quieter as a shadow than she was as a near-god.

"I'm sorry," I say. It's easier to say it to a shadow than a person, which is something I didn't know. I wonder if she hears me. I wonder if she forgives me. I wonder if she believes me. I don't know—there's just silence that I have to fill.

"The constellation," I say. "We should finish it, right? Because we're—I guess we're both going up there soon?"

I wait for an answer that isn't going to come.

I look down into the river and snag a star. It's a big one, and I show it to Dorothy, who can't smile at it or ask me to let her put it in the sky. The ladder is a struggle too— wobbly and scary without someone doing it alongside me. But I do it. For Dorothy. For Penny. The sky isn't all the way dark yet, and Dorothy keeps getting longer and narrower and stranger. She climbs the ladder with me, her color fading to a soft gray in the almost-night. And when I'm at the top of the ladder, by our cluster of stars just starting to glow in the near-dark, I look for Dorothy and I see her legs long underneath me.

I start to place the star but something looks a little different. The shape our stars are making in the sky is the same, almost, but there's one small, glowy star in the center that wasn't part of our plan at all.

"Did you do that?" I ask Dorothy. But when I look down to find her, she's gone. "Dorothy?" I call. I move a hand so that she can move hers. The ladder wobbles, the stars blink, but Dorothy isn't there.

"DOROTHY!" I call out. Louder this time, so loud that I think maybe I've woken up some birds, who start chirping. I don't know much about shadows. Maybe they don't like trips up to the sky. Maybe shadows don't like starlight or ladders or that one particular moment when day turns into night, when it's undeniable. When there's no avoiding the dark, quiet fact of it.

I don't like that moment either. I don't like any of the moments lately, where things flip from one way to another, from sunny to starlit, from alive to gone, from familiar to brand new. I place the stars haphazardly, the shape of Penny a little lopsided all of a sudden, but that's okay, Penny herself was a little lopsided, all crooked smile and shaggy bangs and buttons that sometimes weren't matched up right, shirts that fell over her shoulder or socks in different patterns.

"I'm sorry," I apologize, to Penny or the stars or Dorothy or just myself, the person I wanted to be. And I rush down the ladder, so sloppily that the whole thing slides and sways and almost makes me fall, and then at the very end does make me fall, just a few rungs, but enough for me to hurt my hip and my wrist, which I land on all wrong. I look for my shadow, for Dorothy, who should also have a hurt wrist to cradle, a bruised hip to rub. I stand up and jump, my limbs making me into a star shape—all splayed legs and V'd arms. But Dorothy isn't there. I am suddenly shadow-less.

I am suddenly without my best friend.

It feels every bit as awful as I thought it would.

22.

"Sweetheart?" Mom says as soon as I come in. "Sweetheart, it's late." Mom's in the kitchen with her arms crossed over her chest and she isn't alone. Next to her is Dorothy's dad, looking tired and sad.

"Hi, George," I say. "Hi, Mom."

"It's late," George echoes my mom.

"Sorry. I was at the river." It's true enough.

"Oh, thank Zeus," Mom says. "See, George? They were at the river. Dorothy headed home, Apple?"

George and Mom look at me hard, waiting for me to say the right thing, which I almost always do. But I can't say the right thing today. I shift my weight back and forth and our floors squeak. They've been squeaky lately, the kind of thing Mom usually solves with magic in spite of the way Penny used to tell her not to. Penny liked squeaky floors. And doors. The human-est things.

I look at Mom, thinking she'll fix it right this instant—it's easy for her to do that kind of miniature magic—but she doesn't. She just keeps watching me for signs of what is happening.

"Dorothy didn't head home," I say. I look at the ground. I think I see her shadow hand, the crook of a shadow elbow. I try to move in a way that hides her.

I hadn't thought about this part—the what-to-say-to-Mom-and-George-and-the-rest-of-the-world part. Once we're in Olympus maybe it will all make sense to them and to me, too, but right now I can't find words that will sound right to them.

"Where'd she go?" George asks. He looks like he knows, but of course he doesn't.

I should have had a plan. Chloe and I could have come up with one together. Maybe even Eric would have had some suggestion. But I was so focused on the one thing that I forgot to think about anything else.

"I don't know," I say, trying to make it sound real. "She said she wanted to stay at the river. And I told her that wasn't a good idea. You know, it was late and I figured you guys would worry and everything. But you know Dorothy. She gets an idea in her head and just doesn't listen. So." I straighten my back and it's actually not as hard as I'd have thought, saying something not exactly true in a way that sounds very true. It starts to *feel* true—it *is* the sort of thing Dorothy would do—and my shoulders and my heart relax. It's basically true, I decide. It's true enough.

"I better go look," George says.

"You want me to come?" Mom asks. George tries to say no, but Mom doesn't let him. "Don't answer, we're coming. Right, Apple? You'll know where she is." She gives me a look that says I am only allowed one single answer.

"Sure," I say, even though it's the last thing I want to do. I haven't eaten dinner. I haven't had a chance to just sit and think about all that has happened. I have more to say to Dorothy. I need a moment to myself.

But instead Mom grabs me a piece of bread and smothers honey and sea salt on it, and we head back into the night. It feels all kinds of wrong—the lie of it I guess, but also me being alone with our parents—the missing pieces are too loud. Penny should be leading the way, bird-calling to whatever chirpy birds she hears, telling us what kind of flower is what, pointing out the constellations no one knows very well. And Dorothy should be here too. Quiet and thinking and sometimes walking step in step with me, sometimes smiling with me at something our moms say or do.

I look down below me to where she should be now.

She's not there.

In the dark, there are no shadows. I hadn't known that, hadn't known anything about shadows, never thought of them at all really, except I figured that they're with you all the time and even that doesn't seem to be true.

They leave you. I crunch my toes when my heart starts to ache. I wish away the tears that want to come out. Things keep getting ruined in new and impossible ways.

We get to the river and I see George's shoulders droop at the absence of Dorothy. His face falls and his voice shakes when he says, "She's not here." I look at Mom, to try to exchange a glance or share in something, but she's marching around the trees on some sort of mission and I'm alone.

"Well, we will find that girl, that's for sure. She's a wanderer. Curious. Unpredictable. Like her mom. Like Pandora." Mom sounds exhausted and annoyed instead of affectionate like she used to be about the details of Penny's personality.

"*Mom,*" I say, sharp and sudden, because it isn't the right way to be talking to someone whose daughter is missing.

"Apple. My gosh. Calm down," Mom says.

"Dorothy is Dorothy," I say. I want to say a bunch of stuff—that Dorothy isn't Penny or Pandora and I'm not my mom or Hera and all of us are just ourselves or something, but it's not the kind of thing I would ever say. It's maybe the sort of thing Dorothy would say, or at least think or whisper to me, maybe, here at the river when things are quiet and we're alone and we can say that sort of thing.

"Of course she is. That's exactly who she is," Mom says, her voice all tight and held back and promising, again and again, that there is really only one way for each of us to be. George looks up at the sky, then toward the ladder. For a moment he looks hopeful—but Dorothy's not there, of course.

"Where is she, Apple?" he asks at last, turning to me a little too swiftly, a little abruptly. His eyes narrow like he knows I know something, but I keep my face neutral.

"I don't know," I say.

"Where is she?" he asks again.

Mom must hear something she doesn't like in his voice, because she swoops in, puts an arm around me, and juts her chin in this particular way that means the conversation is over. "She doesn't know. Now, it's late. It's cold. We should all head home. She's fine, that much we know. The gods look out for us. Her decision hasn't been made yet, so she's not—" Mom clears her throat instead of saying the word *dead*, a word we don't say anymore, now that we actually know someone who is dead. "She climbed the ladder last solstice," Mom says, and this too sounds mean. "She did what she was meant to do last year. So you know she's safe, George. I think it's time we go home."

I don't know if she means all of us or just me and her. A line feels like it's forming between us, one Penny wouldn't have liked one bit. She liked that we had keys to each other's houses. She liked baking cookies and sharing them with us, as if we all lived together, as if we were all one funny-shaped family. Penny liked the ways our families collided, that at town events we'd go together, Dorothy and I tagging along in the back not talking, but not *not* talking either, just being, just comfortable with the way we weren't comfortable together. Not friends, back then, just two girls connected by someone else's friendship.

But with Penny gone, all Mom can think about are lightning bolts and ladders and probably a hundred other things that feel important to her but weren't to Penny.

Or to Dorothy.

I look down to see her. But it's dark, so she's not there.

If I had known how quickly she would leave me every time it got dark, maybe I would have had another wish.

Mom pulls me away from George, who isn't speaking, who's just looking at the trees, at the river, at the moon, and at me. And we walk home in silence.

I wish the moon were brighter so that my shadow could appear. So that I didn't have to do this all alone. I wish I hadn't wished at all.

Because even if shadow-Dorothy were here, it wouldn't be what it was meant to be. The thing about shadows is that they don't know anything about moms who walk fast and dads who can be heard singing at trees in the far away distance. They don't know anything about the ridiculous and sad and embarrassing and funny and inescapable ways parents act.

They are right there, shadows, but they're not very good, after all, at making you feel any less alone.

DOROTHY

December 20

23.

Heather Montgomery is rarely in pajamas. I knew this when I was in my human form too—Apple and I had sleepovers when we were littler. Not the kind with popcorn and giggles and, I don't know, fake tattoos? Is that what the human girls do when it's midnight and everyone is the loopy kind of tired but no one wants to actually fall asleep?

Apple and I slept in the same room—hers, usually— and we'd listen to some kind of music that Apple liked and I could easily ignore and I'd draw faces in a notebook—not the ones they have us draw in school of Zeus and Poseidon and Athena and Persephone. But the sorts of faces we'd see on our trips to human towns. Apple would paint her nails and sometimes talk to me but also just the air about whatever thing was going on with her friends, and eventually we'd fall asleep and wake up and eat pancakes but none of it felt like friendship, back then—it was just the way things were. Our moms dropped pomegranate seeds in the pancakes, and slices of almonds, and sometimes the ground-up peels of lemons, and all of it tasted delicious and strange. Those mornings were sort of delicious and strange—our moms laughing about something and everything and me and Apple all quiet and waiting for our actual days to begin, the sleepover and the morning after being a sort of pause on regular life.

I smell pancakes now.

I didn't know shadows could smell. Or hear. Or think, even, but we do all of it. Everything but the walking around and actually *being*. Maybe, somehow, this is right for me. To get the senses and not the body. To be on earth but not seen.

Except I won't be staying on earth. And last night Dad's voice was all broken and scared. And still, here, in a notbody, I miss Mama.

And hate her too, in awful, jabby moments where my brain insists everything could have been good if only, if only, if only. I didn't think shadows would feel anger, especially the kind you're not supposed to feel at all, at a person who is gone.

The pancake smell gets stronger as Apple and I walk

down the stairs, all of Heather coming into focus—blue-dressed and perfect-haired and flipping pancakes the muted almost-yellow color of a gray-sky sun.

"Apple. No. You need to get dressed," she says instead of good morning, and Apple startles at the tone. I do too. Shadows, I guess, can startle.

"For breakfast?" Apple says. She looks down at her pajamas—blue, silky, comfortably perfect.

"It's a special breakfast. Your friends are coming. Any minute now, in fact. So please go put on something presentable."

I watch Apple's face try to parse the words. She's maybe still groggy from sleep or from the strange heaviness of last night or from the anticipation of solstice being tomorrow.

Tomorrow. An impossible fact that is also somehow true.

"Dorothy's coming over?" she says, and I guess the grogginess is something even sadder.

"Not that I know of," Heather says, her words so quick, ready to fly right past me, pretend I might not have ever been. "I'm talking about your best friends."

"Dorothy's my best friend," Apple says. She's cleared her throat and her voice is her own again now. Clear and ready and top-of-a-lightning-bolt sharp.

Heather sighs. Before this past month, I'd only known her as the Heather she was with Mama and the Heather she's been in the almost-year since Mama died. Warm to me and funny, usually, and good at doing all the right things at all the right times. This person in the kitchen making pancakes is more like the awful Heather who stood on a crystal box and announced what a failure Mama was, the person who demanded the town be with her or against her and nothing in between. It never occurred to me that she might be this Heather at home with Apple, too. But Apple doesn't seem surprised at all.

I don't think I like it very much.

I don't think Mama would have either, and that thought makes my heart want to swallow itself up a bit. She should be here—for me, but for Apple, too. For all of us.

The flattened feeling of being on the floor matches the way I've felt all year, and there's a comfort in that but also a terribleness in making a feeling into a reality.

"I'm talking about Dawn. And Reece. Come on, Apple. Dorothy was your— I get it. I miss Penny too. But your whole life you were best friends with Dawn and Reece and that was as it should be, and now it's time to repair those friendships. They're going to Olympus. They're your forever."

Unexpectedly, Heather's voice hitches on the word *forever*, and I think for a moment that she misses Mama and maybe misses the person she was able to be around Mama, but she shakes her head like it's time to let all that go, and the knot in her voice untangles into something smooth and a little bit lifeless. "You love them," she says. "They were so happy I invited them over. They miss you."

"I see them every day," Apple says. She's looking intensely at the ground. For me, I guess. I'm not quite formed yet, my shape needs the exact right amount of sunlight and shade and the balance is off in Heather's home.

There's a knock at the door. Apple's shoulders tense and I watch her try to catch her mom's eye, but Heather only rushes to the door, grinning harder than anyone would ever need to.

There's the smell of pancakes and the chill in the air and the mess in the kitchen that's never been there before. And there's the weight of *forever* pressing down on all of it—tomorrow was just an idea until today, when tomorrow started to feel real, inescapable.

So heavy it hurts.

I wonder if I'd feel that all, see it all, if I were a girl in a body again and not a shadow on the floor.

"Finally, you're back!" Reece says, bursting into the house like it's hers, grabbing Apple like Apple is hers too. Dawn follows. Even her footsteps are softer, and she smiles smaller. She's genuinely happy—I can see it in the way she waits for Reece to be done with Apple before pulling her

245

into a hug that is shorter but bigger, too, somehow. There's so much I never noticed before taking on this shadow shape.

"I've been here the whole time," Apple says into Dawn's shoulder.

"No, some other weirdo has been hanging out in your body and now here you are again. Right? I mean, right?" Reece never used to be the one in charge of their little three-some. It was always Apple who seemed to lead the way. But I guess something has shifted, or maybe I shifted something, or, I don't know, Mama did, or Pandora a billion years ago, or all of us just shift things over and over and over again.

Heather lays out three plates and three forks and three knives and a pile of pancakes that looks almost like it could fall. There's something in the pancakes making them smell extra delicious—cinnamon or vanilla maybe. Or just magic.

Dad loves pancakes with cinnamon, so the smell makes me think of him and I get an urge—big and reaching—to get up from the floor and go find him and tell him I'm okay and make our own batch of pancakes together. I start the movement in my head, but my body can't do anything about it. *Go check on my dad*, I try to telegraph to Apple, but of course she can't hear.

"You're excited, right, Apple?" Dawn says, serving her-self the least fluffy pancake from the tower. "Do you think you'll hang out with Hera a lot? Or, like, learn how to tend to the tree? I heard you and your mom are going to get the most amazing place to live, you know, because of who you are and everything."

"Oh," Apple says. "Yeah, I guess a new house will be nice."

"We'll make things better, I bet," Dawn says. She looks like she believes it, and I try to remember all the times the gods have made things better. I think Apple's thinking the same thoughts, because her mouth makes this *hmm* shape, like there are words she'd like to say but isn't sure she should.

"We probably should have never even been down here," Reece says. She throws some hair behind her shoulders, tilts her chin like her face is looking for the sun. "I mean, a hundred years ago or whenever it was, it was probably a mistake. Like. We're gods. Right, Heather?"

I'd almost forgotten Heather was still in the room, sipping coffee, eyeing the girls and the pancakes maybe just as fiercely as I am.

"We are," Heather says, which is agreeing with part of what Reece's saying but not all of it.

"I wouldn't change anything," Apple says. Heather lowers her head, like she doesn't want to let anyone see what she's thinking either way, but I can feel the way they are both thinking about Mama.

Mama's not here, but the thinking about her is, and

it's in the exact lean of Heather's body—how it looks like it needs someone to lean against, how it's missing Mama's shoulders, perfectly aligned with her own. It's in the way Apple looks outside like she's searching for the sun, which is just another way of searching for her shadow. It's in the quiet, and how wrong it feels when Reece breaks that quiet.

Mama did this to us. The feeling squeezes and releases. Mama gave us these new shapes and then left us to deal with them, and it turns out we aren't very good at being left behind.

The floor feels cold. The pancake smell is starting to bother me. I want to leave the room. I also want to stay right here, on earth, dealing with cold floors and irritating smells. But I'm a shadow. I don't have a say in any of it. On Olympus, everything smells like flowers and apples. On Olympus, the floors are warm.

Reece and Dawn keep talking, debating our time on earth and how much syrup to put on pancakes and what to wear for school.

I'm not even here.

Mama's not here.

Soon, Our Hill won't be here at all.

A cloud passes over the sun and I vanish for an instant. It's almost what I wanted—to disappear into the grief. To stop having them talk about me and Mama. To stop having to decide if I wanted to be like Apple or like Mama and to just be this.

It's almost what I wanted, but not quite right.

"We really did miss you," Dawn says, somehow not noticing that Apple's not really here either.

24.

"Oh. Finally," Apple says on the walk to school when she catches sight of me. I am short in the beginning of the day. Short but clearly defined, and Apple looks relieved but nervous. Near-gods don't have shadows, a basic fact she seems to keep forgetting and remembering over and over again.

I know what that's like. It's a little like the way I remember and forget that Mama is gone.

"Finally what?" Reece says. Her eyebrows keep doing this thing where they look like they are trying to touch but just can't reach. As a person in a body, I never noticed eyebrows. Or much of anything, really, outside of the river and Mama's voice and whatever it was we were eating for dinner. I noticed the stars and the length of the grass and which statues of Athena were where, but not what anyone's faces or fingers or ears did. Not eyebrows.

I missed a lot.

Maybe I was made to be this way—walking in time with Apple, seeing all the little things that no one else is but not having to do anything about it. Not having to feel much about it either.

"Nothing," Apple says. "Never mind."

"You're still being weird," Reece says.

Dawn jabs her with an elbow, but Reece jabs her right back and Dawn quiets.

"I like walking to school," Apple says. "I was just thinking about that. I'll miss that, I guess."

"No one likes that." Reece walks a little faster, like she's running away from the things Apple's saying that don't line up quite right with the things she wants her to say. In the stories we've learned about the gods, they're like this sometimes. They're not always so good at hearing what other people feel or need or want. They turn them into birds and trees or they make them fall in love with this person or that, or they take revenge even if they don't know the whole story, and maybe Reece will be good at being a god.

"Olympus is super pretty," Dawn says. She touches Apple's wrist with this kindness that is almost too delicate to see. Dawn will be a different kind of god up there. Maybe

251

the kind the other gods make fun of for being too soft or something, but the humans will worship her.

Or take advantage of her kindness?

I don't know. I'd have to ask Chloe, I guess, who would know exactly what we should expect from Reece's coldness and Dawn's sweetness.

But of course I *can't* ask her about it. And Apple won't. And it doesn't matter anyway if I'm just a shadow.

In school, I'm able to hide under desks mostly, though I watch as Chloe darts her eyes in my direction every few moments, like she can't look away. She finally approaches and Apple looks down at her desk, like even having Chloe nearby makes her feel something bad.

"You did it," Chloe says.

Apple pauses. Chloe knew, I guess, what was going to happen to me. Maybe everyone knew. I wish I could look around class to see who else is looking our way, but I can't. Apple doesn't move so I don't move.

"I told Eric no," Apple whispers. I get a jolt of nerves at Eric's name. Honestly I can't even picture him ever talking to Apple, and the idea makes me feel like I don't know the world I live in at all.

"But," Chloe says, jutting her chin at me on the ground.

"I guess I did it myself?" Apple finally, finally looks up at her. Her eyes are big, wondering, really not knowing. "I was holding a star. I wanted it. I guess that was enough."

Chloe squints. Apple grips her hands together. I am an accidental wish. I am a plan that wasn't meant to happen. I'm glad no one can see the way it hurts.

"You did it yourself," Chloe repeats, not quite believing it. But there's no time to talk about it, because Mr. Winters is at the front of the class instructing everyone to sit down and be quiet. His voice is harsher than usual.

"It is the last day on earth," he says as if we didn't already know.

Apple is quiet in class, not raising her hand, not bossing people around, telling them where to sit or what to do, just occupying her front-of-the-classroom space with silence and something else.

Sadness, I guess.

Without the pressure to *be*, I like class. Mr. Winters is going over myths that are less known, ones he thinks we're finally ready for, and it's easier to hear him without having to worry about being seen by everyone, without being expected to talk or smile or react a certain way to a certain sentence.

I'm confused, about how something can be right and wrong in the same moment. I wanted this, sort of, but I also wanted not this at all. I like the way I can hide and listen and watch. I don't like the dusty feel of the floor or the way I am trapped into Apple's decisions.

Maybe this is how Mama felt. Happy and sad about her choice. She always seemed sure, but the idea that it wasn't so clear soothes something in me. I wish I could talk to Apple about it. And also I'm glad to get to keep it to myself.

Before lunch, Mr. Winters gestures to Apple to join him at the front of the room. The rest of the classroom empties, with Dawn promising to wait for Apple outside the door and Reece correcting her with a cool *maybe*. Apple doesn't even seem to hear the infraction, but I want her to. I want her to be her Apple self again. Short months ago she could stop Reece's mouth with a brutal flutter of her eyelashes and nothing else, and there needs to be someone who can do that.

I don't have a mouth to open or a voice to shout with or even a little pinky finger that is my own to raise, though, so I can't remind her of who she is, I can't tell her to snap out of it. I can't move a single muscle without Apple doing it first.

We walk to Mr. Winters's desk and surely he'll notice me on the ground right next to him. I try to straighten myself out to make sure he does. If he notices me, he can tell Dad I'm okay. If he notices me, maybe he'll know what to do. The sun streams in in this certain way at this time of day, and his desk is at the perfect angle to expose me, but he's only looking right at Apple.

"Dorothy's out of school," he says. "Her father hasn't checked in. Do you know what might be happening there?"

Apple stares at him like she hasn't heard the question.

He tilts his head and tries again.

"Has she made a decision about Olympus and maybe thinks she doesn't need to be here anymore?" He's speaking in a whisper, like staying on earth is a secret that no one should hear.

"Um," Apple says, and then a long impossible pause after the nothing-word. "I don't know."

"You're the kind of girl who has influence, Apple. You need to talk to her. I know her family is— Well, I know she's a little unusual, but we don't want to lose her senselessly, do we?"

"No."

The light shifts, a cloud covering the sun I guess, and I fade a little. I can feel it when it happens, like a slipping-away from myself, like the moment before you fall asleep but you aren't asleep quite yet because shadows don't sleep, they just are.

I just am.

"The way we lost Penny . . . the way she lost herself . . . I care about Dorothy. I don't want her stuck here while we all get to live up there. Her family has done wrong, yes, but she doesn't deserve that."

"Right." Apple doesn't correct the statement, so it lingers and pinches.

"So you don't know anything," Mr. Winters says. When I was here in the real way, Mr. Winters pulled me aside after class sometimes too. To tell me that I needed to speak up. To remind me that there were lessons I needed to learn and that to learn them I needed to pay attention. To ask me if I'd managed to make any friends lately, and why or why not. He noticed me in all the worst ways. He saw a few parts of me and decided who I was and what I needed to fix from those slippery, separate parts, and I don't miss that way of being seen one bit.

The ground is really so dusty. I sort of want to tell him to sweep it up, to leave the world lovely even if you're not staying in it, to care about the beauty of things even if you are abandoning them.

I would like to say that.

But I can't. My shadow-self tries to tell Apple to say those things, but shadows don't tell their people what to do or say or think.

"I don't know anything," Apple says, so quiet he should notice, but he doesn't.

Reece and Dawn aren't waiting for Apple when she leaves the classroom. She's alone. Except for me, but in the dim hallway lights I'm not really there either.

"What am I doing?" Apple asks no one.

"I hate this," Apple tells no one.

"What do I do?"

No one answers.

*** ***

She walks to lunch slowly and when she gets there, there's no seat at the table with Dawn and Reece. Dawn tries to pull one up for her, but it's lodged between table legs and chair legs and her body barely fits. She has to cross her legs in some weird way and try to make her shoulders smaller than they are.

Everyone chatters on about gods and ladders and clouds and what it will be like to live on top of them, but Apple is quiet and no one really notices her anyway. She looks for me on the ground, and I'm there when she moves her elbow or fingers a certain way, so she does that a few times. I want it to make her feel better, but I don't think it does.

Apple wanted this. She chose it for us. But she doesn't look very happy about it at all.

I'm a shadow, so the easiest place for me to look is right up at the sky, which I do. I wonder if the gods up there ever wonder, the way I am wondering right now, why it is that we have all this power and all this magic and all these wishes that come true but still never feel quite right.

We learn about all the ways gods and humans are so different, and I guess they are.

But somehow none of us seems to know what will happen, when we make a wish, when we make a choice, when we finally decide to change the world.

25.

After the very last ever day of school, Heather is packing. Dad calls, looking for me. Then a few minutes later he calls again. "No," she says, "I haven't seen her. I'll ask Apple again. But Apple hasn't either. You'll find her, George. And if you can't, the gods will."

When she hangs up, she looks closely at Apple, searching for our secret.

"He's worried," she says.

"I know. Me too," Apple says, looking at the floor. Heather nods. It looks like she has a lot to say.

"She's Penny's daughter, so she could be anywhere, I guess," Heather says at last, and it almost sounds mean except she sounds too sad to be mean.

Apple's home doesn't look the way it does when humans move, I don't think. I have seen humans with cardboard boxes and packing tape that makes a loud zipping noise and thick black markers that smell a little like gasoline. They bring everything from one home to another—books and clothes and lamps and quilts and pots and pans.

It must make sense to them, but it's always looked odd to me—the way they are bringing their whole life into a new home, so that they're barely even moving at all, really. They're not exactly starting over, with their same toaster and bookcase and collection of plates that they don't even seem to like very much.

Heather is only bringing a few things up to Olympus, from the looks of it. A silver pen. A ceramic wall hanging of Apple's baby feet pressed into clay. A ring I've never seen before—emerald and diamond and romantic-looking, like Heather was secretly in love at some long-ago time that is now impossible to imagine. She picks up a photograph that sits on the mantel. I know the frame. It isn't gold or silver or wooden. It is a metallic pink color, covered in glitter like some little kid with too much glue made it, but it wasn't a little kid, it was Mama. The photograph is of her and Heather, looking not entirely like gods. Mama is sticking out her tongue and Heather's head is thrown back in laughter and they're both in pajamas, the slightest ring of hot chocolate around Heather's mouth, a dusting of flour on Mama's top. I remember the year that Mama made the frame and wrapped the whole thing up for Heather's birthday. Heather blushed at the photograph—it wasn't who she was supposed to be, it wasn't a side of her anyone but us really knew. But she kept it on her mantel, so Mama must, for a while, have been more important than that embarrassment.

I remember the morning the picture was taken because I took it. Grabbed this heavy camera Heather had and snapped. The camera was one of the few truly human things that Heather loved—that camera, her garlic press, and this wobbly old wagon that she used to pull me and Apple around in when we were little. That morning, Mama and Heather made us a feast for breakfast—mostly Mama, of course. Heather stirred the hot chocolate and kept offering to just *whip something up*, her way of saying they were gods and could just swipe a hand in the air to make food appear. They were in a goofy mood—staying up late and talking all night did that to them. Apple and I happily watched their happiness.

The feast was delicious, and Mama and Heather's joy was a little bit contagious, the way enormous things often are, and I was glad to have gotten a photograph of it all, the way it looked to me. The way it *felt*.

I'm so relieved Heather's going to bring the frame and the photograph that I almost feel I can breathe again, except shadows don't breathe. Apple's body leans a little in the direction of her mom, too. That photograph is hope that we are all trying to hang on to something that was, together.

Heather touches the glitter and some comes off on her thumb, falls to the ground like snow.

"They wouldn't approve," she says to Apple or to no one.

"Who?" Apple says, startling out of her passive state. "What?"

"The gods. They don't want to see Penny. Obviously. And we don't need to— This isn't befitting."

"Befitting?"

It is awful, the way it feels to be here and not, to listen and be unable to speak. It is awful—the way Heather doesn't answer Apple and Apple doesn't ask and the photograph and the frame gets set down in a pile of things that aren't needed on Olympus—sweaters and sneakers and Apple's old report cards.

"We have responsibilities," Heather explains to Apple, who should be reaching out to grab the photo from the pile, who should be reminding her mother about who we all used to be and who that still means we are, somewhere, deep deep down. "We have to be ready to be what they expect us to be."

It sounds awful, and I watch Apple take in the awfulness of it too.

"That's what you tell me down here, too," she says,

finally, after a lake-sized pause.

"Well. It's even more true up there," Heather says. Her voice is clipped and she's sorting through old papers, throwing them away one by one. They float from her hand into the trash can, like a bird losing feathers watching them drift down to earth.

Apple squirms so I squirm, too. It feels good, to be feeling the same thing in the same moment as Apple, so that I can, for one instant, line up in movement with the way that I feel.

I should have appreciated that more when I had the chance.

Apple sits on their enormous puffy couch. Our bodies sink into it and I get lost in the folds of fabric but without the feeling of comfort and coziness and everything else that used to come with curling into that couch.

I should have appreciated a lot of things more.

"What if I don't want to be exactly who they think I should be?" Apple says. Heather's body screams toward her. When she lands, she covers Apple's mouth with her hands.

"They could hear," she says in a whisper.

"You always said they don't pay attention to us."

"Back then!" Heather says. "Things are completely different now. Do not ever say something like that again. Don't even think it."

Apple sinks farther into the couch. There isn't a trace of

262

me to be seen. Heather doesn't move. Keeps a hand tight on Apple's thigh and squeezes, squeezes, squeezes. "Don't ruin this for us, Apple," she says in between squeezes.

I'm surprised by the gruffness of the words, but Apple doesn't seem to be. She nods. "Okay," she says. "Okay, Mom. I'll be good."

That's another thing about being a shadow. It isn't just sitting back and watching the world as you knew it. It's having to notice new things. The hidden things. The things that only shadows ever know.

After Heather has gotten Apple's agreement, she gets up to finish sorting and placing and throwing away the life we all used to love. She answers another call from Dad. I can hear his voice on the other line, loud and urgent now. I want to tell him I'm okay, but maybe I'm not. And it doesn't matter, because I'm not really here anyway. Apple sinks farther and farther into the couch. Her knees pull up to her chest like she really might be able to disappear into it.

And there's nothing I can do about it.

Tomorrow just keeps pressing down, promising that it's coming.

And when the night is at its darkest, Apple still isn't sleeping, she's pacing, so I'm pacing too. I am just a faint idea of myself, from the light of the moon coming in through Apple's window. She looks out at it, and then at the stars, and we both see it at the same time. The constellation.

I'm a shadow for Apple's body but not her thoughts, so I'm surprised by what happens next. Apple putting on a sweater. Shoes. Opening her bedroom window. And climbing out of it. Her body stretches from the windowsill to a tree branch. Her foot finds a lower branch, the other foot follows, and then we jump from branch to ground.

She's done this before, but probably for other reasons, ones maybe I'll never know. Maybe if we could have stayed best friends, I would have heard stories of her being mischievous with Dawn and Reece, maybe I'd learn she's tried to run away before, or just secretly likes climbing trees. But we can't sit down and talk. I know everything she's doing today but nothing she's thinking, nothing she's thought before.

"We have to finish," Apple says. "I should have finished before. I'm sorry." It's funny how Apple whispers when she's talking to shadow-me. She was always so loud when I was in my body.

We get to the river, where she starts digging for stars. I want to tell her she doesn't need to do this. Apple's idea of what Mama should look like in the sky is different from mine anyway, and the incomplete version is okay with me. But Apple is determined. She has stars in her hands and pockets.

She hesitates before the ladder. I've done it alone before too. It's frightening. You can practically feel the gods watching and judging and waiting to punish you. There's a wind that feels a little too strong, a little too cold to just be normal wind. Apple shivers. "You've done this too," she says. She's talking to the gods now, not to me. Apple points at Ursa Major, the constellation Zeus made from Callisto, a nymph that Hera turned into a Bear when she was angry at her.

I wonder if the gods are listening, remembering the things they've done, the people they've chosen to remember.

Maybe they are, because Apple climbs the ladder without a problem and places the stars around the constellation of Mama and the bread. She makes two tiny forms—two little girls helping with bread. One holds a bowl. One holds a spoon. Me and Apple.

It's sweet, a memory captured in the stars. It's the way things were sometimes, Mama teaching me and Apple something simple and human, Heather in the background somewhere, shaking her head at the whole enterprise.

Apple climbs back down the ladder to look at her hard work. An hour has passed, maybe more. It's a nice memory of the way things were, once.

But it's still just that—Apple's memory of Mama and not who Mama was, not who Mama wanted to be. It is not a constellation of what we need to remember most of all.

But of course I can't tell Apple that. Apple smiles. I hope Dad sees her work, figures something out, realizes that if I'm imprinted on the sky maybe I'm not actually on earth after all.

Tell Dad to come up to Olympus too, I try to say to Apple, like the river's magic might be close enough to let me speak, just once. But it doesn't.

"Okay," Apple says. She sighs. She nods like she's finally done the right thing. "Okay."

26.

And just like it promised it would, just like the gods insisted, tomorrow becomes today and solstice has arrived.

Outside Apple's house for the last time, I am so stretched out, I really am starting to look like a tree's shadow and not a girl's, and Apple notices it too. "I looked it up," she says. I can hear in her voice her wish that I could respond. "Shadows get longer in the winter. And the longest at solstice. It's because of where the sun is in the sky." She pauses, like she always does when she's talking to me, like she wants to make sure there's space for me to say something back even though I can't.

She wants to listen to me more now than she ever did

when I was able to speak. Back then, she talked and talked and answered for me: *Obviously you love this dress. Of course you're going to sit with me at lunch. You remember what our mothers were like. We are best friends.*

Heather bursts out of the house like a storm, all energy and force and readiness, I guess, for what is about to happen. But something else, too. Nervousness. Mama used to say that Heather hid her nerves with loudness. Mama would laugh when she said it. "It's not a very smart way to hide something," she'd say. "Usually, I'd suggest whispering." And she'd wink at me or Heather or Apple or whoever, because there was love underneath the bemusement. Love is knowing the strange and wonderful and absurd things people do. It's the delicacy of noticing, and Mama was an expert noticer. Heather's practically screaming on her way out of the house, "Apple, are you ready, you don't look ready, you need to look ready for today, you need to *be* ready, you need to stop hanging your head like some sad girl and hold it up high like the goddess you are about to be."

At mention of Apple's hanging head, I watch Heather's gaze follow Apple's all the way to the ground, to see what leaf or flower or bit of nothing she's all lost in, but instead she sees me—gray and twiglike on the ground. Her eyes squint and she looks back and forth from Apple to me, and back again. "Apple," she says, a warning to tell her what she's seeing, or maybe not to tell her, it's hard to say.

"It's fine," Apple says.

I hate the word and the tiny voice Apple uses to say it. I hate the sun and the ladder and how everything is about to change, and now I'm losing everything, and they are too, they just don't know it.

Heather's eyes keep doing their shimmying dance, and if I could say something, it would be that this is not fine, nothing is fine, everything happening is the exact opposite of fine. I would say I want to stay, and be a human, even if being a human is uncomfortable and sad. I would say that they could stay here too, that it isn't about giving up being a god, it's about celebrating being a human. I would say that humans mess up their bread dough and it doesn't rise but then sometimes they get it right and it *does*, and don't they remember the look on Mama's face when that would happen, when it would come out all golden brown and steaming after so many failures? I would say that humans trip and fall and their knees bleed and someone cleans it up for them, with gentle pats and warm water and bandages with cartoon characters on them, and they walk around with an ache in that joint that is also a happiness, because of the pink and blue bandage and the way a stranger or the person they love most or someone in between helped fix them up when they needed it.

I would say that humans wear clothes that don't fit and they look in the mirror and feel all wrong, but also feel alive, because being alive is also that, is the way things can feel wrong, your whole body can feel wrong, even though it's your body and it's always been your body and always will be. And there's something alive and real and true in that wrongness. There's the promise that another day you will feel right, or that you'll keep feeling wrong but you'll learn that someone else feels wrong too, and then your body will still feel wrong but your heart, your heart will feel right.

I would say, if I could talk, if shadows had mouths and breath and throats squeezing with tears for how desperately I want things to be different, that I know all of this, because I knew Mama, who was human for a short while, but also for the whole time she was here on earth. I would say I know this, because the way I miss her is the worst and the most beautiful feeling, in the same ragged breath. The missing hurts and hugs, it is the wanting her here more than anything, and the gratefulness that I got to love someone so much and have them love me too.

I would miss the missing, is the thing.

Maybe Heather and Apple will go to Olympus. They probably will in just an hour or two. And maybe I'll be dragged along too. This shadow-me, who I thought it might be easier to be, and maybe it is easier, but easier isn't better, isn't happier. And maybe being gods will mean that they can forget dirty dishes and how annoying it is when flies are trapped in the house, buzzing in your ear when you are trying to sleep. Maybe they will forget all about buttons that fall off your favorite coat and rushing out the door to not be late only to realize you forgot the one thing you absolutely had to bring with you. Maybe they will forget, even, the way it felt to hear that Mama was gone. Not gone for a little, not gone to the store, not gone on vacation, but gone in the way that never ends.

But then they will forget to miss her. And miss this. And they will forget when the dishes are clean and you've swatted the fly out of the house and you are early, with everything you need packed into a backpack, and you get to spend a little extra time in the sun on your walk to wherever you're going, a tiny gift of a moment that you didn't know you'd get.

Shadows can't cry. They can't scream or talk about their favorite terrible things about being human.

But I would if I could.

I just didn't know, really, until right now when we're walking away from it all.

"Let's go," Heather says. She seemed to know it was me before, seemed to know Apple's secret. But she doesn't want to know. Maybe in an effort to forget, she steps on me and I brace to feel it. But I feel nothing. The way gods don't feel pain and don't die and don't have to be human at all, and I think gods aren't so unlike shadows after all, are they?

Are they?

27.

We are up by the ladder before everyone else, but the time alone doesn't last. Apple leans against a tree and stares at the ladder like she's still trying to make a decision that it is too late to make. Heather fluffs her hair and adjusts her sky-blue toga. It is one-shouldered and flowing and she looks like she is already a perfect god.

I am long and lean and un-hide-able on the ground. The sun is moving from low to high and I grow with every inch of progress it makes. It feels inevitable people will notice, until I see the crowds of them walking up the hill to the ladder, and understand that they won't be looking anywhere but up and up and up.

It's cold—no one has shifted the weather today, the

almost-gods are letting it be—so the chill in the air is sharp and everyone's breath is visible. People shiver and smile and bounce a little on their toes, waiting for what happens next.

I scan the crowd to look for my dad. Just in case. I don't know what to hope for—I don't want this place Mama loved abandoned by all of us, but I don't want to go up to Olympus without him, so I feel impossibly stuck in something wrong. And I can't talk to him about any of it—I can't even tell him I'm here, I'm okay, I just have to know that he is running all over Our Hill searching and searching and searching.

I see classmates and friends and parents of friends and friends of my parents and the shop owners and statue-makers and river-swimmers that I pass by day after day without knowing much about them.

I see everyone I've ever known, but not my dad.

"Welcome, all," Heather says. She finds a rock to stand on so that she hovers just the smallest bit over the crowd, and she makes her voice just loud enough to be the loudest one talking. Apple sinks farther into her leaning tree. She must have known this was coming but wants to escape it anyway.

Ever since the screeds flew to earth on the tips of flaming bolts, she has been this Heather. The one who won't let you forget that she is descended of Zeus and Hera, the one who has mapped out exactly where each of us lands on the

273

map in her head of how much we matter and how much power we deserve.

"Today is the day," she goes on. "It is our day. The day we move into our rightful places. I know that at first, this decree felt like a punishment. But as the solstice has inched closer and we have had the time to contemplate our place in this universe of ours, I know we have all come to understand that this journey is a gift from the gods. An invitation to be who we were always meant to be. A celebration of their power, and now ours. And I am so thrilled to see all of Our Hill making the right choice. The only choice." She bows her head to the applause that scatters then thunders around us, and she steps off the rock, her work done.

I wonder if she has noticed my missing father.

I wonder if any of them has. They don't seem to be asking about him. Or me. Or where we have gone, their neighbors, their friends who they have known forever.

Heather puts a hand on the ladder. "Apple, honey, here we go," she calls out. Apple looks down at me. I am so long now that my head gets a bit lost in the rest of me, like I am ready to detach from myself.

Apple slumps to Heather's side. She tilts her head all the way back and squints at the sky.

"I liked it here," she whispers to Heather, who pretends not to hear.

Heather puts one hand on the ladder, then the other. A

foot, and the next, and starts to climb, and Apple, swallowing over and over and over, looking up and down and up and down in some effort to make it all make sense, follows. And others follow her. Heather gets four rungs up, five, and the ladder starts to shake and wobble. Apple grips harder and bites her lip. The ladder leans to one side and then, too quickly, shifts back. The ladder is so thin, its connection to the sky so shaky, I wonder for the millionth time why the gods don't make it easier, why they don't give us something more sturdy to hang on to.

The ladder shakes again and then, in a move so sudden and violent, I imagine myself screaming, it thrusts us all from its rungs. Heather, the highest up, lands hard on the ground, and Apple rolls a bit when she hits. She moans, rubbing her hips, her back. Others tumble from the lower rungs, a pile of people forming then quickly un-forming, everyone gathering themselves up, dusting themselves off, looking at the ladder for answers.

"What was that?" Apple asks.

Heather runs her fingers through her hair and brushes off her toga. She clears her throat. "Well. An unexpected—but an understandable, really . . . I'm sure this is a sort of gauntlet. The gods want us to take this seriously. We've been here for generations and an invitation to spend eternity in Olympus is . . . there aren't words right for the enormity of it. So we should have expected some challenges. Some proving of ourselves." Her shoulders move back and back and her chin tilts to the sky. The clouds don't move. No lightning bolts come down affirming her idea. But heads nod and the crowd readies itself to try again.

"We have to hang on tight," Heather goes on. "And be brave. It might not be easy. It won't be like every other climb to the top, because of course it wouldn't be."

Apple looks down at me. I am crisp and defined in the noon light. I am here but not. I can't be whatever it is she wants me to be, but for a moment I wish that I could. It felt good—not always, but sometimes—to be Apple's friend. And she needs a friend right now. Nearby, Reece and Dawn are standing together laughing at something, maybe at Apple herself, and farther away there's Eric and his family, ready to go up too, allowed just as Hades has always been allowed. They're smirking at something, maybe at the confusion, the chaos. Chloe is pacing away from the crowd a little, and she glances over at Apple every so often, but not in the way a friend might. More like she's waiting for something, but I guess we're all waiting for something.

Except maybe Dad, who called Heather again this morning, who I've heard people whispering about: *He's going to miss his chance, looking for Dorothy. That family, what a mess. He's a good guy, he can't go up without his daughter. He doesn't look good, he's come by, he's asked if I've seen her, he's frantic, well, who wouldn't be. But still. Poor guy. Poor guy. What a fate to have. Orpheus's descendant, of course. Destiny, you know.*

I wonder if he'll come up here, but he knows I'd never go without him. He must be at the river, hoping I'll show up. He must be scared.

I'm scared.

I wish we could be scared together. I wish he knew I was thinking about him. I wish he knew everything I've figured out, being a shadow.

"Let's go," Eric's mom calls out, her voice piercing and impatient.

"She doesn't need to rush it," someone else calls back. "Let's do this the right way."

"We don't know the right way," a third person interjects, sounding tired and angry and like they are already missing Our Hill and how easy life has been here, all glowy sunrises and chirping birds and this sort of slow pace of living a life that won't ever end.

Heather approaches the ladder again. She shakes off the words of everyone shouting suggestions at her, and she starts the climb once more, gripping harder now, moving slower.

Apple hesitates. "Is something wrong?" she whispers, and I wait for someone to answer her, but she's asking *me*, her head tilted all the way to the ground, her voice so quiet it is nearly unhearable. She looks so sad and so scared and so unsure of what she's doing, and she is asking her shadow for guidance and I can't say a single word, but I wish I could.

She starts the climb again, and an awful sorrow grips me, a sort of panicked sadness at leaving my home behind, and maybe it is that—maybe it is the force of me wanting to stay that makes the ladder shake again. Heather and Apple hold on longer this time, but only seconds longer, and then they are on the ground once more, breathing hard and watching as the crowd starts to move away from them, starts to make room for them to be on the ground, by the ladder, alone.

"A gauntlet," Chloe's father says. It's somehow not a statement or a question, more like a mirror he's holding up to Heather, asking her to see if she's thinking the right things.

"We'll try again," Heather says. She lifts herself onto her feet, less poised this time, less concerned with the knots in her hair or the dirt on her dress. She doesn't wait for approval or conversation or anything else—she just thrusts herself at the ladder again, and again is thrown off. On the next try she pushes Apple to the ladder, as if the order we climb it is the thing that will make the difference, and Apple doesn't want to—she is a tangle of nerves and *no*, but she does it anyway because you don't refuse Heather Montgomery even if she is so clearly wrong, even if something is so clearly, clearly all wrong.

The ladder thrusts Apple off even quicker and harder

than it did her mother, and she rolls a little on the ground, so I roll too, both of us having a hard time gathering ourselves back up.

There's a grumble of talking and then a silence that stretches and I don't know which is more uncomfortable. Heather approaches the ladder again, and someone tells her to stop, that it's obvious something is wrong, we will not be climbing the ladder to be with the gods today, but Heather shoos them away and tries.

And tries again.

And again.

Maybe this is what it felt like watching Sisyphus push his boulder, a bit of history we learn when we are five and six and being told how things are in the world, and what we came from, and what it all means. Maybe this is what it is to witness the making of a myth, to be a part of a story that will get told forever as a warning and a lesson and a map of the way things have to be.

Heather tries again.

The crowd doesn't go back down the hill, but they don't move toward the ladder, either. They watch and wait, I think for the gods to appear and tell us what is happening, but gods like you to figure it out for yourself.

"I think we all know why this is happening," Reece's father says. He is broad-shouldered and mean-faced.

"I don't think that we do," Heather counters. She is

looking at the ladder like she is about to try again, but it's only making her look weaker, not braver.

"You still love her. Penny. Care about her. About them. That's fine. But it doesn't change the facts. This is because of Penny."

"Penny's not even here," Heather says. Her voice strangles Mama's name, and I'm struck by the pain she's still in over her being gone. She's been so good at pretending it away, I'd almost believed her.

"Neither is George. Or that strange little daughter of theirs," Reece's father says. "Of course they're the one family who won't do what is expected. And of course we are all forced to pay for their mistakes."

Eric's mother nods in agreement. She rises and makes her way closer to us. "They're still punishing us," she says to Heather and to everyone. "As they should. Penny broke the world and then, what, we just let her daughter and husband do whatever they want to do? Surely that's not what the gods asked of us. Surely we had another duty besides looking good for the gods today, don't you think, Heather?"

Heather's hair is still perfectly braided despite her battle with the ladder. Her toga is streaked with dirt, but it fits her perfectly. She has gold bangles around her wrists and thick black eye makeup lining her eyes. A goddess.

"I'm not responsible for Penny," Heather says. "Or George or Dorothy. I don't even know where they are. I'm here. I've gotten us all here."

Above me, Apple's body jerks toward her mother, like she wants to do something to fix the moment. But her feet stay still and so I do too.

"Oh yes," Eric's mother says. "You've gotten us right here. To the bottom of a ladder that we can't climb. Thank you so much for that."

There's a flurry of comments thrown Heather's way, and then a call to find George. Find me. Find those who are really at fault.

"We have made our decision," Reece's father says. "We can't be kept in limbo over some descendant of Pandora, of all people." Not every head nods, but enough do for me to know that maybe there was always a feeling that an ancestor of Pandora's shouldn't be among the near-gods on Our Hill. That maybe there was a reason that Mama's tapestry is in our attic and not hung up in the center of town.

"We have to find them," Chloe's father chimes in. He isn't angry or insistent, just calm and sure. It isn't complicated for Chloe or her family. It is clear—a series of events in the past that led us exactly here. "We have to bring them with us. We have to all choose to leave together. That must be why they're not letting us up now."

People listen, because they always listen to him. Because he knows all the stories by heart, every inch of our history, and it makes us feel safe and sure. So those who had taken a seat in the sun get up, those leaning on trees straighten up off them, those who were facing Heather, ready to leap at her, ready to rattle the ladder or muddy her dress or undo her perfect hair, turn to follow Chloe's father down the hill.

Everyone except Chloe.

Her face is twisted up with thought and something else—a wishing things were different. She looks at Apple, waits for her to catch her eye, and when their gazes meet, Chloe mouths something. *Tell them.* Apple turns away. I don't know if it's because she didn't understand, or because she did.

A moment passes, people grumbling down the hill, listing places me and my father might be. But a voice rings out above the rest, stopping them.

"Consequences," the voice says, and the voice is Chloe's. It is strong and powerful, different from the voice she uses in school. Different even from the voice her dad was using.

"What's that, Chlo?" her dad says, reaching for her hand like he too knows how strange this moment is.

"History is about consequences," Chloe says. "Intended. And Unintended. Pandora. And Zeus. And everyone in between. And I don't know every rule the gods have made, I don't know much about us leaving the earth. But I know about consequences. Unintended ones."

Everyone has stopped. I don't think they know why, exactly. No one on Our Hill is usually very interested in what kids have to say. But Chloe isn't a normal kid and this isn't a normal day.

"Apple," she says, her voice steadier than I would have ever guessed it could be. "Stand here." She points to a place in the sun. "Everyone else, move back. Make room."

They listen to her. It's sort of amazing, if it wasn't also awful, how everyone is doing what she says. Little Chloe, with her buttoned-up dress and oversized glasses and all her enormous knowledge and power.

It is a strange and impossible day.

The crowd moves back and back.

There is nowhere to hide.

I am undeniably here, without the cover of dusk, without any other shadows occupying the landscape. I am just me, shorter than other times of day, but unmissable anyway. A short shadow in the noon sun. A shadow attached to a god, a thing that isn't meant to be. A wrongness in the world.

An unintended consequence.

There is a gasp. And then there is a rage.

But I'm still just a shadow, so there's nothing I can do about any of it.

Next to us, the ladder, the rickety, willowy, silvery ladder, crumbles to dust.

APPLE

28.

The whole hill gasps at the dust, at the way our connection to the sky disappears in one single moment. They stay still for a long time before speaking, then there's no speaking at all, just yelling, screaming over each other, blame and anger and fear and chaos.

And a retreat down the hill, away from the dust and the shadow and the mistakes that have been made.

Soon it is me, Dorothy the shadow, and Mom on the top of the hill, next to the piles of dust that used to be the ladder.

"What did you do?" Mom says at last.

"She wanted to stay," I say. "And I wished it. Just for a little while. But the wish came true." I don't know how to tell her the long version of the story. It's too much.

"Who? Stay where?" Mom says, but there aren't that many answers to those questions, and she must know it. In the sky, clouds start to come in, and I'm pretty sure they're for me. Dorothy lightens, parts of her vanishing entirely. "Don't turn into some teenager now, Apple," Mom goes on. "You're twelve, not fifteen, so you need to keep talking."

Mom has a thing about teenagers and the way they talk or don't talk to their parents. Maybe it's something she reads about in books or remembers from when she was young. Lately, she has been eyeing my closeness to teendom, taking note, I guess, of my body and size and skin and the way I talk, judging if it sounds enough like kid-me or if it's turning into something else.

Sometimes I do feel like I am turning into something else, but I don't know what, exactly.

"Penny told me to look out for Dorothy," I say. I want it to make sense to her the way it made sense to me. "She knew things would be hard after the whole . . . after last solstice. And she asked me to make sure Dorothy was okay. At school and stuff."

Mom's eyes close. Her body moves a little in the wind like it's a branch of a tree. She used to be sturdier.

"And then she died," Mom says. It's the first time she's ever used those words, and I can tell she hears it too. Her face falls.

"And then she died," I say, like Echo, unable to find my

own words for a moment.

"And then what?" Mom says. She wipes her eyes that are not crying but maybe want to, and she tightens the strap of her toga. I think she wants to make sure that something stays together while everything else falls apart. The knot in the fabric is strong. It will stay.

"Then Dorothy said she wanted to stay on earth. She was going to die too."

"Someday," Mom says. "Not like Penny. Penny was— It was terrible luck. It was impossibly bad. It wasn't supposed to be like that, so sudden. She was supposed to live a whole—"

"I didn't want to be alone like you," I say. I'm saying things I've never said before and maybe never even really thought.

"Like me." Mom is Echo too, and the story was always told as a sort of curse the gods placed on her, but maybe it wasn't so bad, to never have to figure out what to say next, to always get to say someone else's words as you try to untangle what they might mean.

"She was my best friend," I say. I hear the past tense of it, the way a shadow isn't the same as a person, how she is already gone, and not just because of the afternoon clouds. "I didn't want to go up there without her. When Penny left everything changed and I needed something to not change. She was like, the person I could hold on to if everything else was all swirling and weird."

"You two barely even liked each other," Mom says, as if the last month has meant nothing. As if growing up side by side means nothing. Memories aren't frozen things. The way we were together three and four and five years ago doesn't mean the same thing it did then. Maybe then it seemed like distance, but after we got close, those memories looked different—warm and glowy and welcoming, like the very best part of life that I had sort of somehow missed but I was getting a chance to see differently.

Like a star in my hand instead of in the sky.

The memories changed.

I bet that's one more thing the gods don't understand about life here on earth. All those little moments with Dorothy when we were little seemed like nothing at the time but are now something huge. They are evidence of how much friendship matters, and they are the heartbreak of what was lost, and they are, mostly, above all else, the promise I made to Penny Hardy.

Those moments of me and Dorothy and our moms used to be the thing on the side, and now they are all that matters, the best part of our time on earth, the very thing I need the most.

"Being Dorothy's friend made me feel better," I say, which doesn't capture any of it, which is the stupidest thing to say, a nothing of a sentence.

"And how did you make her feel?" Mom asks.

The wind picks up and the clouds move along, Dorothy coming into focus again below me.

I am trying to answer a question I never thought to ask.

"It was an accident," I say. "I didn't know wishing would make it true. I didn't know."

Mom keeps looking at the sky, waiting for the gods to tell her why we are on earth and not up there, how it all connects. But I'm down here trying to answer that one question about how I made Dorothy feel. I look at her, who is now just me, really, the threads of me, and my stomach turns.

Mom walks down the hill, eventually, after maybe an hour or a minute.

But I stay up here. Me, the ladder dust, and a shadow that actually isn't Dorothy at all.

29.

I stay at the top of the hill until the sun sets and Dorothy disappears, the way she always does as darkness sets in, leaving me alone. And I hate being alone.

The walk down the hill feels longer than the walk up. Colder, too. I think it might rain.

"You told us to choose and we chose," I say to the sky, even though I'm sure the sky isn't listening. I've been trying to talk to the sky since I was little, wishing my hair straight instead of curly, wishing myself taller, wishing my mother nicer, wishing the days longer so I could avoid the night.

Then only one wish came true. And I don't really understand why.

Because they never answer, those gods up there with

their tridents and the flowers in their hair and thrones so big they almost look like they're being swallowed by them. They watch and laugh and get angry and judge and set up impossible obstacles and make up new rules that we're supposed to follow without knowing why or how. And maybe I'm a descendant of the most powerful gods in all of Olympus, and maybe that almost meant something, once, but if the ladder to the sky is broken and I can't climb it, am I really one of them at all?

I walk and walk and I end up at Dorothy's house, knowing she won't be there and Penny won't be there but George will, and I knock until he answers.

"Apple? What are you doing here? Why aren't you up there?" He looks exhausted, and I know he's been up all night, and probably more nights than that. He limps a little, like he's walked and run so much, been back and forth over every inch of Our Hill for so many days that his legs are starting to give out. He's holding a list of places Dorothy might be, and he's sweating.

"They didn't let us go up," I say.

"Ah." George doesn't ask why.

The thing about George is that he understands things about the gods that I don't. Because he's descended from Orpheus, he knows about the ways the gods can hurt you. Orpheus learned it all those generations ago, when they took away his love just because he looked back to make sure she was okay walking behind him, and George is learning it again now.

"I know where Dorothy is," I say, even though I don't want to. His face changes completely, wakes up and moves through a hundred feelings at lightning speed. "I did something. I turned her into a shadow. Into my shadow."

George stares at me for a while. Longer than anyone has ever looked at me before. I sort of thought twelve was old but now it feels young, and I'm this little kid who doesn't understand anything and George is waiting for me to catch up.

"I'm sorry," I say, which is nothing, which does nothing.

"And now what? You'll make a constellation of her in the sky too? You'll let me look at some pattern of stars that is her and you'll think that's enough?" He's angry, and I've never known George to be angry. Then the anger slips into sadness, and he folds over, like his body can't stand up to hear the news.

It seemed right, at the time, and powerful, to do something all by myself that Mom would hate. But now it's all wrong. Dorothy shouldn't be on the ground next to me and she shouldn't be up in the sky either.

He looks out the window to see the Penny constellation, and he sees what I've done.

"I'm sorry," I say again, but it doesn't mean anything because I can't fix it. I made Dorothy a shadow. And a constellation. And it was all wrong, wrong, wrong.

We both stare at my mistake. Penny in the sky looks like Penny, in the sense that she's the shape of her—hands and arms and a torso that all looks the way Penny looked, except also not. She looks like Penny frozen in some photograph of herself that she hates. She looks like Penny posing for a picture where she's pretending to be some imitation of some other person who is a little bit like her but isn't really her at all.

And Dorothy in the stars looks like my memory of Dorothy as a kid. But she's not Dorothy either.

I shiver.

It's wrong.

I am wrong.

"I'm sorry," I say for the third time, but each one just feels weak, airy, empty.

"You did it all on your own?" George asks.

"I was holding a star," I say. "I made a wish and I didn't really mean it but I sort of did and then it happened." I know the words aren't good ones. Aren't sturdy, sensical ones.

George squints like it doesn't quite make sense, my story of what happened, which is right. It doesn't.

"And Dorothy?" he says.

I try to remember what Dorothy was doing.

"We were arguing," I say. "I don't know, she was upset?"

George leans down so that we're face-to-face. "And did she have a star too?" he asks. I reach for the memory of

295

the moment. The sky. The river. The look on her face. The panic I felt. The wind in the leaves.

The star in her hand.

I nod. George closes his eyes. He nods too. He sits down and buries his face in his hands. I stay, then move away from him to another part of the house where I can't hear him crying or singing sad songs. Eventually, I find my way to the attic.

There's a tapestry on the loom, which there always was, but this one is nearly finished.

Pandora.

30.

It is Pandora but also not.

In the paintings and drawings we see of Pandora in textbooks, she is stunned and sorry. Sometimes she is screaming. She might be crying or hiding her head in her hands. She is watching the misery she's unleashed, and she is desperate to put it back in the box. Sometimes she is the littlest bit dopey, this woman who is doing something enormous but doesn't understand it at all.

Every once in a while, the books will show her as a little bit cruel—this smug smile on her face, like maybe she's done this because she's awful, because she's careless. Like her curiosity also means she's just sort of a terrible person.

This Pandora doesn't look wrecked by what's happened.

The Pandora in this tapestry is looking into the jar. Around her, the misery is swirling—it's gray and thick and everywhere. But Pandora doesn't seem worried about that. She's gripping the edges of the jar and searching in there for something else, for some last thing to come out.

And she is smiling at whatever is at the bottom. It glows.

This Pandora looks like Penny and Dorothy. She has the straight nose and eyebrows just the littlest bit out of line with each other. She is big-eyed and pale-skinned and wispy-haired. She looks—it is the only word that is right for the expression on her face and the curve of her neck looking into the box and the reach of her hand in and in and in—hopeful.

"A story is just a story," Penny said when I asked her about Pandora a million years ago. "It could be interpreted a hundred different ways by a hundred different people."

We were sitting in Penny's kitchen eating ice cream. It was a human tradition that she particularly liked—ice cream sundaes where she put toppings in little glass bowls and we took our vanilla scoops through the lineup, piling on cookie crumbs and sprinkles and sauces. Other things too, that maybe humans wouldn't think of—berries and honey and flower petals, the kind you can eat if you know which is which. Fresh maple syrup and sea salt and basil leaves chopped into tiny bits of green confetti.

Mom never liked the sundaes much. She'd squeeze a squiggle of chocolate syrup on and call it a day, and Penny would make fun of her rigidity and Mom would make fun of Penny's silly interest in messy human things, and they'd both roll their eyes with these big goofy grins on their faces, like it was a little fun, to have a friend who wasn't like you at all.

"It's not a story," Mom said, taking the daintiest bite of ice cream, then immediately wiping her mouth with a napkin. "It's history, Penny. Don't get these girls all muddled up."

"Well, what's history?" Penny said, wiggling her eyebrows. Her sundae was absolutely loaded with tastes. Cookies and rose petals and raspberry jam and a sprig of rosemary. "A collection of myths. Stories someone's told us, but they can't tell us how to feel about it all, can they?"

The light came in at funny angles in Penny's kitchen. For some reason, Penny hated curtains, so there was nothing to do when the sun was coming in too strong, hitting you right in the eyes. Mom made a visor of her hand, squinted, then got up from where she was sitting to stand in a shadier corner, alone.

"The story of Pandora is one they always use as this warning of the worst thing that happened," Penny said. "But what if it wasn't the worst thing?"

"Penny." My mother's voice was a warning. A stern one, to stop talking immediately.

"You know it too, Heather," Penny said. Her voice had its own sort of soreness. "There was something at the bottom of that jar or box or whatever it was that we all needed."

"We should go," Mom said. I was only halfway done with my ice cream—a perfect mix of three different syrups and enough sprinkles to give every single bite a rainbow crunch. "This isn't appropriate conversation for the girls."

Dorothy looked at me and I looked back. She raised her eyebrows and I shrugged. She shrugged back. This happened sometimes, with our moms. Everything would be fine and then it suddenly wouldn't be. Then we wouldn't see each other for a few weeks, and when we all came back together it would be as if nothing happened.

Dorothy and I never talked about these little glitches. Not then, when we were just the bored witnesses to our moms' friendship, and not when we were in our own friendship either.

"Hope is always appropriate," Penny called while we were walking out the door. I remember, because it was such a weird sentence that it sort of made me smile, and then Mom gave me a death stare to shut me up.

"Penny is the sweetest person in the world and my best friend," she said. "But she's not exactly a muse of history, is she? She doesn't always see right and wrong very clearly."

"And we do?" I asked.

Mom looked confused by the question. "Of course," she

said. "That's what leaders do."

I mostly forgot about the whole conversation until right now, with this new version of Pandora in front of me all sunny and sure, reaching still for something good in the midst of the horrors. She unleashed death and illness and jealousy and cruelty. Wars and selfishness and suffering and natural disasters. She shouldn't be smiling.

But.

But.

Our Hill has been without those things. We haven't had to take on the human toll of terribleness, the unpredictable and unforgivable parts of life on earth. We have been promised living forever and cloudless skies and a ladder to Olympus and the gods smiling on us.

As long as we did exactly what they told us to do.

As long as we didn't ask any questions.

As long as we were only who they wanted us to be.

Now I don't know who I am anymore, but I want to be someone who matters, the way Pandora did. The way Penny did. Then they both died mortal deaths, a similarity I'm only just seeing now, but one that surely Penny saw all along. I don't want that for me. Or for Dorothy. But I don't want to leave either—at least I don't want to leave Dorothy and the memories of Penny and the hope that Pandora left behind for us.

I want to be where I will matter. I want to be a leader,

maybe, like Mom says we are, but maybe not in the way she envisions it. I want to be somewhere that I can drum up hope and give that glow and be myself, if I ever figure out who that is.

I bring my hands to the loom. And between my hands and Penny's leftover magic and all the feelings pulsing inside me, I finish the unmade bit of tapestry that was left. There she is. Pandora and all her hope, unapologetically on display.

"APPLE!" Mom's voice is loud, booming from downstairs, where George's soft, sleepy voice is bumbling underneath hers. "Where are you? Come down here."

I take one last look at this version of Pandora, who did something she wasn't supposed to do, who was who she was, and who made mistakes but who searched for hope anyway. I look at the glowing orb she is reaching toward. She brought that out too, didn't she? Hope wasn't here before. Maybe because it didn't need to be. Or maybe because hope is more complicated than things like immortality and easiness. Hope is heavy and bright and strange and sacred.

There's a glow in me now too. Hot and sweet and mine. It's something I've never felt before. Maybe because I've never needed it, or maybe because it took someone doing something we weren't supposed to do to make it appear.

It feels just the way the glow looks in Pandora's jar.

It feels like an impossible hope in the midst of so many terrible things.

It feels alive.

It feels inappropriate, sort of, to feel anything but awful about the day. Except Penny's voice rings in my ears, reminding me, *Hope is always appropriate.*

31.

Mom drags me home and puts me to bed like I'm some little kid who can't be trusted to stay under the covers, and I surprise myself by sleeping hard. I thought the mixture of panic and hope and whatever else is happening would keep me up, but the day was so long and so strange and so impossible to untangle that it's morning before I know it.

"School," Mom says when I walk down the stairs in my pajamas. She is only speaking to me in one-word sentences now, I guess.

"School?" I almost laugh. Mom keeps looking out the window as if a lightning bolt might strike with a message for us at any moment, like Zeus himself might appear to tell us what we need to do to set the world right.

"That's what's been decided," Mom says. I have a hundred questions about who decided and why and what it means, but Mom's arms are crossed and there's no breakfast or coffee on the counter, no sign of anything familiar or okay, so I keep the questions to myself and go back upstairs to get dressed in another blue dress on another blue day. I catch sight of my bracelets around my wrist. I don't notice them often—they're always there, which means I never remember they're there. Two names wrapped around my wrist—Dorothy and Hera. Two beings I don't know how to see again.

The walk to school is lonely. Dorothy appears from time to time on sidewalks and in piles of leaves—a shadow hand or foot or loose strand of hair, but it doesn't make me miss her less.

"There she is," Reece says when I arrive. The doors haven't opened yet, so there's a crowd outside the building, huddled around the largest Athena statue, as if she might do something to protect them. We all talk so much about Athena and her wisdom, how she helped human heroes. How we are searching for a fragment of what she had. Mom says maybe Athena understood humans better than anyone. But a statue of Athena isn't any better, really, than a shadow of Dorothy, so I don't know what exactly they're waiting for.

"Tell her," Reece says. Chloe is next to Reece, and she

looks uncomfortable. Eric stands a few feet away, legs wide, hands on his hips, the stance of someone who knows what is happening and why it's happening and will be fine, no matter what happens next. I squeeze my legs tight together and look at the hint of my shadow on the grass in front of me.

"It's the shadow," Chloe says.

"It could be anything," I say, which I think I want to be true more than I actually believe it could be true.

"Gods don't have shadows," Chloe says. Her voice is kind but firm. I wonder what it would feel like to be Chloe—wise and calm and passionate about knowing all sorts of things about the world. "Near-gods don't have them. We've never had them."

"Okay," I say. It's weird that no one else is talking, like they've all elected Chloe to be Spokesperson of Telling Apple Why She Is the Worst.

"We don't have them for a reason," Chloe says. I get the feeling she wants me to make some connection on my own, to understand something without her telling me. But the world feels upside down and inside out, or maybe I'm the one who's all twisted around.

"Okay," I say again. Clouds move across the sky and obscure Dorothy on the ground below me. Maybe the gods are watching this conversation. Or maybe it is just the weather. It's impossible to know anymore.

"Shadows tie us to earth," Reece interrupts at last, tired, I guess, of Chloe's slow and gentle pace. "That's why the trees have them and the buildings and the things that are meant to be here forever. But we don't have shadows. We never have. I mean, why did you think the humans had them and we didn't? Just coincidence? Just a random little hiccup in the system? There are *gods*, Apple. There is order. We aren't meant to have shadows. We aren't meant to be tied to earth. We are from the sky. Did you even think?"

It's not like Reece knew any of this two days ago. If I'd asked her, then, why near-gods didn't have the shadows that humans do, she would have shrugged and asked me if her hair looked okay. Now, though, she's talking like it's a fact we've known all along.

"It's true," Chloe says. She looks at me and the ground and the sky. "It wasn't something I knew anything about but when we got stuck I sort of—I asked Eric and I talked to my parents and . . . I should have known. I'm sorry."

I shake my head. It's not Chloe's fault, or Eric's, even, though he knew what I was thinking about doing. It's my fault. It's mine. I don't even have the excuse of being Pandora's great-great-great-whatever. I'm just a selfish person ruining the world.

I'm a near-god making god-sized mistakes and paying human prices for them.

I'm tired of the in-between, I realize. Maybe it worked for a while, but it's too hard, being both god and human. I'm not any good at it.

The doors to school open and Reece and Dawn push right inside, without looking at me. No one is really looking at me. It's weird, to be the girl no one wants to sit near. But that's who I am. When we're in the classroom desks are pushed around—back and to the sides, in odd directions and making strange formations—so that no one has to sit too close to me.

"How the mighty have fallen," Eric says from his spot in the back of the room. He's still mostly alone, but with the new setup he is closer to others than I am. I could spread out my arms wide and not touch anyone. I am in the front row, center, as always, but the rest of the class is in a chaotic mess behind me.

"Well. This is new," Mr. Winters says. He doesn't look at me either. "I know we weren't expecting to be here today. But here we are."

Mr. Winters paces and starts teaching a lesson about what makes a god and what makes a human, and why it matters, who is who. It makes my skin itch and he manages to avoid walking near my desk even though it's the only one in the front of the room.

"Our job here on earth was to respect the gods," he says. "To celebrate them. Which we've done." He gestures around the room at paintings and sculptures and embroidered fabric we've made over the years, all featuring the gods' faces, favorite colors, words.

"Then what's the point of being here now?" I ask by accident, as if Penny has overtaken my body and I'm not even me anymore. Which in some ways I guess I'm really not.

"The point?" Mr. Winters says. I notice, then, that he's sort of seething underneath his normal calm. "The point is we have nowhere else to go, Apple. The point is you turned us human with your selfish, thoughtless actions. The point is, we had the opportunity to live forever as gods in the most beautiful place imaginable, and instead we are tied here, humans who will die." His eyes are narrow and his words are sharp, tiny stings on my skin.

I want to tell them about the warmth and the glow and the tapestry and the things we have never quite understood about the differences between humans and gods. About hope, and clinging to it even when things are terrible. They always miss the point about humans. If I could be a god, I'd be the kind that understood them better.

Because when I really think about it, about who I am and where I want to be, as much as I am in awe of humans and their hope, I am meant to be in the sky. I want to be surrounded by clouds, eating grapes and roasts and the most unbelievable chocolates. And I want to be helping humans locate hope when it seems hard. I don't know how to be a good human. But I think I finally know how to be a good god.

I understand Penny's choice. I do. And Pandora's before her. I even maybe understand the choice Dorothy wanted to make, although I hate it.

But I am meant to be a god. This whole year, I've been trying to understand who I am, and who I am supposed to be. I'm not Mom and I'm not Dorothy or Penny and I'm not Hera or Zeus, either. I'm sitting by myself while desks are pushed all the way to the walls and Reece and Dawn are wearing matching white flowers in their matching braids. The flower is especially pretty in Dawn's dark hair. It almost gets lost in the white-blond of Reece's.

I forgot to brush my hair, and I don't hate the way it is wild and wandering all over my neck and shoulders. So I am not the old Apple Montgomery. Or I guess I'm not the Apple Montgomery everyone told me to be.

But.

I loved pinning Penny and my memories to the sky with stars. I love the taste of the apples of immortality. I loved the ladder, even, the way it was both delicate and strong, and that first breath of flowery, cloud-flavored air at the top.

I want to rewrite the myth of Pandora and her box so that the humans know what came with that misery. I want to make constellations in the sky that show things humans might not notice, might forget, might be unable to see because they're so worried about everything staying the same, or being beloved, or being in control, or making someone they love stay forever and ever, even if it's not what's right for them.

I want to be a god. Not the kind I thought I'd be. Not the kind they tell us to be. But a god in the sky who can help. Who can hope. Who can undo the mistakes that have been made.

The mistakes that have been made by me.

"I want to be up there too," I say. "I want to go up there to help everyone who is down here."

I don't know why I'm saying it aloud, interrupting Mr. Winters showing us a new technique for painting Athena's hair. I look at my shadow, who can't do anything but what I do, who can't tell me *good job* or *bad idea* or just give me one of those looks Dorothy used to give me, like she wanted to figure me out but couldn't quite manage it.

"I made a mistake," I say. "I made a hundred mistakes or, like, a thousand. Because I'm not a god here on earth and neither are any of you. We're part human, too. We wanted to see what it was to be human, right? That's why we're here? This is what it's like."

We are never supposed to call ourselves humans. It's a quiet rule we made up among ourselves. We are near-gods. But underneath that word is the other word that has to be there, too. We are near-*gods* because we are part *human*.

I guess if you can't say the truth when the world is

splitting apart, when can you?

The rest of them can keep hating the humans, thinking them small and scared and silly.

But the humans lose what they love and find a way to keep going. The humans hold on to hope even when it hurts, even when it is barely possible. The humans make their mistakes and have to stay here on earth, forever, figuring out how to make the world right again.

It is not the worst thing to be, part human.

It is a little bit beautiful, actually.

32.

It is not a lightning bolt this time, but a whoosh of wind so strong that it wobbles the windows and we all rush to see what is outside. It is exactly the same and completely different as the day with the thunderbolts scorching Our Hill. We press our noses against the window, our hands, too, our breath fogging it all up so we can't see what has made its way here for us, except that it is fast and colorful and startling.

When the windows clear and the clouds and dirt fade to reveal what's underneath all that ferocious speed, we rush away from the windows.

The gods have never traveled to Our Hill to see us. Until now.

There are two of them, and years of studying the gods means we know who they are immediately. Iris is draped in every color of the rainbow, Hermes is covered in clouds, only his head and his winged sandals peeking out. We turn to Chloe, like she'll be able to tell us more than we know, but we all know the same few facts. Iris and Hermes are the messenger gods. They're here to tell us something from Olympus.

My heart shudders around in my chest, and the rest of the class, too, look sweaty and scared.

Hope is like that. It's scary. Hope means you care. It means you'll be heartbroken if things don't go your way. It is heavy. It's maybe what humans are most scared of in the whole world, I think. There's no risk without it. No care. No love.

I choose to do it. I choose to let myself hope. In honor of Penny and Dorothy and the things I would change if I could, and the mistakes I understand I've made. In honor of humans, and their ridiculous and beautiful and often unanswered hope.

Mr. Winters opens the windows. He does a sort of bow-curtsy and we'd all laugh if the moment wasn't so clearly serious.

"You are not gods here." Iris speaks first. Her voice is loud. Booming. "And you are not humans. And the gods decided that was not tenable."

We know this. We hang our heads and I think of Penny, but maybe other people think of other things, other ways we have failed at being god or human.

"We gave you a choice. But a shadow was created that made that choice untenable too."

Now they are all looking at me. I don't know how to explain that I didn't know I was tying us to earth, I only knew I was trying to tie me to Dorothy, and that I didn't even really know I was doing that. I held a star. I made a wish. I changed the world.

"A shadow is a delicate creature. And the untying of a shadow from a person is delicate work. Intricate. Complicated. But not impossible," Iris goes on.

There it is again: hope. I look around to see if others feel it or if they're not brave enough to. Because hope, I am finding, is a kind of courage.

"Make me a shadow too," I say. The words come out before I have a chance to think them through. "Tie me to earth, but not everyone else. It was my mistake."

It's not what I want, but I have done what I wanted this whole time, and it hasn't done anything good for me.

"Apple," Mr. Winters says, like he's about to stop me from making this decision, like he's going to step in and save me from myself. But as soon as he steps forward, he steps back. "Whatever you think is best," he says.

There it was again—hope, that he would do something

to help. And the heartbreak at being alone in this room with no one to stop me or tell me if this is a good idea. But still. It feels right. Maybe I'll be a myth they tell, about selflessness and sacrifice and goodness in the world. Maybe I will be Apple Montgomery who saved Our Hill, who let near-gods become actual gods. Apple Montgomery who changed the world, the right way this time.

"It's my fault," I say. "How can I undo it?"

Hermes still hasn't spoken, the clouds around him still haven't cleared. Iris tilts her head at me.

"Are there special scissors? Can I pull her up from the ground and, like, mold her into a person again? I know there's something I can do to show I understand." My eyes well up with tears that burn with heat and urgency.

"It is difficult work," Iris says at last.

"The gods want you to know it is easy to do and hard to undo. It's a lesson you should have all learned by now," Hermes says, speaking at last. His voice is unexpectedly hoarse, like he has delivered too many messages in his life.

"No kidding," Reece says. Her white-blond hair swings when she speaks. I try to remember a few months ago, when I would have called her my best friend, even though it makes no sense now and probably made no sense then. We were best friends, if the calculation to becoming a best friend has to do with hours spent sitting a little bit away from everyone else, talking about what makes you better than them. The hours added up, I guess, and we thought they meant something.

I got the tiniest taste of the other kind of friendship—where someone can do or say something you don't like and you love them anyway. Where they know what you look like when you're unsure what your mother wants from you, or they show you how to lift stars from a river because you both care about the same things so deeply that you have to write it into the night sky.

I got the tiniest taste and it was everything.

It was love, the real kind, until I ruined it with being a god and making her mine. I didn't know that friendship was the best kind of love—a big kind with enough room for two people to be whoever they need to be. I should have understood—I'd gotten to see a big, beautiful friendship my whole life until it vanished.

But now I know. I made it small when it should have been big. I made it mine when it should have been ours.

"Whatever I have to do," I say.

Mr. Winters nods like I've done something right, at last, and that's fine. He can think I'm here to save the near-gods of Our Hill, but really I only care about righting the world by bringing Dorothy back into it.

"The top of the hill," Iris booms. "Tonight."

"Before the dark," Hermes says.

And as quickly as they came, they are gone, flying fast

back up to the sky, away from this place they'd never been before. I wonder if they liked it. I wonder if it looked to them the way it looks to me now—like a dream we've woken up from, an in-between place that was never meant to last.

33.

I imagine it is Dorothy as a person, walking me up this hill. She'd be quiet. She'd place her feet carefully, avoiding flowers in her path, never wanting to disturb any bit of nature. Maybe she would point out a star she likes, or remember something her mom used to say.

I knew so little when I made her a shadow. I didn't know that shadows can't tell you their memories, can't help you remember the person you're scared you'll forget. Maybe, if I ever go to Olympus, I'd tell them that humans do the strange and impossible things they do because they have to live with loss and this other kind of love that lasts and shifts and hurts and lets you grow.

But I don't think I'll ever get up there now.

When we reach the top of the hill, the ladder is still gone, silver ladder-dust sprinkling the grass. We feel so far away from the sky now. So human.

"Okay," I say, watching my shadow, my Dorothy, and the way she is long and lean here and now, a little like a ladder herself. "Okay, I'm ready," I say again, louder this time, because I don't know exactly what has to happen for this to work—I don't know exactly what the gods are waiting for.

The wind blows harder, like a warning, like the promise of something to come that I don't know much about yet.

My shadow seems to sway, and that seems like a sign too, that they've heard me, that they know I'm ready, that our agreement is taking place.

I take another breath and expect to smell water, but I smell apples, and I can't help it: The apples make me do it, I swear. It is always the fault of the apples.

"Wait!" I cry, so much louder and clearer than the first call-out to them, which was small and soft. "Wait. I can't."

The shadow of Dorothy stops in a way that I am not stopping, and I'm sure she's heard and maybe she's angry, or something else, whatever the shadow version of anger might be.

There is a flash of lightning in the sky. Humans call it heat lightning, but it is always, always Zeus. And with that flash comes Iris and Hermes again. Iris's face is mad. Hermes is carrying a pair of golden scissors.

"You can't?" Iris asks, like she's been here all along, like we are mid-conversation.

"I need to know what happens," I say.

"You cut her free with these scissors," Hermes says. They are so direct, it almost knocks me over. Mom says things in a roundabout way, like she's waiting to be sure of her own words before she'll let them all the way out. But Iris and Hermes are sure.

Gods are sure.

"And then?" I ask.

"When you cut her away from you, she'll be human. Earthbound. You will be letting her go." Iris looks a little sad for me, like she knows it will hurt. "You will go to Olympus. She will stay on earth as a human."

"Wait. I go up? And she stays here? No, that's not— I could just stay here with her," I say. "My mom will be— But I could do that."

Iris shakes her head. "You're a god, Apple."

"Not yet."

"You made your friend a shadow. You changed the way the world works. You are descended of Zeus and Hera. You are Apple Montgomery, and you are a god. And Dorothy is a human. And you have learned something about love that gods are always trying to learn. You are ready to be a god. A powerful one, who does things that matter. And this is part of that. Athena taught Arachne about humility, and you have learned it too. A humble god is a powerful thing. Rare." Iris's voice isn't loud up here. It is gentle, like she knows me, like we are already something to each other.

"And Dorothy?" I ask. Iris smiles, like this is the right question.

"She's rare too," Hermes says.

"So I just cut and then she's back to herself?"

They exchange a glance, these two gods, these strange creatures who know more than me and have lived forever and will keep living forever and seem calm in that forever-ness.

"She has to get herself up," Hermes says. He sounds sad, like there's pain in this too.

"Just, like, get up from the ground?"

"It takes strength. And wanting. She has to want to be here," Iris says.

"She never wanted to leave," I say. "She didn't want this. It was all me."

There's a glance between Iris and Hermes, like there's something that has to be said that they thought maybe they'd never have to say.

"A near-god can't make a person into a shadow," Iris says. She speaks slowly, as if I need to understand some-thing important that is just beyond my reach. "Think back to that day."

I think back, just like I tried to think back the other day.

The river. The words. The worry. The stars.

"She wanted to be my shadow?" It doesn't make sense, the words they're saying—except it makes a tiny bit of sense when I strain to remember not just the beautiful and long and smiling days with Dorothy but the other ones too, when she pulled away, where she was swallowed up by grief, when she let me tell her who to be, even though before she had always been so squarely herself. How she never changed her hair back. How she shrugged instead of speaking.

How she held a star that day too. How we were both holding stars so tightly.

How maybe I wasn't the only one who made a wish. It never felt right that my one wish would change so much. But two wishes made by two near-gods holding two stars . . . that's something else.

"Maybe she didn't know what she wanted," Hermes says. "Humans are like that."

"But she'd have to know now. To fix it," Iris goes on.

"And if she doesn't know?"

"She stays."

"With me?"

"No, Apple. Here. Alone." Iris looks a little sad to have to say more, but she does. "A shadow without a person. Just a shadow sitting at the top of the hill."

"No." The word comes fast, the wrongness of what Iris is describing so stark, so clearly awful, that I have to expel it from the conversation. My throat feels like it's closing at the idea, the impossible sadness of Dorothy being stranded up here alone, the rest of us earthbound or in the sky, and her just a flat shadow of who I used to be, in between.

"That can't happen," I say, looking for some other way out of the mess I've created. But Iris and Hermes just look back at me, wordless, waiting for me to decide.

I look at my shadow for answers that aren't going to be there.

The scissors glint.

DOROTHY

34.

It is cool tonight on the top of the hill, and the sun is starting to set. Sometimes, as a shadow, it is my favorite part of the day. It is the moment before I'll disappear entirely, where I can be here and not-here.

Sometimes, I want to miss Mama under the cover of night, where it can be just me and the way it hurts.

That's why I thought it.

That's why I wished it. *It would be easier to just be Apple's echo*, I thought that day at the river. *It would be easier to follow her around and do what she wants and disappear into that.* I remember I looked at the trees. From the leaves to the place their trunks met the ground. And then their shadows. *I wish it could be like that*, I thought. And I squeezed the star, not knowing what Apple was thinking. Not knowing what we were doing.

Apple takes the scissors from Hermes's hands. She hesitates. I can't speak and I can't tell her if I'll be able to lift myself up, and I don't know what the world looks like after this, and if it's a version of the world I even want.

The sun dips a little bit behind the trees, a promise of what will happen to me soon if Apple doesn't get to work. And so she does. She starts to cut.

When we were little, Apple and I liked to make Valentine's Day cards. Apple liked to have the cards to hand out to whoever she deemed most important at school, the sizes of her cut-out hearts in direct proportion to who she was closest to. I liked the cutting and gluing, the searching outside for petals and berries and pine needles to make my cards look the way I felt about the world. I gave them out to everyone, trying to match colors to how they made me feel, but that wasn't the point. For me, the point was putting our world on a patch of red paper and sitting next to Apple while she glittered and glued and tried to write poetry.

It's a good memory.

There are a lot of good memories, but so many of them have Mama in the background, peering over our shoulders to tell us how pretty our cards were, bringing little bowls of nuts and fruits as snacks, making her own valentine, enormous and smothered with glitter and rose petals, to leave on Dad's side of the bed, no matter how embarrassing I told her it was.

Rejoining the world means rejoining the world without her.

And without Apple, too, which I sometimes thought I wanted, but now feels impossible.

Somewhere, at the bottom of the hill, Dad's missing me and Heather's mad at Apple and everyone I've ever known is waiting to see if we can fix this thing we broke, and all I have to do is decide I want to, I guess.

Apple is almost done with her cutting. It doesn't hurt. There's a shiny metal feeling along my shadow arms and legs, and my neck feels goose-bumped and alive. But the pain is something deeper down. Difficult and harder than I want it to be.

"I finished the tapestry," Apple whispers to me. She's cutting near my heart, talking into my ear. "I get it now. What your mom did. What Pandora did. What I want to do, too." She stays where she is, stopping her snipping. "There's something beautiful about life here. It isn't for me. But you—you'll sit at the river and I'll tell the gods what it really is to be human, and you'll have a whole life that is different from the one you thought you'd have. But that's the most human thing of all, I guess. The not knowing how it's all going to be. And then doing it anyway." She still doesn't snip. I want to tell her that I'm not sure, that maybe this shadow life is better, that maybe I should have become a god too, that maybe I never deserved to be on Our Hill, that I'm just a descendant of a muse who made a mistake, and that's not something to celebrate. I want to tell her I'll never know things the way she knows them.

I want to tell her I miss her. Even the bad parts. Especially those parts, maybe.

It's how I feel about Mama. I miss her. The parts that were easy to love and understand, and the rest of her, too. The parts that made her leave me here, the parts that kept everything a mystery. The parts that I still don't get, that still hurt, that still make me feel angry. I miss it all.

"Pandora did the most important thing of all. Your mom, too," Apple says, as if she can hear my thoughts. Her whisper is lower. Closer to me, so that she's practically lying all the way on the ground. I am the lightest shade of gray now, the sun is almost gone, so I am almost gone, and I can feel that this is it, this is the only chance we have, and it is so, so hard to take it. If I get off this ground, all those things—hating Mama and loving her; hating Apple and loving her; staying on an imperfect earth instead of traveling to the perfect sky—will be real. I'll have to deal with them, live with them.

I'm scared. I hadn't thought of that word, since all the other words—angry and grieving and confused and lonely—loom so large. But under all that, the thing I am most is scared.

"Pandora. Your mom. You. You made it matter. The world. You all made it mean something."

Memories are funny. They live in your heart but they're sleepy sometimes, they get lost along the way and they're impossible to find, like keys and missing socks and that one hair clip that you liked the most that should be in your pocket but somehow isn't.

And then someone says something and the memory is bright and sunny and so real you could touch it.

I remember Mama and me at the river. It was a few days before she was gone and I was trying to work up the courage to ask her why she'd done what she'd done and what it meant and if I'd lose her and if I should stop climbing the ladder too, and a hundred thousand other questions that I needed answers to but was too afraid to ask.

"Some people are here to make things beautiful," Mama said. "Some people make it hard. Some people want to make it *theirs*. Gods do that. They want to make it make sense. The world. Life. The things that are nonsensical." I remember thinking that sounded nice. I wanted it all to make sense. I almost said as much, but Mama put a hand on my knee to quiet me before I spoke.

"We come from Pandora," she said, telling me a secret I was too overwhelmed to understand. "Our job is to make it matter."

35.

The last place Apple and I are connected is our shoulders. It's funny, because our shoulders have been touching for years, pressed into bed together at forced sleepovers, sitting in booths smushed next to our mothers, walking down streets, sitting side by side at the river.

And now. Me as her shadow.

The snip is loud. Apple lets out a tiny, strangled cry, like she doesn't know what she's done. She stands, and moves, and I stay still below her. Instantly, I miss the dance we were in before, where my movements were decided by hers, where I was a mirror and didn't have to think or decide what would happen next.

"Dorothy. Come on," Apple says in a quiet voice. Iris

and Hermes each put a hand on her shoulders and I think they're reminding her that no, the gods can't do anything about this. This is between me and the world.

The sun is still peeking out but just barely, the sky a perfect pink-gray, and I have only moments to decide before I fade to nothing and the offer disappears. I don't know all the rules, which is probably on purpose. I have to make the decision on my own, not knowing everything it means for Apple and the rest of Our Hill. I have to make it the human way.

"Aren't you curious about what will happen?" Apple says. Her eyes are bright on the word *curious*. And my heart lifts to meet that word too. *Stay curious*, Mama always said, even though it was a dangerous thing to be on Our Hill, a dangerous thing for her to say. We were supposed to be the opposite. Mama and I were supposed to be apologizing for where we came from and trying to do better.

Mama never wanted that.

I look up at the sky. Her constellation is just starting to appear. If I stay on this patch of earth, I'll be looking at her forever like this, and there's a rightness to that. Mama in the sky, and me lying down on the earth, the both of us looking at one another for eternity. There will be nothing to decide. I won't lose anyone else. I won't get hurt or mad again. I won't be scared. I'll just be here loving Mama, missing her, remembering what was. It lines up with the hundreds of myths I've had to memorize over the years. It's how love works, for gods and humans and muses and people who have made mistakes that can't be righted.

Okay, I think. *Then that's the answer. I stay here as a shadow. Mama stays up there. We look at one another for eternity, missing each other. And that could be enough.*

Apple shakes her hands out, like they're holding all the worry of what I'll do. Iris and Hermes hang their heads, feeling, I think, my decision getting made. The neatness of the ending of the story of Our Hill, the story of Apple and Dorothy, the warning about friendship and love and curiosity that the gods need the next generation of humans to heed.

It will make a good myth.

Except.

The constellation of Mama is all wrong, still. Apple added me and her, but that's not what was missing. We don't need to be there. Mama's hands are busy with bread and she looks calm, like the world makes sense to her, like everything is going the way it is meant to. She doesn't look like she has any worries, any questions at all. She doesn't look curious. She doesn't look like Mama at all.

If I choose to stay a shadow, I won't be lying in the grass for eternity looking at Mama as she was—strong and questioning and hopeful and here. I'll be looking at this idea of her, Apple's idea of her, the person Apple needed her to be.

A memory that isn't even mine.

It's not enough.

Apple's right. I'm curious about what will happen next.

And Mama always said that's enough, that's all you need, really.

The last of the sun's beams dims, and Apple starts to cry. "She can't do this, she can't," she says. But it's not the tears that make me do it. It's not the way Apple is hurting, even though I care about that—I'll always care about that.

It's curiosity. Which, in the almost-gone light on the top of this hill, looks a lot like hope. It's a new wish, one I know I'm making, that there is something for me, in the world, without Mama. Without Apple, even. Just something for me.

I lift myself up off the ground, still a shadow, just moving upright now. It hurts, the lift, the choice, the having to be a person again, a real one, with everything that comes with that.

Apple gasps.

And painfully, slowly, I turn back into a body in the world. Before I can take a full breath, Apple thrusts herself at me, her arms around my neck, her body shaking and sobbing and trying to say all kinds of things she doesn't have to say.

"I'm here," I say. "I'm here."

36.

The ladder reappears from a snap of Iris's fingers, as if it never crumbled at all.

"Okay," she says. "It's time. Gather the town."

"Wait, what?" Apple says. She's out of breath even though she's barely moved.

"It's time," Iris repeats. "This was the deal. You separate from Dorothy. You go to Olympus. You let her go and you join us where you're meant to be."

We both heard it before, of course, but it sounds different now, with me upright and made of skin and bones.

"In a few days," Apple says. "Or the next solstice? Not now. Not right this second."

"Yes, right this second," Iris says. Hermes looks up to the sky, where storm clouds are brewing. They appeared so suddenly, they can only be from the gods. There is a rumble of thunder and a burst of light. Lightning bolts, a dozen of them at least, zoom to the earth, striking ground as they did that day so long ago or not very long ago at all.

Down below, people walk out of their homes, startle at the now-familiar scent of the burning earth, look at the sky with hope or terror or something else. They read the screeds, and immediately there is a rush of joy, a clamoring of shouts and calls to one another and then feet, furious, running up the hill to where we are. It isn't the elegant ritual they tried days ago. It is messy now. Desperate. But happy, too—friends and neighbors are crying, hugging themselves and each other, talking so fast they can barely breathe. And when they see the ladder again, they crumble into more tears, more exclamations. Some of them run up to touch it.

Then they see me.

There is a pause in the thrill.

"I'm staying," I say. "You can go. We fixed it." I look at Apple, whose head is hanging, who looks scared and sad and all sorts of things Apple almost never is. "Apple fixed it. She had to be brave. She had to let me go."

Their eyes blink but they don't seem to know how to respond. I look for Iris and Hermes to explain it more, but they're silent, no more messages to deliver. I guess we're not supposed to have any questions now. They'll all climb the ladder. I'll stay here.

I don't know exactly what will happen next. My eyes search everywhere for Dad. I want him to see me, I want him to know I'm here, I'm safe, I'm staying, he isn't alone. And I want to stand next to him while we watch Our Hill leave.

But Dad's not here. Just people who used to be friends and neighbors, but I guess aren't anymore. Gods, even near-gods, don't like mistakes. They don't like the confusions of being human. They don't like me and Mama and Pandora and curiosity and bravery and hope and how it all mixes together to become living.

They don't say thank you or ask me questions or even reach out to hug me. These are people I have known my whole life, and was meant to know forever, for a hundred lives, but they don't have anything to say to me now.

They're gods. Gods aren't meant to concern themselves with human things. And I'm human.

Then Dad appears, running up the hill, crying, sprinting, breathless. He pulls me into a hug so big I get lost in it, so big I believe in what I'm doing, in who I am, and what we've decided.

"Thank you," he says. And I think he means for staying, but he means for just being me, too. And for being a little bit like Mama. For being brave and curious to see what will happen next.

"I'm sorry," I say, and he shakes his head like it's nothing, the last few days of worry for him, and I know we will be okay here, he and I. We will be a couple of humans trying to understand what life has given us.

The stars are brightening now, and I look up at Mama again and realize I can't fix her. I'm not a near-god anymore. I am a human. A regular one. I won't be able to reach into the river and scoop up stars to place in the sky.

"You have to fix Mama," I say, turning to Apple. It's weird. I am now a human asking a god for a favor. I feel the history of that in my bones. I am part of a new myth now, a new story of gods and humans and the ways we wind ourselves around each other.

"Fix her?" Apple asks. She looks worried, like I'm asking her to bring Mama back to life, but I know that's not possible.

"The constellation. Make her look like Mama. Just Mama. The way she really was. Okay?"

Apple nods. She looks in the sky. I know she still sees the Penny Hardy that she loved in the shape we made, but I think she is letting that go, too.

"I'll make her look just like you," she says with this smile that tells me she is already a god, already a little bit different.

The climb up the ladder begins. I don't know who goes

first or second or third. They all rush up: Eric and Reece and Dawn, Chloe and Mr. Winters and all the people I've known forever who I won't know any longer. Everyone Mama knew and loved. Everyone from Our Hill.

Everyone except Apple and Heather.

We hold hands and watch the climb. The ladder sways. Sometimes it looks like it might throw someone to the ground, but it doesn't—it rights itself every time. We have to lean our heads so far back to watch, and even then we can't see them beyond a layer of clouds. We just have to trust they made it.

We don't have to say anything. Apple's hand is hot and mine is cool and we are so different, she and I, but so the same, too, in the way we want the moment to last, in the way it feels like holding on to a hundred perfect memories that we're both so scared to lose.

Heather comes over to us before her climb. She pulls me in for a hug and I think it's meant for Mama more than for me. "You were always human," she says. "You and Penny. It's better this way." I think she means it as an almost-insult, but I decide to hear it as a compliment.

Mama and I have always been human, which means we have always been curious and complicated and ourselves. I have been a near-god. I have been a shadow. I have been a maker of constellations. I have been a friend to the most powerful girl on all of Our Hill. But I have liked being human most of all, in spite of everything.

Heather gives Apple a warning look, a *Don't do anything else unbecoming of a descendant of Hera* look, and then she climbs up too.

And then no one else is left on earth. Just my father and me and Apple and the two gods who are making sure we seal our agreement.

"Now, Apple," Hermes says. I would have liked to get to know him, I think, if I'd chosen to go up the ladder myself. He seems solid and secretly kind. I like the wings on his boots and the crowd of clouds around him. I like his eyes.

"I can't," she says, and I hold on tighter too. I squeeze. I want to keep all the good parts of me and Apple and figure out how to get rid of the rest, but maybe this is it, this is the only way. Maybe we are meant to be memories to each other.

The thought catches in my throat, and I'm crying too.

"You never cry," Apple says. I love her knowing that about me and hate that some new friend someday will have to learn it. I hate that any new friend won't have known Mama. Won't have seen the way Mama used to dance and sing and bake bread and brush my hair and tell me to be brave. A new friend won't have seen the way Mama walked away from the ladder, the way she smiled up at it after, like it was an old friend she missed but knew she had to let go of.

"You're going to be amazing up there," I say, pulling

Apple into a hug, wanting to be as strong as Mama looking at that ladder.

"You're going to be amazing down here." Her tears are heavy and make her words messy. Hermes, I swear, wipes a tear too.

"Best friends," Hermes says. He smiles, like he wants a best friend himself, like he had one once too. Later maybe I'll look through my books to remember more about Hermes, who is said to be a trickster but is so serious here and now that it's hard to believe.

Maybe we aren't always exactly what the stories say we are.

I wonder what the stories will say about Apple and me.

"I can't say goodbye," Apple says.

"You have to," Iris says, and Hermes clears his throat, shuffles. She gives Hermes a look like he knows better than whatever it is he's about to do. She shakes her head. I think she maybe smiles a little, because that's what it's like to know someone really, really well. You know what mistake they will make moments before they make it, and you love them a little for it anyway.

"Once a year," Hermes says. "You can come be with her once a year. Summer solstice. At noon. The shortest shadows of the year." He gives Apple a heavy glance at this, as if the short shadows will stop her from trying anything foolish.

Apple lights up, and I do too. Once a year. When shadows

are shortest. We'll meet right here. It isn't the friendship we started; it is something else, maybe something better.

We hug one more time. It's a sturdy hug, and I miss her before it's even over.

Then she climbs the ladder into the sky to become a god. I watch her go. The climb seems easy, for her. The ladder is still. She's strong.

She's Apple Montgomery, and she is doing what she was always meant to do.

37.

Dad and I sit on the porch at night. The hill is quiet with no one else on it but us. The quiet isn't so bad, really. It makes it easier to hear birds and crickets and this little hum in the background of it all that I sometimes think is Mama.

He's hung the tapestry of Pandora in our living room, and I can see her through the window now, glowing, filled with promise of something good that will come. Not the kind of good thing you prepare for. The other kind, that kind you could never expect.

"I miss Mama," I say. It's funny, but I hadn't said it quite that way before, all laid bare and clear.

"I do too," Dad says, and I wish we'd said these exact

words in this exact way months and months ago. "I missed *you*."

"I'm sorry," I say, like I said on top of the hill. Because I know I made the wish to be a shadow just as hard as Apple wished it. I know I wanted to disappear, forgetting that disappearing meant disappearing from Dad.

He doesn't say it's okay, because it isn't really, but we're both here now and that's good.

It's scary. It's sad. It's strange.

But it's good.

"Should we stay up?" Dad asks. I don't know why the decision feels so massive, but it does. As a shadow, nothing mattered. As a human, everything does. Mama was right. We are here to make things matter, whether as gods or as humans, whether for everyone or just for us.

"Stay up," I say. "It's a pretty night." I say it because it won't always be now. The weather will be what it is—the nights will be cold or rainy or warm and sticky and we won't be able to change it. For a moment, I wonder if we've made a mistake, if maybe we were meant to be gods, deciding if a night was going to be the perfect temperature. Sitting in the clouds, watching other people's lives.

But no. We're meant to be here, letting the weather happen, and deciding what we're going to do in the midst of it. Maybe the gods think they decide everything, they have the power. But that's because they've never been human. We have it too. We have it right now, on the porch, deciding to make a hot chocolate and tug our hats on tighter and stay outside because it's a mild winter night and we don't have anywhere else to be.

We watch the sky, all of Mama's favorite constellations, and the one Apple and I made, too, and it's nice. It's enough, somehow, for right now.

And then. It is more. The sky begins to shift. Not the whole thing. Just one corner of it.

"Dad? Are you seeing—"

He puts his hand on my knee like if we aren't quiet we'll lose the moment. We lean forward.

The stars move. My stars. The ones I placed up there. And I know it is Apple, keeping her promise. I want to shout something to her—*Thank you* and *I miss you* and *I'll think about you all the time* and *This is right, it really is, even if it will feel wrong from time to time,* and *Thank you for being my friend, even though it turned awful and weird, it was still so real and it mattered so much and I learned everything I needed to learn.* And I want to say *Remember* and then list a thousand memories, good ones and horrible ones that only we share, from watching our moms, from witnessing the way friendship is love, and is struggle, and is knowing someone so well.

But I don't say anything at all. Because she's a god. She can't hear me.

The stars start to still, deciding what order they're going to be in.

Dad and I leave the porch to get a better view. We lie down on the front lawn. If anyone were here, they'd think it strange, probably, but anyone who could judge us is gone.

Mama is in a new shape. A star-smile. A glow of hope, like Pandora sees in her jar. She is Mama, next to a ladder of stars. She has turned away from the ladder, and she is facing something new, something unexpected in the distance she can't quite see yet, and neither can we, but something that she trusts will be beautiful.

And I do too.

It is Mama, exactly as I want to remember her.

And it is me, too. I'm sure of that.

Because finally—at last—Apple, up in the clouds, sees me.

And down here on earth, looking at what she has made for me, I see her too.

APPLE

Summer Solstice

EPILOGUE

Mom tells me not to go. "We're done with all that," she says, gesturing to the world below. Up here there are castles and thrones. We eat sweet fruit every morning and we float on clouds and we watch the world below. Mom likes to sit next to Hera and discuss how to teach the humans the lessons they need to understand—humility and caution, especially. She finds humans like Penny, like Dorothy, and she tries to change them. She wants them to be safer and smaller.

But I go in after her and let them be messy. She takes down a tree a little girl likes to climb—*too dangerous, too high*, she says. And I let a new one—taller, wilder—grow in its place. I watch the girl climb it, fall, climb it again. She is bruised and knee-scraped. She reminds me of Dorothy. Mom tries to lead someone to make friends with the simplest person, the one with the wide eyes and nice smile who shrugs when you ask them what the bravest thing they ever did was. Then I seek out the goddess of friendship, Philotes, who is mostly left alone because everyone's always looking for Eros, the god of love. And we let the other friendships' flames burn brighter. We watch the rocky friendships, the mismatched ones, the ones where they fight and make up and they hurt and they love and they don't like what the other one is doing or how they're doing it but they stay friends anyway. We let those grow.

"I'm going," I tell Mom now, and my voice is clearer than it used to be, louder, too. "She's my best friend."

"You have Philotes," Mom says, though she doesn't like her so much either. She's not important enough, barely known at all, really, rarely mentioned in our myths, rarely even thought about, though that doesn't seem to bother her. "You have Dawn and Reece," she goes on. She likes when I'm with them, which is occasionally, when I want to think about what used to be. And she likes when I cozy up to Hera, gardening with her. Or when Zeus invites me over for tea and asks me to tell him more and more about what it was like, being a near-human, for a while.

"This was the agreement. It's summer. It's time to see my friend."

"While you can," Mom says, and it sounds like a threat, but it's also the truth and it is a truth she knows too well.

"I'm coming back," I say, because she looks so sad. "That's the deal. I go once a year. I return up here." Mom nods. She's not happy about it but it is an arrangement with the gods, and there's no arguing with that.

It's easier than I thought, not being who she wants me to be. It seemed impossible on earth. But now I'm just Apple, a god who lies on clouds and makes mischief and kisses Mom on the cheek when she lectures me on who she thinks I have to be. "I'm not you," I say as nicely as I can. "I'm not your shadow." I say it again now, and Mom clenches her jaw but doesn't say anything back. Then I take the ladder. This one is rope. I unfurl it from my favorite cloud, unwinding and unwinding until it touches the tippy-top of Our Hill, which isn't Our Hill anymore. Humans have been moving in, slowly. I watched from Olympus as George and Dorothy met them in neighboring towns, showed them the beauty of the hill, told them magical stories about her friends who moved up into the sky. The humans laughed and shook their heads and said *But no, what really happened?* and Dorothy just smiled. She asked if they might want to join them in community up there. Everyday humans, in our homes, on Our Hill, making it their own.

Some days it's nice.

Some days it hurts.

Today, I will finally be there again. I climb down. One foot at a time, just like all the years before. My body remembers the way. The rope ladder is swingier, but I'm stabler. I won't fall. I can't.

Maybe she won't be here, I think, when I'm halfway down. Maybe she doesn't want to see me as much as I want to see her. Maybe she doesn't forgive me. Maybe she doesn't need this. Maybe we were never best friends at all. I try to prepare myself for the possibility the rest of the way down, so that by the time I step one foot and then the other on the ground, I'm a little teary and scared.

I look around. It's colder than it should be in summer, and I think of changing it, but Dorothy wouldn't like that. Penny wouldn't have either. So I let it be rainy and foggy and oddly chilly. Everything is the same and different. The hill is the same shape, the trees, too, the sun hitting them in all the same places, the same flowers growing in the same random patches. And then there is Dorothy. She is sitting cross-legged on the grass. I can only see her in profile. She's got a worn T-shirt on, and her hair is blowing all over. Her yellow rain boots are muddy and her cheeks are freckled and she looks different—not older or bigger. Just more like a human. She is not a god anymore. She is not my shadow. She is Dorothy, exactly as she was always meant to be.

"Hey," I call out, and I step toward her, the earth giving a little under my feet, the ladder swaying, the sun so bright in my eyes that I have to make a little visor with my hand. "You're here."

And Dorothy, a smile just starting to make its way to her mouth, turns to say hello.

ACKNOWLEDGMENTS

With every book, it becomes ever clearer just how many people are necessary to turn an idea into a story into a real, tangible book. My heart is full from the care and time and brainpower that contributed to this one.

A massive thank-you to my editor, Mabel Hsu, for your patience, your vision, your heart, and your willingness to go on my winding book-writing journeys with me. This book would truly never have been without you.

As always, thank you to my agent, Victoria Marini, for the wide-ranging and infinite ways you keep me steady and inspired.

Thank you to Katherine Tegen for years of support and a home for my books. I am so glad I got the honor of working with you over these years.

Thank you, Julia Johnson, for your hard work and meaningful feedback.

And so many starry-eyed thank-yous to the thoughtful and clarifying work of Alexandra Rakaczki.

Thank you to designer Amy Ryan and illustrator Karl James Mountford for beautiful ideas and a truly perfect cover.

Thank you for all you put into my books—Vanessa Nuttry in production, Alison Kerr Miller, the entire marketing team, and Patty Rosati, Mimi Rankin, Christina Carpino, Josie Dallam over in school and library marketing, where I know my books are always treated with such care. I feel so lucky to have so many brilliant people giving time and energy and thought to my work, and helping readers find it too.

Thank you to all the friends and family who offer so much support along the way. Most especially Frank, Fia, and Thisbe, who make it all fun, make me fearless, and give everything an extra bit of heart.